Glutton for Punishment

THE BEELER LARGE PRINT MYSTERY SERIES

Edited by Audrey A. Lesko

Also available in Large Print by Cecile Lamalle

Appetite for Murder
Prepared for Murder

Glutton for Punishment

Cecile Lamalle

BEELER LARGE PRINT
Hampton Falls, New Hampshire, 2002

Library of Congress Cataloging-in-Publication Data

Lamalle, Cecile.
  Glutton for punishment / Cecile Lamalle
    p.   cm.—(The Beeler Large Print mystery series)
  ISBN 1-57490-432-9 (alk. paper)
    1. Cooks—Fiction. 2. Art thefts—Fiction. 3.
Restaurateurs—Fiction. 4. Antique dealers—Fiction. 5. New
York (State)—Fiction. 6. Large type books. I. Title.

PS3562.A4185 G57 2002
813'.54—dc21   2002010434

Published in Large Print by arrangement with
Warner Books, Inc.

BEELER LARGE PRINT
is published by
Thomas T. Beeler, Publisher
Post Office Box 659
Hampton Falls, New Hampshire 03844

Typeset in 16 point Times New Roman type.
Printed on acid-free paper, sewn and bound by
Sheridan Books in Chelsea, Michigan.

Prologue

Article in *Albany Star-Register*

A ONE-OF-A-KIND REGENCY CABINET MISSING FROM a residence in Klover New York, was one of over seventy antiques reported stolen in upstate New York, southern Vermont, and western Massachusetts in the past six months. Police speculate that this may be the work of a ring of antiques thieves operating on the East Coast and possibly nationwide.

Investigators from the State Police Bureau of Criminal Investigations Major Crimes Unit, who have an ongoing investigation of the antiques-theft ring, got wind of the Klover heist when the owner, returning from an extended stay in Florida, noticed the piece missing from a seldom-used guest room in his seventeen-room house. Other antiques appeared to be missing, as well, though there was no sign of a break-in. Police speculate that the theft was committed by the ring they are currently investigating.

Senior Investigator Thomas Gault said the antiques-stealing ring has been operating for three or four years, but it has only come to the attention of local investigators recently. He asks that anyone with information regarding the theft of antiques from private homes contact the State Police in Albany.

Dinner Preparations at La Fermette

TIENS, CHARLY POISSON THOUGHT AS HE FOLDED THE newspaper where he'd been reading about an antiques-theft ring. *What will the crook think of next?* He hurried from the chef's office into his big spotless restaurant kitchen, all stainless steel and white tile.

"Take four big shallots," he told Benny Perkins, his nineteen-year-old sous-chef. "Peel and finely chop them, *bien entendu,* and saute them in beef dripping with a handful of chopped garlic . . . "

It was just after eight o'clock on a frigid Friday morning in February, grey and blustery, looked like more snow. Charly, the owner of LA Fermette, the finest French-American restaurant in Van Buren County, upstate New York (well, the only French-American restaurant, the county tended more toward Italian and steak houses), was guiding Benny through the intricacies of Marchand de Vin sauce, the accompaniment to the most expensive dish on the restaurant's menu, *Côte de Boeuf Marchand de Vin.*

"If it snow, cancellation all over the place," Charly prophesied, "but sauce, he will keep." As he spoke, Charly idly spooned some of the congealed beef dripping onto a piece of stale baguette. "It need salt," he muttered, reaching down for the coarse sea salt. Who needed the Proustian madeleines? The rich, greasy taste took him right back to his Tante Jeanne's kitchen in Bourg-en-Bresse in the Jura Mountains in France. Dear Tante Jeanne, mountainously obese, a glutton to be sure.

Charly sighed, munched his bread, and looked out the window at the grey landscape. Just three more months and the fields would be alive with buds and greenery, and he would be planting his garden.

"Fridays aren't so bad," Benny said with a smile. When Charly fussed and worried, Benny wanted to comfort him. "There's the skiers and the weekenders."

Benny, born in Van Buren County, looked like a Breton fisherman with his short, squat body, his pink cheeks, his dark, straight hair. He looked so French that Charly, in his philosophical moments, wondered if it was karmic. If Benny was the son he'd never had. "And," Benny continued, "you always do lots of takeout on Friday nights, snow or no snow."

La Fermette was located on Route 65, one of the main roads that led from New York State to Massachusetts. Over the twenty years that Charly had been operating La Fermette, he found more and more customers veering toward takeout. They'd leave the restaurant armed with a big bag of Charly's frozen soups, ragouts, pâtés, sauces, and perhaps one of Patty Perkins's (Benny's mother and Charly's pastry chef) spectacular pies. Even the locals patronized Charly's takeout service. A hostess might wish to cook her own entree and dessert, but might serve Charly's *pâté de campagne* with cocktails, or Charly's Madeira-laced mushroom bisque as an appetizer. This worked well, not the least for Charly's supplier of foam and cardboard containers, who embellished the boxes with a stick-on French flag and the logo: "La Fermette, the little farmhouse, where the foods are country-fresh." The supplier also provided bright red shopping bags. Charly's years as a New York City waiter, headwaiter, and restaurateur stood him in good stead. He knew that presentation is everything in

3

the restaurant business. If it looked good, it tasted good. Voilà.

"I get it," Benny said, sliding the chopped shallots into the hot beef fat with his stainless-steel bench scraper. "The shallots and the garlic have to be sweated, first, to bring out their natural sugars, and that's what gives the sauce its sweetness."

"That is correct, Benny. I am proud of you. The food, it talk to you, and you know what it is saying. And after the sweating, we will sprinkle with just a bit of flour, then we pour in the hot wine and the beef stock, and we reduce. Reduction is the secret of the fine sauce."

Benny looked around La Fermette's kitchen: the stainless-steel stoves and refrigerators and grills, the burnished copper pots hanging overhead, the scrubbed wooden butcher blocks and chopping surfaces. He enjoyed working in such a clean and orderly place.

"I've got the marrow bones in the oven," Benny said. He loved Charly's little speeches, though he had heard most of them many times. "And while the sauce is reducing, I'll get the pea soup going for lunch. You want me to make the egg pies?"

"No, Julius is coming in, soon. He can do that," Charly said. "I am so happy that Julius is coming on Fridays too, now. We have become so busy."

Julius Prendergast, the fortyish stockbroker from Albany, the state capital thirty miles north, had been working Saturdays and Sundays at La Fermette for over a year. Julius's aunt—Charly's good customer, the aristocratic Honoria Wells—had asked Charly to give Julius a parttime job, for Julius was tiring of the stock market and wanted, in a few years, to open his own country inn. This apprenticeship at Charly's was meant to give him practice. A strong bond had developed

4

between Charly, Julius, Benny, and old Mick Hitchens the dishwasher, and Charly hated to think of the day when Julius would leave them. Julius had become one of the family.

Now, since January, Julius was taking Fridays off as well to work in Charly's kitchen. Friday nights were becoming as busy as Saturdays and Sundays, and Charly needed the extra help. He'd certainly never gotten any help from his partner Maurice Baleine who was, at this very moment, winding up his stay in an exclusive rehab spa in the Adirondacks, his bout with cirrhosis not cured, but in remission.

"Here's Julius now," old Mick cried, peering out of the window, where he could see Julius's ancient white BMW pulling into the back parking lot. Mick hobbled over to the prep station and gathered up some bowls to wash. Charly frowned at the old man. "You are looking tired, Mick."

"Can't seem to get my breath these days and the cold makes my legs ache. The work's good for me. Gotta keep going."

"And Bruno, he is hokay?" Charly asked. Bruno was Mick's big black Labrador mix. Bruno took care of many of the restaurant's leftovers.

"Bruno is wonderful," Mick told them. "He's like my child."

"Snow forecast, I heard it on the radio," Julius said, sweeping in with a blast of icy air. "Morning, everyone, Charly, Mick, Benny. Mmmm, this place always smells so good."

Julius, tall and thin, shrugged out of his yellow down jacket and shook the golden curls that surrounded a balding pate. He looked like an aging archangel, gentle and a bit remote. Charly, who often read the illustrated

5

Petit Larousse, that noble dictionary, told Julius that when he lost all of his hair he would look like Alexis Carrel, the French doctor and author of *Man, the Unknown ("L'Homme, cet inconnu")* which had won him the Nobel Prize in 1912. He even showed Julius the Larousse picture. Julius, bemused, would answer that he had no intention of losing all of his hair.

"Is Marchand de Vin sauce you smell," Charly said. "In an hour, you can taste, tell us what you think." To Benny, Charly whispered, "We will not tell him you made. We will see what he say."

Julius reappeared from Charly's office, where he had hung up his outerwear, shrugging into his white chef's jacket. Then he tied a white apron around his waist. "There's a huge grey car pulling up by the kitchen door, looks like a pimp-mobile. That's Rex Cingale, isn't it?"

Charly, chopping onions, chuckled. "That is Rex Cingale. Important man must have important car." Rex owned the bar and restaurant Steak Heaven up the road. "The best steaks and the longest bar in Van Buren County" was Steak Heaven's logo. And rightly so. "We must make some more coffee. Very strong for Rex. Benny? You will do it?"

Rex Cingale, corpulent and prosperous-looking in a fawn camel-hair overcoat, walked into the kitchen. As a fellow restaurateur he had kitchen privileges. "Charly, Mick, Julius, Ben." He nodded glumly.

"Why, Rex"—Charly hurried over—"you look . . . not good."

Rex took off his overcoat and hung it on the back of a chair, then sat at the big pine table in the corner of the kitchen where the staff took their meals. "Julius? Ben? Mick? This is in confidence, right? Like, you won't spread it around?"

6

"Right, Mr. Cingale," the men agreed.

"I got so much indigestion, Charly, I don't believe. It's Bobby."

Bobby was Rex's nephew, and his barman. Bobby was a gambler—always confident of one day winning the lottery.

"For Christmas I gave Bobby a percentage of the restaurant, like I give my other nieces and nephews. You know, make them members of the team.

"Well, this morning, he comes to me, tells me he's in hock to some pretty bad people, I mean, like fuckin' scum. He's been gambling at Ugo Buonsarde's place across the river, The Country Squire, they have illegal gambling on the side but everyone knows, even the cops."

Rex rubbed his fingers together, indicating payoffs. "Bobby owes them ten grand, he borrowed money, can't pay the vig, so what does he do?"

"What does he do?" Charly echoed.

"He gave him his percentage of the restaurant to use as, what the fuck's it called"—Rex snapped his fingers—"collateral. Ever since he tells me, my stomach's been crampin' something awful. Thanks, Benny." Benny had placed a mug of coffee in front of Rex, with a sugar bowl and a quart container of heavy cream. "Bad move, Charly."

"You right, is bad move."

"Oh, sure, I knew Bobby gambled," Rex went on, adding a royal amount of cream and sugar to his mug. "I knew about the horses and the numbers. But I didn't know about his gambling across the river. That place, it's supposed to be run by the mob, for Christ's sake. How could Bobby be so dumb? To get in hock to creeps like that. Italians, too. They're an insult to every Italian-

7

American." Rex took a swig of coffee and said, "Ahhh."

Charly got up, reached into a cupboard. "Coffee is no good with upset stomach, here is what you need. Fernet Branca. Is Italian. Is made from herbs." Charly grasped the small bottle, got a glass. He poured a generous measure. "Drink this, Rex."

Rex sniffed, made a face, then sank the shot and shuddered. "Jeez, Charly, you trying to poison me? My Aunt Philomena drinks this stuff."

"No, no, Rex, is good for you."

"You could unclog a sink with it."

"It will help. Not with your problem, but with your stomach. For your problem, I do not know . . . but I would talk to my lawyer."

"Yeah, I got a call in to Angie Vongola, he's calling me back. But I'm disappointed in Bobby. You believe it? Ten grand, the kid owes. And now they've got a share of my restaurant. I gotta pay, no two ways about it." Rex shook his heavy head so forcefully that his plump cheeks quivered.

Charly cleared his throat. "And once you pay, that will be the end of it? Bobby will never gamble again? Bobby will learn the lesson?" Charly's voice was heavy with meaning.

"Who the hell knows?"

"You pay today, tomorrow Bobby is gambling again, is a fact. Wait, Rex. Talk to your lawyer. Do not do anything for a few days."

"You think so, Charly?"

"I know so."

After Rex left, Charly tasted the simmering Marchand de Vin sauce. Perfect. He smacked his lips and looked over at Benny. Benny was staring at the saucepan. He appeared to be holding his breath.

"Julius? You want to taste a good sauce?"

Julius came over, dipped in a spoon. Tasted. Savored. Then tasted again. "It's always good, Charly, but this one's sensational."

Benny was not a gambler, but he looked like he'd won the lottery.

"Benny made it," Charly said proudly. "Benny made the Marchand de Vin sauce."

Patty's Story Served with Chocolate Cake

BENNY SAID, "BOBBY CAN'T JUST GIVE HIS SHARE OF the restaurant to those gamblers, can he? I mean, that's crazy."

"Of course he cannot," Charly agreed. "Unless the lawyer is an idiot, there is always a clause to say that the co-owner gets first refusal."

"Then why didn't you tell him?"

Charly shrugged. "Is good Rex should worry little bit about Bobby. Signor Roberto is a very foolish young man. Rex should worry more."

"Charly's our Machiavelli," Julius said. "You ever read *The Prince and the Discourses*, Benny?"

"I've never even heard of Mach—whatever his name is."

"Charly has, haven't you, Charly?"

Charly gave a shrug. "Is possible. But Julius is right, is important book. It tell how to stab people in back in politics. Good to know."

"Certain things like what, Charly?" Benny pursued.

"The art"—Charly frowned—"of dealing with people

9

who do not want the best for you. Which is everybody. Like these men who lend Bobby money, knowing he cannot repay. You come across many people like this in life."

"You better believe it," Julius snorted. "Everyone's out for number one. I am, you are too. What are you into now, Benny? Vegetarianism? The I Ching? The Tao?"

"Some of the guys at Tae Kwon Do are eating vegetarian, drinking only water. One guy used to drink six, seven Cokes a day, now he drinks none and his whole face changed. He used to have a fat face, now his face is real thin. I'm also reading up on Zen Buddhism."

Benny was discovering the wisdom of the East, mainly via his Korean martial-arts classes that Charly was paying for.

The back door rattled, and plump, motherly Patty Perkins staggered in under a mountain of pies. "Benny? Julius? Can you help me? There's three boxes of cookies, more pies, and two cakes in the back of the car."

Benny and Julius hurried out. Charly followed Patty into the dessert room that adjoined the kitchen. Here was where Patty made the fragile desserts, the mousses, flavored creams, sorbets, and ice creams.

A long time ago, when Benny was still a baby, Patty had appeared at Charly's kitchen door. Her husband had recently been killed in a car crash; she needed money but wanted to stay at home with her baby. She brought Charly samples of her apple pie, cookies, blueberry turnovers. Would it be possible, Patty asked, to make certain desserts for the restaurant?

Charly tasted and recognized a pro. Patty's selections were countrified, but her hand was delicate and she knew how to capture flavor. He hired her on the spot. Today Patty's desserts were far more sophisticated, and she'd abandoned *Good Housekeeping* for dessert books by pastry professionals.

"You have tried to make the chocolate cake?" Charly asked. Charly and Patty were trying to develop a chocolate confection, a cake that Charly remembered from a pastry shop in his hometown of Lons-le-Saunier.

"I've made a first version," Patty said. "It's very rich, not at all to the American taste, Charly. And it has a food cost of forty percent if you charge $7.50 a slice. Callebaut chocolate, ground hazelnuts, rum, almond paste, buttercream icing—it's too much. I can make a much simpler, cheaper version. Food cost on the other desserts are less than twenty percent."

"We will see," Charly promised. "Can I have a slice, now?"

Patty smiled at Charly's gleaming black hair (courtesy of a French hair dye) and his pencil mustache. "Of course. Oh, and I saw an old friend this morning, Amanda Kendell. She's going away tomorrow. I invited her to come to the kitchen and taste this famous cake. I hope you don't mind."

"Excellent," Charly said. "Kendell. I do not recall that name. They do not come to the restaurant, I think."

"I'm sure they don't. They have money, but they're . . . odd. She's a poor thing, her husband beats her. You remember I asked you for the name of your therapist in Albany? For a friend who was real depressed?"

"Yes, of course."

"Well, that's Amanda. Dr. Metz really helped. She's gotten up the courage to divorce Matt. She's leaving tomorrow for her sister Catherine's in Worcester. The divorce papers will be served while she's gone."

11

"And how will she live, poor lady? Will the husband give her money?"

"Amanda's not asking for alimony," Patty said. "Both Dr. Metz and her lawyer agreed that all the properties Matt's put in her name for tax purposes are legally hers. Matt owns a trucking company. He's a rich man."

Charly pulled a long face. "Ah, I do not like the sound of that. Monies in her name. There is much danger. But, she is leaving tomorrow, you say?"

"First thing in the morning, Charly. It's a three-hour drive, and the divorce papers will be served Saturday afternoon. She'll be well away when Matt finds out. Don't worry."

Benny and Julius entered the dessert room. Julius said, "I tasted a rum *tuile,* Patty, it's great. You still cooking for old Wes? I bet he doesn't like those rum things. Probably thinks they're communist *tuiles.*"

A year ago, Patty had started going out with Weston Hinkley. Hinkley, a Van Buren County native, respected member of the Town Board, worked for the County Highway Commission. He detailed snowplow routes, determined which roads needed repaving, where new flood culverts were needed, and so on. Wes's wife Esme, a friend of Patty's, had died of cancer. Patty and Wes spent weekends together—as much as her job with Charly allowed—and recently Patty had begun cooking Wes's meals.

Neither Charly nor Julius had ever met Hinkley. Patty refused to bring him to the restaurant. Later Patty admitted that Wes didn't like what he called "fancy foreign food" and was opposed to Patty's working at La Fermette. He wanted Patty to work in an American restaurant.

"What do you think of Wes?" Julius once asked

12

Benny.

"I don't know what she sees in him," Benny replied. "He thinks working as a sous-chef is for faggots; Tae Kwon Do is, I quote, 'an Asian terrorist plot.' Guy's a small-town tight-ass. But, hey, she's my mom, right? She says he's a comfortable person and a pillar of the community. He's got an arsenal, runs around shooting animals. That's what a real man does, old Wes says. But I think she's finally seeing the light. She refused to spend last weekend with him. Too busy, she said."

Charly would clear his throat nervously whenever Patty mentioned Wes's name. Julius said xenophobe Wes sounded slightly to the right of Genghis Khan, but for Charly not to worry.

"You right, Julius, things will work out," Charly would say dubiously.

"Well, yes, I'm still making Wes's snacks"—Patty frowned—"but the last meat loaf he said was too spicy, and asked me to follow Esme's old recipe, you know, powdered onion soup, all that yucky stuff. And Wes's favorite soup is, let's see, you take cans of cream of chicken, pea, tomato, mix 'em up. And you eat it with toasted Wonder bread. That's the only bread a real American would eat." Patty sounded disgusted. Charly's smile broadened.

Charly, as always before a meal, dropped some Bach flowers onto his tongue, to calm his mind. Patty's affair with Wes Hinkley was driving him to distraction. Ah, the good homeopathic Dr. Bach, what a pity he was English and not French. For the English, as everyone knew, had burned Joan of Arc at the stake and were a wicked people.

13

A Fresh Start

ABOUT FIVE MILES AWAY FROM LA FERMETTE, Amanda Kendell sat at her desk in the little alcove off the kitchen, writing a letter. This was hard work. She'd dropped out of school in the tenth grade. Her spelling was atrocious. Four pieces of her good writing paper had already gone into the bulging wastebasket. She was writing to a friend in New Hampshire.

"*Dear Bobsie,*" Amanda wrote. "*I'm goin to visit Catherine & fam. tomorrow and hope you can drive down to Worster and visit me!!! I'm divorsing Matt!! Finally got up corage, only he doesn't know it yet. I'll be living with Catherine & Tom & kids until I can find a place of my own.*" End of page one. "*So oftin I've wanned to kill myself, just end the wole mess. And now it will be all taken careuf. I cannot take it any more and it will be so good to end it. I have been so dipresed.*" Amanda reread what she'd written. It looked awful. Why go into it all in a letter? She dropped yet another sheet in the wastebasket and got out a new piece of paper.

"*Dear Bobsie, I'm coming to Worster and hope to see you. Will be staeing with Catherine. I have lots of news!!! maybe we can have lunch next wek.*" Then she signed, Amanda Winlove Kendell, with several hearts and Xs. She wouldn't be signing Kendell much longer. Thank God.

Writing the letter exhausted Amanda. It would be easier to call, but Amanda often wondered if Matt had bugged the phone. He knew about her lending money to Greg, that one time, and she'd never told Matt, only

14

talked to Greg about it on the phone. She slid the letter into an envelope, addressed, sealed, stamped it, and put it in her purse. She took one of the discarded sheets from the wastebasket (Amanda, despite her husband's wealth, was thrifty) and wrote on the back: *"stek, oven frys, sandwich meat, visit Patty, get gas."* She washed her hands, applied more mascara and lipgloss, and touched up the corner of her eye with makeup where the bruise was still an ugly yellow. Then she brushed her wavy brown hair.

Amanda admired herself in the hall mirror. Her hair fell to her shoulders in ringlets and her skin was creamy white. Just like the heroines in the romance novels she loved. She had on her favorite ruffled pink wool dress, her gold locket, her pale grey snow boots. Now she put on her baby-blue polyester-filled winter coat and her pink wool cap embroidered with forget-me-nots. Should she bother to change her brown purse for the grey one? Not today. No time. Too bad. Amanda loved for everything to match.

Amanda slammed the back door and jiggled the knob. Matt was furious when she left the door unlocked. She shook her head to clear away the cobwebs. She'd taken a tranquilizer several hours ago. It made her feel tranquil, all right, but it made her mind fuzzy. Still, it was better than shaking all the time. Now, she'd forgotten something. What. Probably nothing important. Oh, thank God this marriage would be ending soon.

Amanda started her car, a pale blue Oldsmobile Aurora, and carefully backed out of the garage. Now, where should she go, first? Maybe to Patty's restaurant. Patty was the one person she wanted to keep up with. A very kind woman. Amanda envied Patty. Lucky girl— her husband had been killed in a car crash. He used to

15

beat her too, she'd heard. Another drunk.

Amanda knocked on the kitchen door of La Fermette. Benny opened the door and Patty hurried over. There were three other people in the big, airy kitchen and Patty introduced them: Mr. Poisson, the owner, who took Amanda's hand and kissed it, just like in the romance novels; a tall man with twinkly eyes; and a smiling old man washing dishes. Everyone seemed so friendly, and it was warm and smelled good. So clean, too, with those beautiful pots hanging up near the ceiling. And she and Matt had never had a meal here. Amanda wished she'd confided more in Patty, her friend.

"We are just tasting a cake that Patty has made, it is filled with good thing," Mr. Poisson said in a funny accent. He peered at Amanda. Was that a bruise at the corner of her eye? Patty had said the husband hit her. She'd tried to cover it up. Disgusting, the husband must be. "Ah, here we go," Charly said as Patty came over with a slice of chocolate cake on a plate and a fork.

Amanda laid down her handbag, gloves, car keys, and list on the big table, where Charly had just opened a tin of dried cepe mushrooms. A handful would be soaked in water, then used to make a wild mushroom sauce. "Linguine with woodland mushroom," Charly told Amanda. "Cepe, portobello, white mushroom, and shiitake, mixed with butter and cream and Madeira." Amanda didn't know what all that stuff was, but it sounded good.

"This is delicious," Amanda said politely, tasting the cake.

Charly returned with another small slice for himself.

"I cannot resist," he told Amanda. "It bring me back to my childhood. Patty tell me you are leaving for

Massachusetts tomorrow. I wish you a good voyage."

Amanda laid down the cake plate arid gathered up her belongings. "It's thanks to Patty and to you, Mr. Poisson, for recommending Dr. Metz. I may never come back. I'm beginning a new life. Dr. Metz is a wonderful man."

"He will be your friend forever," Charly said.

"He's got offices in Springfield, too, close to Worcester. I'll keep on seeing him. Good to meet everyone, and thanks for the cake."

"I'll walk you to your car," Patty said, pulling on her jacket.

Charly shook his head as he idly closed the mushroom tin. *A curious woman*, he thought, *with the little-girl voice, the little-girl dress all pink and frilly, the long curly hair like a schoolgirl's. And if she is Patty's age she is forty. Women who try and remain little girls, they are strange. And her face is a mess. Ah, la la, Dr. Metz has a job with this one.*

A Stranger Crosses the River

POOR AMANDA, ALL THOSE BRUISES," PATTY SAID, back in the kitchen. "Isn't she a lovely person, Charly?"

"Lovely," Charly lied. Amanda made him uneasy. A little girl at forty. He had customers like that: they ordered "girlish" cocktails like The Pink Lady (apple brandy, gin, lemon juice, grenadine, egg white) that looked innocuous but packed a terrible punch, and after three or four they'd turn either quarrelsome or tearful. They also loved nursery foods like creamed chicken,

17

demanded separate checks, and were terrible tippers.

"Matt's a brute," Patty continued. "I'm so glad she's getting out. She's not too smart, but she has an awfully good heart. Now, Charly, to get back to your cake. I know you love it, but everyone in the kitchen thought it too rich. And the food cost is horrific. Why don't you let me cut out the almond paste and halve the sugar, and sprinkle it with a few of those pignolas instead of mixing in all those powdered hazelnuts?"

"You could try," Charly said doubtfully. He couldn't understand the American palate. Desserts couldn't be too rich, yet people swilled the sugary Coca-Cola with their meals, and the child's favorite sandwich was heavily sweetened peanut butter and jelly. And they thought his cake rich? *Voyons.*

"We've got twenty reservations tonight, about forty-eight people," Patty said, having just checked the reservation book. "Count on—what?—five tables of walk-ins? Maybe not even that, it's just started to snow."

Charly peered out the kitchen window. Great fat flakes were spiraling down from the darkening sky. Yes, sure to be cancellations. "My poor lobsters," he lamented. The stylish Friday night dish, this winter, was Mediterranean lobster stew (last year's had been bouillabaisse; they were similar). A lobster was cut up, sautéed in olive oil, flamed with brandy, simmered with garlic, shallots, saffron, tomatoes, white wine, and fish stock.

"If people do cancel," Julius pointed out, "you can boil them up, then tomorrow you can halve them and serve them cold with herb mayo. Or hot, with Newburg sauce—heavy cream, mushrooms, sherry, butter."

"Hmmm," Charly said, "is idea. Where you get these

18

thought?"

"Well," Julius explained, "you know how I'm always looking for old cookbooks? I found one from the New York Women's Exchange, dated 1940. My grandmother loved the Women's Exchange. I thought it was because of the genteel food, creamed everything with sherry, but the real reason was because the Women's Exchange served the biggest martinis in New York. My grandmother took me once. All those blue-blooded old dears, tweed suits, felt hats, swilling enough gin to slay a football player."

Charly chuckled. "I have never been to this famous place. And that is what they serve? All foods with cream and sherry?"

"Yep. All of this was B.C., before cholesterol, you understand. Creamed chicken, veal, lobster, bound with egg yolks, heavy cream, and sherry."

"The 1940s were the war," Charly mused. "Was there no rationing? Sugar, cream, butter, you could not find in France. The Nazis took everything."

"Well, they did have some rationing here," Julius recalled. "I remember my mom said they ate a lot of Spam, but I don't think they were deprived too much. This cookbook does have a recipe for War Shortbread: eight ounces of oatmeal, four ounces each butter and sugar."

Charly shook his head, remembering the bad old days. "Butter was *un luxe*, like the diamonds," he said bitterly. "To mix four ounces with some horrible cereal? *Pas vrai*. It cannot be true."

"Well, Charly," Julius said, "we were never invaded. We never understood what war really was, to have the enemy camping in your living room, raping your sisters, crapping on your Aubussons. My dad was in the Second

19

World War. He understood what it was like, over there. A horror."

"Ah, let us forget," Charly said. "To remember, bring pain to my heart."

"There's another old-fashioned sauce my parents' cook used to make," Julius quickly changed the subject, "sauce à la king, sautéed peppers, mushrooms, and pimentos, then you added cream and egg yolks and sherry. Lots of fat ladies then, just like today. I have a book of New Yorker cartoons dated 1937. 'Helen Hokinson ladies,' Dad called them, she was the cartoonist who drew them, ladies with enormous bosoms and tiny feet."

Good, he'd made Charly smile. "Fat lady, always funny," Charly agreed.

"I remember," Julius continued, "my grandmother telling us about a country auction. The auctioneer, Mr. Mitchell, was famous. A huge chair was put up, and Mr. Mitchell said, 'And here's a chair for a lady with a broad understanding.' My grandmother loved to tell that story."

"My Tante Jeanne, she was fat, too," Charly reminisced. "She taught me how to cook. I think she was never sober. *Les cerises à l'eau-de-vie,* cherries in brandy, that was her favorite drink."

"Did she die young?"

"Not so young, not so old," Charly said. "Seventy-nine. A good death. She rise from the dinner table, and she drop dead. *Patapouf.* Just like that."

Benny, coming in from his martial-arts practice, said, "I saw Mr. Crozier in town, he said put aside two orders of Shrimps Charly and two orders of lobster stew for tonight, and to reserve a table for four for tomorrow night."

"I wonder who are his guests?" Charly mused.

Benny hung up his jacket and left a book on the pine table. "I've finished your book, Charly. I enjoyed it."

"Thank you, Benny, will you put it in my office?" But just then there was a knock on the back door and Benny went to answer it. Charly glanced up, and seeing a stranger at his door, he hurried over.

What he saw was a gentleman about his own age and height, stocky, with a luxurious black mustache and a head as bald as an egg. The man wore a beige cashmere overcoat and a yellow silk scarf. Both were costly. Snowflakes drifted onto his bald dome and melted there.

"Come in, sir," Charly urged, pleased by the man's obvious prosperity.

"Ah, what a wonderful aroma," the man said in a deep voice, sniffing the air. "You are Monsieur Poisson, the chef and owner?"

Charly nodded and bowed. "*À votre service, monsieur.*"

"I live across the river. I hear that yours is the best restaurant in the area. Would it be possible to make a reservation for three, for this evening?"

"But of course. For three? At what time?"

"What time do you open?"

"Six o'clock."

"Three for six o'clock, then, monsieur."

"And the name, sir?"

"Ugo Buonsarde," the gentleman said. "This is a beautiful kitchen. It is spotless. Many restaurant kitchens are not clean. They are vile."

"That is true, alas," Charly said, wondering where he'd heard the name Buonsarde recently. "To eat in many restaurants is to invite food poisoning. Monsieur, no good food can be prepared in a dirty kitchen. And

21

here, we have good food. Would you like a little tour of our kitchen?"

Charly guided Ugo Buonsarde around, pointing out the various areas. "A separate dessert room, with its own air conditioner; my office, at the back; the preparation area for vegetables; for meat and poultry; for fish; the door to the cold room. And my staff"— Charly tried to remember the formal Brigade de Cuisine—"my *chef rotisseur* Julius Prendergast, my *sous-chef* Benjamin Perkins, my *commis et plongeur* Michael Hitchens."

The men bowed. Buonsarde bowed back. His eyes lit up as he noticed Benny's book on the pine table: Van de Wetering's *The Empty Mirror*.

"Ah," he breathed, "one of my favorite books. It is yours, monsieur?"

"It is," Charly acknowledged. "My sous-chef has just finished reading it."

"You have a literate young man for a sous-chef." Buonsarde smiled. "Experiences in a Japanese Zen monastery. I remember it well. The author—and I have read all of his mysteries—suffers dreadfully trying to follow the monks, but he persists. That is what I respect. Persistence."

"Precisely," Charly agreed. (Where had he heard the name Buonsarde?)

"Van de Wetering alternates between euphoria and despair," Buonsarde continued, holding up a finger, "and it is his failures which I enjoyed most, as he understood his failures and accepted them. Do you recall when he sneaks out to eat a steak?" Both men smiled at the memory.

"We fail at most thing, a condition of life," Charly said. "Like Icarus, we try to fly too close to the sun. We

22

try to—how you say—master things we have no business mastering. Like cloning that poor sheep."

Buonsarde shook his glistening dome. "If we succeed in understanding our failures, they are no longer failures. They become learning experiences. Good afternoon, Chef Poisson. I look forward to tonight."

Both men bowed and shook hands, and Charly held the back door as his newest customer sailed out into the snowy afternoon toward a large black Rolls-Royce. As Buonsarde approached the car, a man hurried from the driver's seat and opened the rear door, bowing Buonsarde inside.

"*Tiens,*" Charly said. "A man after my own heart."

"Who needs Sartre?" Julius said. "Who the hell is that man?"

"He's kind of scary, isn't he?" Benny asked.

"Just another rich bug, showin' off how important he is," old Mick muttered, and went back to his dishes. "Rolls-Royce, indeed," he snorted.

"His name is most familiar, but I do not recall where I hear it," Charly pondered. "About this man, I have the funny feeling, here." And he indicated his stomach. He cleared his throat. "Of course, we must not speak ill of our customer. Especially a new customer."

Friday Dinner at La Fermette

CONTRARY TO CHARLY'S FEARS, THERE HAD ONLY been two cancellations. At six o'clock customers began pouring into La Fermette. The restaurant was a stately Greek revival farmhouse, built over a century ago by a farmer who had taste as well as money. Back in the 1880s help was plentiful and cheap, and the farmer's wife had a baby a year, some of whom survived. When Charly had bought the spacious, derelict house and outbuildings some twenty-five years ago ("for nothing" as the real-estate agent assured him) the front door was hanging loose and bats roosted in the living room. Charly was charmed. His dream of owning a country restaurant was about to be fulfilled.

Rural New York state wasn't an area for late-night dining. This was farm country, now interspersed with car dealerships, snowmobile and lawnmower showrooms, tractor merchants and Agway stores. People rose at dawn, and six o'clock was the proper dining hour. (Seven o'clock was considered racy; eight o'clock decadent.) Furthermore, Charly's customers knew that he prepared a limited amount of food, and if you weren't on time, the Shrimps Charly would be gone. Weekenders who arrived after nine o'clock found that the kitchen was out of their favorites, if not out of food altogether.

Maurice Baleine's wife Barbara had decorated the restaurant in the current fashion, that is, to resemble an American's vision of an English inn: chintz and pale colors prevailed, with solid American antique sideboards and armoires. Huge urns were filled with flowers in the summer, greenery in the winter. Even the atmosphere was elegant, with Rigaud candles contributing to the air of luxe. Maurice, Charly's invisible partner, might be a ne'er-do-well, but his wife Barbara was a serious designer, and she'd made herself a nice reputation. La Fermette's decor was a good advertisement: it wasn't unknown for customers of Charly's to ring up Barbara and request "a living room like that lovely restaurant with the beautiful antiques."

The dining room and barroom walls were painted in pale apricot, flattering to ladies' complexions, and the tiny, individual table lamps sported pale pink bulbs and shades. The padded brown and pink chintz chairs were easy on ample bottoms, and the pine sideboards and armoires, and the herbal bouquets at each table, bespoke luxury. *Money has been spent . . . and for us*, the flattered customers thought as they dug into amply stocked plates.

Nouvelle Cuisine with minimalist portions might do well in the big cities, but Americans were grossly overweight because they loved to eat. "At Charly's, you always go home with a doggy bag," customers would brag. And if it cost a little more than other restaurants? Well, that was something to brag about, too.

Charly and his kitchen brigade worked nonstop preparing the Shrimps Charly, the *moules marinière,* lobster stew, grilled herbed chicken, that had become the restaurant's signatures. (No one ordered the veal kidneys in Madeira, so they went off the menu along with the calves' brains in black butter and the sweetbreads *financière.)* By adding a few lower-priced items to his menu of guinea hen, lobster, pheasant, salmon, and filet mignon, and becoming well known in the community by contributing to local charities, Charly had succeeded in his aim to attract the townspeople. Charly's lawyer, his stockbroker, his plumber, his purveyors of foodstuffs, all came from the area. And naturally they dined at Charly's. Ninety percent of his customers were acquaintances, if not friends. From his years in New York City Charly knew that city folk moved on to the newest "in" spot: loyalty was not their forte. Whereas the locals chose one or two restaurants

25

and stuck with them. He was proud of his crowded dining room, almost like a club, where friends visited between tables and shouted greetings across the room.

Elton Briggs, a waiter, hurried into the kitchen. "Table nine wants another order of Shrimps Charly, they're eating like it's their last meal on friggin' earth. Three baskets of bread, so far." This was Buonsarde's table. Ugo's tablemates, Charly decided as he peeked into his dining room, were bodyguards. Bulges in their jackets looked suspiciously like shoulder holsters.

"What are they drinking?" Charly asked.

"The bald guy's drinking Barolo, the other two guys are drinkin' Cokes."

"The expensive Barolo?"

"Yeah. Lobster stew for the boss, steaks for the—I think they're his headcrushers. I'm pretty sure that's Ugo Buonsarde, you know who he is."

"Tell me."

"He's the big mob guy across the river. Runs that country inn—which is also an illegal gambling joint, I'm told."

"Are you sure?"

Elton shrugged. "Not a hundred percent. But he looks like Buonsarde and there's a black Rolls in the parking lot and Mr. B drives a Rolls. And the two guys with him are carrying. How many guys come in here with guns sticking out of their armpits?"

At half past seven Charly went to his office and exchanged his soiled whites for a fresh jacket (from Dupont & Malgat on the Rue Coquillère in Paris, the Cartier's and Tiffany's of chefs' gear) and plopped a tall white toque on his head. He admired himself in the floor-length mirror: a noble brow, coal-black hair, and the pencil mustache that looked most debonnair. He looked exactly like what he was, he decided, as he preened a bit: a distinguished French restaurateur and chef.

Charly glided smoothly into his dining room and glanced over at table nine. Ugo and his men were still eating their entrees, he'd visit later. Tommy Glade, the barman, gave him a thumbs-up: all was well. Then Charly noticed Win Crozier (the heir to Crozier Plumbing Supplies) and Morty Cohen smiling at him. Win and Morty owned The Paint Barrel, the paint-and-decorating store, and Win was a great epicure, as you could tell from his girth. The gossip was that Win could have bought out all of Hogton from his Crozier Plumbing money, and that the store was merely a toy.

"Divine lobster." Win smiled. He and Morty were drinking a Châteauneuf-du-Pape. Or rather, Win was drinking and Morty was sipping, being neither a glutton nor a tippler. Both were dressed in turtlenecks and tweed sports jackets, their usual Friday-nights-at-Charly's attire.

"Yes," Charly agreed, "is good recipe. From Chef Reboul, who write *La Cuisinière Provençale,* the bible of the cooking of Provence. But we disagree on one point. Chef Reboul takes the coral and the tomalley and cook them separately in butter, then he, how you say, squiggle them"—Charly made motions of pounding in a mortar and pestle—"with even more butter, and spoon it on top of the dish. This I do not do." He knew that Win was flattered when Charly discussed the finer points of French cuisine with, as it were, a fellow gourmand. Win couldn't even boil an egg, so Morty said.

"What do you do with the tomalley and coral, then?" Morty asked.

"I cook them along with the lobster. They add much

27

richness. Of course, you must always ask for female lobster, since the coral is her eggs."

"Only female lobsters at our house from now on," Morty said. "Okay, Win? No boy lobsters, only girls."

"We'll make an exception for lobsters," Win agreed. "You can make us creamed lady lobster next week, Morty." Win leaned over and whispered to Charly, "I see that you have Buonsarde here. I've not seen him here before."

Charly whispered back, "You know Signor Buonsarde?"

"He buys all his paint from us. Not to mention silver wallpaper and gold leaf, for his Italian workmen to apply. He's got a huge estate."

"I hear," Charly hissed in Win's ear, "that he is Mafia."

Win pursed his lips and frowned. "Don't even think it," Win whispered back. "To us, he's merely a good businessman."

"He'll put business your way," Morty said. "An influential man."

So is the devil, Charly thought. "Wealth will respect wealth," an old saying of his Tante Jeanne's. He would get no truth from these two. Aloud he asked, "May I offer you a digestif of Poire Willem? With pear sorbet?"

Win the patrician smiled. "Most gracious of you, Charly. And did you get the message that we'll be here tomorrow night with two guests? People I knew in New York City years ago. Terrible thing happened, thieves raided their weekend house in Pennsylvania, took a lot of antiques."

"Horrible," Charly agreed. "Barbara tell me there is much theft of antiques recently. No one knows who. *Le grand mystère.* Yes, gentlemen, I have your reservation

28

for tomorrow night at half past six."

"Half past six," Win agreed. "Can we buy a small pâté tonight? We'll have it for lunch tomorrow, with Morty's onion soup and cheese and fruit."

Charly nodded. "I will tell the kitchen to pack one up." Charly moved off, then turned back. "Win, did you buy that washstand you told me about?"

Win beamed. "Yes I did, Charly, and it's a beauty. Shaker. You must stop by and see it. I've got it in the living room."

"I will, I will." Charly moved on. He glanced at table nine. Yes, they had finished. Charly walked up to the table and bowed. All of the plates were as clean as could be, and bread crumbs were scattered everywhere, which to a Frenchman is the sign of an enjoyable meal. "Gentlemen." Charly bowed. "You have enjoyed?" He smiled at the three men and wondered how many people they had murdered.

Ugo looked Charly in the eye and assumed the respectful pose of one eyeing a miraculous relic. His deep voice was reverent. "Not since the death of my dear mother, Chef Poisson, have I enjoyed such food," he declared, hand on heart. "This meal has been a dream." Ugo rolled his eyes heavenward, as if asking the Almighty to attest to this. Now he shook his head, indicating that mere words could not do justice to such a repast. "Such food," Buonsarde whispered, "is sacred."

Charly, whose opinion of his cuisine was fairly high, felt privately that this was gilding the lily, but playing the part of a sage, he nodded. *Another glutton,* he thought, *with whom I must discuss la cuisine.* "My food," Charly intoned, "is made from the finest raw materials available. Organic fruits and vegetables, grown without chemicals or pesticide. Fowl is range-run

29

and fed a diet of corn and other pure grains. Beef from Black Angus steers, grown naturally. Veal is from farm in Virginia, humanely raised and slaughtered. Fish is line caught. Only the best, Signor Buonsarde, for customer of La Fermette." Charly raised himself on tiptoe, puffed out his chest, and looked his customer in the eye. "Is good innocent food, treated with respect." (This speech had been polished over the years. He'd tried it out on Julius, recently. "What horseshit," Julius said. To which Charly replied, "You will see, Julius, when you have your inn. Is the horseshit which make the cash register go trinkle-trinkle.")

"Innocent food," Buonsarde repeated, and smiled. "This is the food that I grew up on, Chef Poisson. My parents had a garden. My mother spent her days cooking for her husband and sons. Her lobster was much like this one. And her tripe! Ah, Chef Poisson, her tripe."

"I am very fond of tripe," Charly replied. "Very few Americans like tripe. The next time I make Tripes à la Mode de Caen I will let you know."

Buonsarde beamed. "That would be excellent, Chef."

Charly bowed himself away from the table, his chest puffed proudly out. It was late. Benny, Julius, and old Mick were putting the food away.

"Signor Buonsarde, he like our food," Charly said.

"You give him your pure innocent foods speech?" Julius asked.

"*Oui.*"

"Innocence," Julius quoted, "is like a delicate exotic fruit. Touch it and the bloom is gone."

"A beautiful line," Charly said, "it is, I think, from Alfred de Musset."

Julius said, "It's from Oscar Wilde's *The Importance of Being Earnest.*"

30

"You are certain of this fact, Julius? *Un Anglais* said that?"

Julius was generally amused by Charly's chauvinism, but tonight he was tired. "No, you're probably right, Charly."

Later that night, a mad thought skipped across Charly's mind: Ugo Buonsarde was a gangster. Gangsters were usually murdered. His last best customer, also a gangster, Walter Maxwell, had tried to kill him. Would his friendship with Ugo Buonsarde end in a bloodbath? *"Tant pis,"* Charly muttered. "That is the nature of our business. We cook for the crook."

LOBSTER STEW

YIELD: 4 SERVINGS

4 1-½-pound female lobsters
4 tablespoons olive oil
4 tablespoons brandy, heated
4 cloves garlic, peeled and chopped
2 shallots, peeled and chopped
Pinch saffron threads (about ¼teaspoon)
2 cups tomatoes, peeled, cubed, and seeded
4 tablespoons parsley, chopped
2 cups dry white wine
1 cup fish stock or canned clam juice
Salt and freshly ground pepper, to taste

Kill the lobsters just before cooking by plunging a knife into their carapace where the body and the tail meet. Heat olive oil in a big pot. Cut lobster into pieces, remove sand sac, and sauté in olive oil until they begin to turn pink. Heat brandy and flame lobsters. Add remaining ingredients, bring to a boil, lower heat, and cook 10 minutes. Remove lobsters, reduce liquid 20 minutes. Remove coral and tomalley and mash with a fork. Add to stew. Season to taste with salt and freshly ground pepper.

Patty's News

IT WAS STILL DARK WHEN CHARLY AWOKE AT HALF past five Saturday morning, two cats on the bed, two cats in baskets in his little bedroom under the eaves. Charly's modest house, about two hundred yards from the restaurant, had been a farmworker's dwelling. Charly had the French peasant's horror of displaying his wealth for every scam artist to see, so he had made minimal changes to the outside. The clapboard was white, the shutters and trim dark green, unchanged in over a century.

Inside, however, Charly had permitted himself a few luxuries. Efficient central heating kept the house toasty warm, and the big hot-water boiler allowed Charly to soak in chin-high water in his six-foot tub. Old oriental rugs covered wide-board pine floors. French country furniture from Charly's hometown in France graced the rooms. There were Hermès towels, Porthault sheets, Baccarat crystal tumblers, and the heavy Daum crystal vases that the bourgeois French love. It was a comfortable house.

"Oh, oh, oh," Charly groaned as he stared at the electric clock that now registered five thirty-two. The cats were waking (*"Arrête-toi, Frère,"* to the old yellow cat who was sharpening his claws near Charly's head).

He reviewed today's program. Today was Saturday. There might be more snow. There would be lunch to prepare, probably for about twenty people. Dinners last night had numbered about fifty, a respectable number for a February Friday, and he was preparing food for two cocktail parties. Fred Deering and Max Helder, his

33

catering team, were arriving at ten to prepare the extra pâtés, salmon rillettes, smoked salmon roses, meatballs. Four sides of salmon gravlax were marinating. Not too busy.

Charly chuckled as he thought of Ugo Buonsarde. A gangster? An underworld chieftan? Perhaps. He really knew nothing about the man, and people loved to gossip. Better not to know, Win and Morty were right. Charly was a businessman. He didn't tut-tut over the morals of his customers, some of them gentle folk, others rednecks with fat wallets. Julius called these last "Cadillac white trash." Why should he worry about Buonsarde? At least Ugo didn't make a big pretense of being law-abiding or religious, and the pious bigots were the ones to watch out for: they told you how honest they were, complained about the food and service, wanted things for free, spoke loudly of their Christian heritage, and were poor tippers.

Next, Charly thought about Patty Perkins and her lover Weston Hinkley. True, he was a pillar of the community, and he offered security and perhaps love. But a small-minded man. Charly hoped that Benny was right, that Mr. Hinkley was being shown the door. Patty deserved better than that.

The clock registered five forty-one. Charly swung his legs over the side of the bed, toed into his sheepskin slippers, grabbed his woolen beret, and plopped it on his head—a deterrent to the deadly drafts that every Frenchman knows cause arthritis, lumbago, sciatica, sinusitis, colds on the stomach. He grasped the bottle of Dr. Bach's remedies and squeezed a dropperful onto his tongue—to help keep him mentally alert. He visited the toilet and made his way downstairs, preceded by four eager cats. The day had begun.

Charly brewed his Puerto Rican coffee extra-strong, and after three cups he felt sufficiently energized to face the day. He peered through his kitchen window into the darkness but could see only the grey-white of snow-covered fields. He opened his back door, let in the cats, sniffed the cold, metallic air, which indicated snow. "So, *mes amis*," Charly said to his cats as he spooned out their food, "the little mouse, she is asleep in her hole."

Later, after a bowl of Les Gaudes—cornmeal mush liberally laced with butter, salt, pepper, and red wine, a specialty of the Franche-Comté region of France—Charly ran a bubble bath. He lay in the bubbles and closed his eyes, making lists in his head—new chicken dishes he might try, new vegetable dishes. Last weekend three customers had asked the kitchen to make them vegetarian platters: Julius had layered a base of linguine noodles with grilled portobello mushroom strips, zucchini tossed with garlic and parsley, sautéed onions and sun-dried tomatoes. This was becoming a trend, perhaps: cooked and cooled cornmeal, for instance, could be sliced, sautéed, and topped with a tomato or mushroom sauce; a risotto of mushrooms and peppers was tasty, and puréed lentils made a handsome croquette.

Sunk in gastronomic musings, Charly used his toes to open the hot-water tap. The hot water was soothing to his arthritic legs and back. He lay in the hot water until his skin crinkled and his forehead sweated. Just as he was wrapping his big Hermès towel around his body, the telephone rang. Charly sprinted to his bedroom. It was Patty Perkins, and she was sobbing.

"Patty, Patty, what is wrong?" Charly imagined all sorts of horrible things, Benny dead on his motorcycle, the Perkins house burnt to the ground, Patty attacked by robbers, or perhaps Patty had been scolded by Wes.

"It's Amanda, Charly. She's dead." Patty sobbed and sobbed.

Silence from Charly. Who was Amanda? "Amanda?" Charly asked.

"Amanda Kendell, the lady who came to the restaurant yesterday, she was going to divorce her husband. She was driving to Massachusetts this morning."

"With the marks on her face where her husband hit her. *Bien sûr*. How do you know she is dead?"

"I called this morning to wish her a good trip," Patty said, sobbing, "she'd told me she wanted to be on the road at half past seven, so I called at seven."

"And?"

"And John Stark answered the phone. He said there'd been an accident and Amanda was dead. Looked like a suicide, a self-inflicted gunshot wound. He didn't want to talk about it."

"Tchah," Charly said reprovingly. "I cannot believe she kill herself."

"Of course she didn't, Charly. That awful husband of hers killed her. But John said she left a suicide note."

"A note," Charly lectured, "is easy to write. Of course the husband kill her. He put the properties in her name, he find out about the divorce, he kill her." Charly remembered his worry when he'd found out that Amanda had properties in her name. If that wasn't a perfect motive, what was?

"Oh, that poor woman, what can we do?"

"For the moment," Charly said, "nothing. There is nothing we can do."

Patty said, "John doesn't know the Kendells, he only

36

knows what he sees. I've got to find out more."

"We will both find out more," Charly soothed. He shut his eyes and saw Amanda standing in his kitchen in her pale clothes, with her little-girl ringlets and her white skin. He'd found her so unattractive, and now he felt guilty. Poor repellent lady, the forty-year-old girl. "We will talk more about this when you come in. You are coming in, this morning?"

"Yes," Patty said, still crying a bit. "I have to make the lemon curd for the tarts. And some more pear sorbet, and ice the cakes and cover the apple tarts with rum butter cream."

"Of course she did not kill herself," Charly said again. "Chief Stark is mistaken. The husband, he kill her. Have you met the husband?"

"A few times."

"And what is he like?"

"He's a big brute. Lots of money and Amanda says he's never sober."

Charly wondered what it would have been like to have pale, wan Amanda underfoot day and night. What had she done all day? What sort of sex life had she and the horrible husband had? She'd been such a passive person. The little-girl woman had turned him off. Had she cooked? Kept a beautiful house? He must question Patty closely. Arid there was another side to it. What sort of man would choose a woman like Amanda for a wife?

But to Patty, Charly merely said, "We must give the matter much thought. Is clear that the husband, he kill her. But we must find proof. Be assured, my dear Patty, that I will put my entire head to the process."

"Thanks, Charly. I always liked Amanda, and now that she's dead, I feel that she's got to find justice."

37

Charly drew himself up to his full height of five feet five inches and clutched at his towel. "I know, my dear Patty, *exactement* what you mean."

Conveniently Charly forgot that Chief of Police John Stark didn't welcome interference. And that the Sherlock Holmesian world where the amateur detective ran rings around the simpleminded police existed only in works of fiction. He hummed a little tune as he put on his layers of clothing. What a good thing the Kendells weren't customers. He would have no qualms about exposing the husband, that vile and cowardly murderer.

Charly Asks Innocent Questions

WHEN CHARLY ARRIVED AT THE RESTAURANT AT EIGHT o'clock Benny the punctual, dressed in his white chef's jacket and checked cotton trousers, was already there, molding hamburgers into the six-ounce softballs that had become a restaurant signature. It was a trick that Charly had picked up from The Jackson Hole in New York City, and though it took a long time for them to cook they looked most impressive on a toasted bun.

"Mom was so upset, I didn't want to stay home. What could I say? You know, Mom identifies with Mrs. Kendell. My dad used to drink."

Charly nodded. "Do you know this Mrs. Amanda?"

"Not really." Benny shrugged. "I knew she and Mom had been to school together. She's married to that weirdo, who beat her."

"Of course he beat her," Charly agreed. "Did you not notice her face yesterday? A big bruise near her eye that she try and cover up?"

Benny shrugged "No, I didn't notice. All that gunk women put on their faces, eye shadow and stuff, they all look bruised to me."

"Why do you call Kendell the husband a weirdo?"

"Well," Benny said, "nothing seems to hang together with him. He's got this big trucking company, drives a Jag XJ 12, I mean, you're talking bucks. But he looks like a bum, and he's got a reputation for forcing cyclists off the road. I'm on my bike, I see him coming, man, I move right over."

"But," Charly persisted, "what makes him a weirdo?"

Benny shrugged. "He's creepy. You ever see him?" Charly shook his head. "He's real big, six feet three or four, goes around two-fifty, looks like a killer moose. He's got this way of looking at you, like he's looking into some other world. Oh, and the guy stinks. Doesn't wash."

"In the cooking world, personal cleanliness is paramount."

"We ever smell in Tae Kwon Do, the master makes us take a shower. Or he throws us out. Says a clean mind is in a clean body."

"I understand," Charly continued, "he have a trucking business?"

"That's right. Kendell Transports. Over on Mill Road. You must have seen it. Big place with a lot of sixteen-wheelers parked all around."

"Do you know anyone who work there?"

Benny shook his head. "Oh, you know something else? Bobby Matucci told me Kendell sneezed once at the Steak Heaven bar and his false teeth—his upper plate—flew out and hit the bar. Bobby said no one dared laugh, everyone's scared of him. Now, Charly, your burgers are all done, I'm gonna cut some fries." The restaurant made its own french fries for lunch. They could never make enough. They were a big draw.

"Maybe I will visit this man—on a pretext which I must think up."

Benny rolled his eyes. Someday Charly was going to get himself killed. Look at that situation when Walter Maxwell nearly shot him. "Suit yourself, Charly." Benny believed that minding your own business was the only way to live. Charly, on the other hand, thrived on other people's business.

Old Mick the dishwasher came in. He, too, was questioned by Charly.

"Nope, don't know 'im, don't want to. Man's got a reputation as a tough customer. I steer clear of folks like that. You're lucky he's never come here for a meal. Old Etta at the diner? She says he didn't like his scrambled eggs once, threw 'em at her, plate and all."

"*Mon Dieu.* What did she do?"

"Made him pay for the plate, told him to get out, come back when he could behave hisself."

Charly thought the man sounded like a cross between the count of Luxembourg, who'd supposedly sold Joan of Arc to the English, and Dracula. Why had Amanda married him? She was so young and innocent. The money, probably. The ladies liked money, and that was a fact. And they liked to rub up against power and danger, too. A tall and powerfully built man would always attract a certain kind of woman. (Thought Charly the short, the plump, the gentle.)

Who else could Charly ask? Just then the telephone rang and it was Win Crozier. He'd gone for a walk early this morning through all that sparkling snow, and he'd felt so invigorated when he got back that he'd eaten nearly the entire pâté they'd bought to serve their guests for lunch.

"Mon Dieu," Charly said, shocked. "You will have the *crise du foie,* the crisis of the liver. This is a terrible thing, Win." Meat was rich and unhealthy, and charcuterie, or processed meats, especially so. Charly's father, Papa Jean, had been a *charcutier,* had his own shop, yet he only let his sons and daughters eat charcuterie on Sundays, once a week.

"That's probably true, Charly," Win said blithely. "But with sourdough toast and Morty's pepper relish, it was so delish I just couldn't stop. Morty's furious. Can we stop by this morning and get another one before we go to the shop? We're only open until noon today, it being Saturday."

"No, I don't know the man personally, but I hear he's a tough one," Win said. It was nearly nine o'clock, and Win and Morty were off to The Paint Barrel. Win had the new pâté in his hand. "I hear he's from Maine. Mrs. K's been in the store a few times, she's a poor creature."

"Poor creature?" Charly asked. "What do you mean?"

"Not to speak ill of the dead," Win said, lowering his voice. "But she wasn't very bright. She'd come in and say, for instance, 'I'd like to buy some paint.' So then we'd have twenty questions: what color, inside or outside, latex or oil-based, matte or shiny, how much did she need, really, it was tough going. She couldn't answer the simplest question."

"The husband, he used to beat her," Charly said.

"I hear he had another wife, and she died," Win whispered.

"A man of mystery."

Win continued, "Ask Joe Okun. He's from Maine,

too, and I think he knows Kendell. Joe does odd jobs around our place. You know Joe?"

"Sure," Charly said. "Once, when Mick is sick, he come and wash dishes. He is a nice man. Perhaps he drinks a bit. He break a lot of dishes."

"He's very careful, now," Win said. "He's been going to AA for over a year, and he doesn't drink a drop. He's a reformed character."

"Hmmm," Charly said, being suspicious of reformed characters.

"Once," Win continued, "I think Joe tried to get a job with Kendell, but it didn't work out, I don't remember the details, you could ask him."

"I could," Charly said. After Win left he made a couple of egg pies. First he cubed leftover potatoes and sautéed them in oil with chopped onion, a pinch of garlic, bell peppers, and Italian sausage. Then he stirred in beaten egg, and poured the mixture into two greased pie pans. Next, he decided, he would make more potato and leek soup. "Ah, Julius," Charly said as the back door opened. "*Comment ça va?* We have bad news."

Julius strode in, shaking snowflakes from his brilliant yellow down jacket. "Bad news, Charly? Another of your famous murders?

"*Oui.*"

"Mom's friend Amanda Kendell, she was in yesterday, remember, Julius?" Benny said. "Mom called her this morning, and . . . " Benny explained.

"You should open a detective agency on the side," Julius said.

"I do not have a license. Ah, here are Max and Fred. Some coffee, gentlemen?" Max Helder and Fred Deering, classmates of Benny's from Tae Kwon Do, cooked lunches at a local private school, which meant

42

that their evenings and weekends were free. Max was short, built like a bull, with straight black hair. Fred was slender, with a pink Nordic complexion and white-blond hair. Charly assumed that they were a homosexual couple (they lived together) but nothing was ever said, and the bourgeois French were reserved about sexual matters. *"Tout le monde a ses petites mouches,"* meaning, everyone has his little flies, or little mannerisms and habits.

"You're going to give Chief Stark an ulcer," Julius said, pouring coffee.

"Tchah, how you talk, Julius. Chief Stark is very grateful to me for catching the arsonist last fall."

"You nearly got yourself killed last fall," Julius accused. Then he looked out the window. "And, speak of the devil, here's Chief Stark right now. He's just getting out of his car."

"So that's the story," John Stark said. "Amanda Kendell was lying on her side of the bed, nightgown and robe on, looks like she'd stuck the pistol in her mouth, pulled the trigger. Note was lyin' on the table beside the bed."

Stark, sitting at the big pine table, sipped at his mug of coffee and bit into his apple pie. "The station got a call, oh, around three, I think, they called me at home, I got out to the Kendells' around half past. Matt claims he'd just got in from a dinner meeting in Albany, went upstairs, found his wife lying like that. Good pie, Charly."

"More coffee, Chief?" Charly placed a third slice of pie on Stark's empty plate, and pushed over the heavy cream. Stark must be tired, up since three.

"Yeah, Charly, just a drop. But what I'm here to ask, is about your impression of Amanda when she came

43

here yesterday afternoon. Patty says she was on top of the world. Husband says she was depressed. So what's your take? Was she depressed, or wasn't she?"

Charly was happy to give Chief John Stark of the Klover Police the benefit of his opinion. He waxed eloquent. "She was beginning a new life, Chief. She was in transports of happiness. Divorcing that husband who beat her, did you see the bruise mark near her eye? And going to live in Massachusetts, near her sister. But she made a grave mistake: she took the monies and property that the husband put in her name. For that he kill her."

"Yeah, right, Charly. But to get back to her being depressed. You say she wasn't depressed?"

"Not depressed, Chief Stark. Excited, pleased, happy, making a new beginning to her life, leaving the horrible husband, a woman on top of the world, a woman prepared to forge ahead . . ."

"Not depressed, then," Stark said, plunging into the torrent.

"My last word, Chief. Not depressed." And Charly made a small half bow, indicative of his subservience to the Chief of Police.

"I hope, Charly . . ." Stark looked at Charly, then looked away.

"Yes, Chief?"

"Oh, nothing." Asking Charly not to pry was like asking the sun not to come up. "Mrs. K has a history of suicide attempts, did you know that?"

Stark, a kind man, was nonetheless not displeased to see disappointment etched on Charly's face. Thinking of the evidence Charly had destroyed last fall—in his quest for justice—erased all charity from Stark's heart. Charly's shoulders drooped, his mouth turned down.

"Ah, I did not know."

44

"Once when she was a teenager, then about five years ago. Pills, both times. The first time her brother called the ambulance, the second time, her husband did. It's all down on the record."

"I see."

"Charly, please don't nose around You'll get everyone upset. Oh, hello, Patty, I'm just leaving. Great pie you made."

Charly drew himself up to his full height and threw out his chest like a general. "It would never occur to me to do such a terrible thing."

APPLE PIE WITH RUM BUTTER CREAM

YIELD: 9-INCH PIE

1 recipe pie crust for bottom of 9-inch pie shell
4-5 cups peeled and finely sliced Rome or other firm cooking apples
½ cup sugar
1 tablespoon cornstarch
½ teaspoon powdered cinnamon

Rum Butter Cream:

1 cup confectioners' sugar
¼ cup rum
4 tablespoons softened butter

Lay pastry on bottom of pie pan. Place apple slices in a bowl and toss with sugar, cornstarch, and cinnamon. When well combined, place apple slices in a pattern in the pie shell. Bake about an hour in preheated 350° oven. If crust starts to brown, cover pie with tinfoil. To make the cream, mix the confectioner' sugar, rum, and butter in a small bowl. Remove pie from oven when done and let cool 30 minutes, then cover with rum butter cream. With a soup spoon or spatula, drizzle cream over the apples. Let set 1 hour before cutting.

The Return of Maurice

"AND BETTY STARK WONDERS WHY JOHN'S GAINED SO much weight," Patty scolded. She was inspecting her apple pie with rum butter cream. There wasn't much left.

"Three piece only," Charly said defensively.

"Then we must have a pie-eating ghost in the kitchen, because when I went home last night this pie was whole."

"Chief Stark is not small. Naturally, the piece I give him"—Charly gave an elaborate shrug—"may have been a bit larger than normal."

"That's eighteen bucks the chief scoffed in five minutes."

"More like ten minute. Besides, is good policy to keep in with the police. Money well spent. The relations public."

"What did John say?"

"He say that Madame Kendell, she try to kill herself two time before, once as a child and once about five years ago."

"Oh, my Lord, Charly, I didn't know that."

"Well," Charly soothed, "it may not be true. And if it is, so what? You know, and I know, that the Mrs. Amanda did not kill herself."

"That's right, Charly. Oh, goodness." Patty was peering out the big window that looked onto the back parking lot. "There's a . . . it looks like a dark blue Mercedes pulling up just outside. That's Maurice's car, isn't it? But he's still in the Adirondacks, isn't he, at that drying-out place?"

Charly looked out the window. It was Maurice's car, all right. Charly looked glum. "I speak to Barbara yesterday, she tell me he has one more week. Ah, la la, Maurice . . ."

Charly inherited young Maurice Baleine when Maurice's father, Charly's original partner, died and left his shares to his son. As co-owner, Maurice, Junior, was entitled to half the profits. But he did virtually no work. After years of heavy drinking Maurice had succumbed to cirrhosis of the liver and a stay at a private sanatorium had been prescribed. Neither Barbara, Charly, nor any of the restaurant staff wanted him back.

Maurice strutted around braying advice, finding fault with everyone's work, suggesting menu items that Charly knew wouldn't work in the country, like fennel fondue, smoked beef rib, salsify flan. A Princeton man, a superior being, Maurice put everyone's back up. His job of greeting customers in the evening had long ago been taken over by Patty Perkins, since by six o'clock Maurice was too overcome by alcohol to do much welcoming.

The back door flew open and banged so hard that a rack of pots and pans shook. Mick sprang over to steady it.

"Hello, everyone, surprise! Surprise!"

Plump, jovial Maurice Baleine swept in, his expensive navy-blue overcoat dusted with snowflakes. Thinner, he would have been a handsome man. But now, small, piggy eyes were embedded in the fleshy face like raisins in round, pink dough, and Maurice's beautiful teeth (a triumph of the family orthodontist) shone white and even, framed by puffy grey lips.

"Maurice," said Charly, forcing a smile. "*Quelle surprise.* We do not expect you until next week."

48

"I told the quacks there was a family emergency and they agreed that I was as cured as I'd ever be. In remission, it's called. So I decided to come down and surprise you all. Not even Barbara knows. Aren't you surprised?"

"We are surprise," Charly admitted. "How pleased Barbara will be," he added dryly, knowing that Barbara did not relish Maurice's return.

"I just stopped in at the house, she's not there. Are we going to drink a glass of non-alcoholic champagne to celebrate my return?" Benny and Julius were looking dumbly at this apparition. Mick, at the sink, ignored them all.

"And what is this family emergency?" Julius wanted to know.

"Ah, my good Julius," Maurice took on a condescending air. "I am about to make the killing of all killings on the stock market. A gentleman I met at the sanatorium, an Italian count, has put me wise to a certain computer stock, and he's having a meeting at his—ah—duplex penthouse in New York tonight for potential buyers. I, of course, must attend. It is imperative."

When Maurice, Senior had bombed one more time on his dubious investments and the restaurant was heading for chapter eleven, thrifty Charly, Maurice's headwaiter, who had invested in sound blue-chip stocks, had bailed him out and become co-owner.

Perhaps it was fitting that Maurice, Junior, should be following in his father's footsteps. Even though old Maurice had begged Charly to take care of his son if he should die, Charly, could never forget the son's remark: "But, Daddy, he's nothing but a waiter." With old Maurice buried, Charly decided to close the restaurant and move to the country, and offered to buy out Maurice, Junior.

But like the proverbial albatross, Maurice hung around Charly's neck: wouldn't be bought out, followed Charly to the country, grumbling. He married Barbara, the plump and well-connected (read, rich) daughter of a local blueblood, Martha De Groot. Barbara, with her smart little plaid skirts, cashmere sweater sets, and Smith College education, might be too snobbish for the locals ("snooty De Grooty" she was called behind her back) but she and Maurice hit it off splendidly. Martha, no fool, was a respected antiques dealer, and after one look at Maurice she called her lawyer to establish a trust fund, thereby protecting the De Groot money. Maurice wasn't able to get his fingers on one penny. His lordly airs, his Mercedes, his expensive house designed by the noted Italian architect Carlo Penci (a college classmate), his Princeton diploma, had at first impressed the local folks, but now merely bored them. They finally saw what Charly could have told them all along: that Maurice was a supercilious ass. Barbara, starting a decorating business, had begun to see the true Maurice, as well.

"Now that's interesting," said Julius. "Are you going to confide the name of this Italian count?"

"It's no secret." Maurice smirked and smoothed down the lapels of his beautiful overcoat. "It's Count Ercole Antonio Buonsarde. He and I spent many hours at the sanatorium discussing investments. He had a bit of a drinking problem, but that's over. He has a seat on the stock exchange."

Silence. Then Benny dropped a knife, and Julius made a strangling sound that might have been a laugh. "Tony Buonsarde?" Julius said. "Tony Fingers, the old mob enforcer? *Tony Fingers?"*

Maurice bestowed a patronizing smile. "Count Buonsarde, who lived on the family estates in Sicily for many years, came to the United States about fifteen years ago and founded a brokerage house. I don't know who this Tony Fingers is, but it has nothing to do with my friend the count."

Julius said, "I see," in a disbelieving tone.

Maurice turned on Julius: "You're simply annoyed that I don't use you as my broker. I don't need a broker. I did a lot of work on my holdings while I was at the spa: I sold Comco at forty-four and one-eighth, and I bought it for twenty-four. I sold Avgo at fifty-four, bought it for thirty-four—and all the money's going into this computer stock."

"Compu Class A," Julius said.

"Yes, that's right. I'm not surprised you've heard of it. Compu Class A. So what do I need a broker for, eh, Julius?" Maurice rocked back on his heels, hands in trouser pockets, his superior smile in place.

"Of course you don't need a broker, Maurice," Julius said smoothly. "You probably don't need a dentist, either, you could fill your cavities yourself with bubble gum. But I'll give you this advice, for free: the Securities and Exchange Commission is keeping a very close eye on Tony Buonsarde's company, and on Compu Class A, as well."

"Ridiculous," Maurice snorted. Now his face reddened with anger and his plump cheeks quivered as he drew himself up to his full height of five feet ten. He still had to look up to tall Julius. "My friend, you don't know what you're talking about. This is all so much nonsense. You're jealous, that's all."

Charly cleared his throat. "We have a busy day ahead

of us, Maurice, two parties we are providing the food for, and a lot of reservation, and now that you are well, you will be expected to do your share. So go home and change, and we will put you to work. There is much to do, and you are, after all, co-owner." Maurice affected not to hear.

"As co-owner," Charly continued, his voice hardening, "you are expected to do half the work if you are to receive half the profits. We have carried you for months while you were—ah—ill, but now you are well."

Since Maurice had never worked a day in the kitchen in his life, it seemed improbable that he would start now, but Charly was disgusted. Mainly with himself, for keeping Maurice on. Maurice had to go. Out of affection for his deceased partner Charly had allowed the Maurice business to simply jog along. No more. "Equal pay for equal work, Maurice. No pay for no work. Like the man in the American history book who say, 'If you don't work, you don't eat.' *Monsieur le capitaine Jean Schmidt.*"

Maurice started to say something but the look in Charly's eye put him off. "I'll go home and unpack," he muttered.

"You can help the caterers after lunch," Charly suggested, "then be back here at five to go over dinner specials, before you greet the customers at six."

"I told you, Charly, I have to be in New York tonight." Maurice hurried off before Charly could say anything else. The back door slammed shut.

Julius widened his eyes. "Oh, my Lord, I just made the connection. Buonsarde, that name was familiar but I couldn't think why. Ugo, your customer last night, and Tony fingers must be related. Ugo's the mob's

52

godfather up here, and Tony Buonsarde, whose money came from the Sicilian Mafia, so the story goes, runs the mob's investments on Wall Street. The SEC's finally figured out that the mob has infiltrated the stock exchange, and Buonsarde and Company is one of their chief movers."

Charly threw up his hands. "Mob, no mob, I do not care. Maurice will have to go. I am disgust."

"When that guy's around, I mess up everything," Benny said, holding up onion rounds that were much too thick. "He makes me so mad."

But it was old Mick the dishwasher who had the last word: "I can't stand that man."

Charly Visits Steak Heaven

SATURDAY LUNCH WAS QUIET, AND AT HALF PAST ONE Charly was sitting at the bar ("the longest bar in Van Buren County") of Rex Cingale's big log cabin restaurant, Steak Heaven. He was sipping an espresso and talking to Rex's nephew Bobby Matucci. Bobby leaned over the bar, speaking in a low voice, not wanting the other patrons to hear. Occasionally he swiped at the bar with a none-too-clean towel.

The bar was still crowded, the jukebox blaring a country-western song about unrequited love; a big television showed a basketball game. The smoke was thick enough to cut, and the odor of stale beer and alcohol was powerful enough to knock you down.

Out of the corner of his eye Charly glanced at the man sitting near him, a bruiser whose fleece-lined denim jacket was open to expose a belly the size of a watermelon. The man was drinking a Van Buren County favorite, a schooner of beer with a Kahlua chaser. Charly shuddered and glanced around the big dark room.

Plastic swags of greenery left over from Christmas festooned the barroom's pine paneling. Strung amid the greenery were winking lights, and the garlands were further enhanced with plastic cutouts of Rudolph the Red-Nosed Reindeer, the red nose a blinking electric bulb. Charly could hear the *ping-ping* of the old-fashioned cash register as Bobby or one of the other two bartenders rang up a sale. It rang constantly.

The room's decor was so horrible that Barbara Baleine, Charly's stylish decorator, would have fainted dead away, but it was cheerful and Charly enjoyed his visits to Rex's place. Maurice called Steak Heaven "the armpit of Van Buren County" but so what? Nothing wrong with armpits.

"You make the best espresso in town, Bobby," Charly flattered. He shifted his buttocks on the well-padded stool at the end of the long U-shaped bar, as far away from the television set as he could manage. Most of the bar's population were intent on the game. Periodically the swinging kitchen door at the top of the U opened and a voice would shout, "Pickup, pickup," while the aroma of fried meat and sizzled onions burst through the cigarette smoke. The bar specialty was the Hamburger Deluxe Platter—two burgers, french fries, sliced tomatoes, onion rings, a dill pickle, coleslaw, potato salad: a tremendous value at $4.95. The bar was going full bore: it was Saturday, and the patrons had no desire to brave the pelting snow. They were guzzling their suds as if their lives depended on it. "Delicious, Bobby."

Charly smacked his lips at the strong coffee.

"Yeah," Bobby said glumly. "So everyone says." Bobby turned sideways and eyed himself in the bar's back mirror: black jeans, a black cowboy shirt trimmed in silver bands, the Elvis haircut that was the rage among the town's movers and shakers. Bobby was Mr. Cool. But not Mr. Happy, today.

"Your Uncle Rex, he stop in to see me," Charly ventured.

"He tell you what happened?" Bobby slapped at the bar with his towel.

"Well," Charly hesitated. "He say you have troubles."

"Everyone's pickin' on me," Bobby whined. "Just because my brother's a police officer, I should be perfect? Rex says I'm a bum."

"Tchah," Charly said. Bobby *was* a bum. Good-looking, likable, cheerful . . . but when your sole ambition is to win the lottery and make a killing on the horses and at poker, you might come off as less than serious.

"People are unkind," Charly offered.

"Unkind? Jeez, I mean, I had a little run of bad luck. Everyone has a little run of bad luck sometimes, am I right?"

"Right," Charly agreed.

"You know what I think?" Bobby took Charly's empty cup and spooned more coffee into the espresso machine's little tray. "I think it's in my stars. You know? Like, I should see one a' them, whaddaya call 'em, astrologists."

"Not a bad idea, Bobby. Many businessmen do just that."

"No kidding. You ever been?"

"Oh, yes." Charly nodded. "The stars have much to

do with our lives."

"And my mom"—Bobby poured out a fresh cup, set it in front of Charly—"she's cryin' all over the place, says she can't face the rest of the family, like I'm some fuckin' criminal. Bad luck is all it was."

"Bad luck, yes," Charly agreed.

"First, the horse. I was told by—well, let's say on very good authority—that the nag, at eighteen to one, was a shoo-in, a winner."

"A banana race," Charly said knowledgeably. "The race, it is fix."

"Yeah, right. But them jokers, they get caught. 'Oh, just a few herbs, Inspector,' they say. Sure, like ephedrine, comes up positive in the spit box."

"Bad luck," Charly repeated.

"And then the poker. The run a' cards I had, bad, really bad. I hadda get out from under, know what I mean? I didn't know the guys across the river were mob, honest. Rex, for Christ's sake, you'd think he'd understand, have more sense of *famiglia*."

Charly sipped the good coffee. "You ever meet Ugo Buonsarde?"

Bobby grinned. "Ugo? He stopped in here yesterday afternoon for about twenty minutes. Sits at the bar, looks around. I look out the window, see his two goombahs standin' by his big black car. I come over, I say, 'What can I get you, sir,' like he's a stranger, he just shakes his head. Like, I'm too low to even talk to. So I move to the other end of the bar."

Charly sipped. "He say nothing?"

Bobby shook his head. "Ugo sits and sits, and finally he gets up and leaves. Not one fuckin' word. So I guess you could say I've never met him. Nah, guy I do business with, guy who runs the inn, his name's Carlo

Calamare. Rex says if Carlo ever shows his nose over here, he'll piss in the guy's pasta. I hear Carlo's a really revengeous person."

"That sound serious," Charly said.

"But, I'll tell you something about Carlo. He's got a fuckin' beautiful daughter. A knockout. This gal, I look at her, my knees get all weak. Kimberly. That's her name. Kimberly. Isn't that beautiful?"

"Beautiful. Are you courting this young lady?"

"Not exactly," Bobby sighed. "I've hung out with her, you know, over there. She's my kind of woman. But her dad, see, he's very strict. And I don't think he likes me much, at this moment in time."

Charly drew himself up. "Remember this, Bobby. The course of love, it never run smooth." He raised his index finger: the teacher. "But true love, it cannot be denied. If it is destined to be, it will bloom, despite all ob-sta-cle."

"That's a very beautiful thought, Charly."

Charly laid some bills on the bar. "Good luck, Bobby. And thank you."

As Charly reached his snow-covered red van in the Steak Heaven parking lot, Rex Cingale's big grey Lincoln pulled up. The window on the driver's side rolled down and Rex stuck his head out. "Hey, Charly, good news. I just come from Angie Vongola's, you know, my lawyer, and he says not to worry, Bobby can't give his shares over, I gotta have first refusal."

"Very good, Rex. I am please for you."

"So that lets me off the hook."

"And what will happen to Bobby?"

Rex shook his head impatiently. "Aw, fuck him, the little squirt. He knows what I think of the mob, I've told you before, they're an insult to every Italian-American.

57

Someone mentions Italians and right away people think, ta-da, the Mafia, you know? Hey, and something else Angie made me aware of: if I pay off Bobby's debt, you know what'll happen?"

"But, yes, Rex. Bobby will do it all over again. I told you that."

"Fuckin' A, Charly. You got it pegged exactly correct. Bobby's got the brains of a fuckin' stone."

"I agree, Rex. But you must remember, Bobby is family. And his brother is a respected policeman. And the men who come to your bar, they like to talk to Bobby. He has a nice way about him, always friendly, always happy."

"You tellin' me I should pay? Ten thousand clamolas?"

"No, no, Rex. But we must think about it. We must reflect."

"Two cancellations, Charly," Julius announced as Charly walked into his warm kitchen, noting with approval the shiny copper pots and the gleaming white tile. "I'm only going to marinate two racks of lamb and four orders of chicken breast."

"Yes, yes, Julius, that is wise. Now, tell me about this business with Maurice. The stock that he is going to buy from the man Buonsarde."

"Anthony Buonsarde, according to the rumors I've heard, used to be known as Tony Fingers. He was an enforcer for the New Jersey mob, and he used to break the fingers of people who couldn't pay their loans. The story is, he moved to Sicily as a young man, I think the feds were after him here, then he came back some fifteen years ago with bags of money. He started a firm called Buonsarde and Company and they've made a

58

pile. The gossip is that he's being bankrolled by the Mafia in Sicily."

Charly looked nervous. "Where you hear this from?"

"Well," Julius said with a shrug, "it's just gossip, you know. But that's what's being said. I wouldn't touch the firm, personally. The SEC doesn't look kindly on Buonsarde and Company. They recently bought up a lot of shares in a little high-tech computer firm called Compu Class A in Ohio. The story—and again, Charly, it's just hearsay—is that Tony's company will wait until the shares get a little higher, maybe push the price way up by getting a lot of people to buy, then Buonsarde will sell out and the shares will drop. They've pulled this before."

"And Maurice, he does not know this?"

"Obviously not. You heard him say he never uses a broker, so he doesn't hear all the stories going round the brokerage business. I also heard that Tony had a little drinking problem and he went up to a spa in the Adirondacks to dry out. So it's clearly the same man. He pretends to be an Italian count, and that impresses the hell out of innocents like Maurice."

"And Maurice loses his money," Charly sighed. "I ask my investment man Jimmy Houghton about Compu Class A, he say, do not touch it."

Benny came into the kitchen, stamping his feet. "Forecast says snow's stopping this afternoon," he told them. "So you're all set for tonight."

"Is still coming down," said Charly, peering outside. He went into the dessert room, where Fred and Max were working on the cocktail party appetizers. "Everything hokay, gentlemen?"

"We're all set, Charly. Almost ready to roll. We'll pack the van at four, leave by half past, a little early, but

59

we want to allow plenty of time in case the roads are slippery. Both houses are off Route 32. You going to drive?"

"I will drive," Charly said, "and I will help unload. I like to speak to customer. Little personal touch. Show that I care." It also allowed Charly to collect his money over and above the deposit that had been paid when the contract was signed.

"Of course, Charly. When we're done here, we'll help Julius and Benny with dinner, until it's time to load. You going to stick around?"

Julius said, "Everything's pretty much done, Charly. The crab bisque, onion soup, entrees are all ready to go, and Patty's done the desserts."

"Then," Charly decided, looking at the clock, "I think I run over to old Doc Ross. Take him some soup, cold ham, little rice pilaf, little dessert. I want to ask him some question. I call, now, make sure he is there."

Doc might be old, but he had a good memory for Van Buren County scandals, old gossip that might date back twenty, thirty years or more. And his head was screwed on right. Old Doc knew who was who and what was what.

Old Doc Ross Undergoes an Examination

CHARLY DROVE CAUTIOUSLY DOWN ROUTE 65 UNTIL he came to County Route 18—some three miles. The roads were gritty with sand. The snow had stopped falling and the fields were white with brown stubble sticking through, the tops of wild grasses and flowers, dried and scattering their seeds for the coming spring season. *Just two more months,* Charly thought. He recalled the old saying, "Snow is the poor man's fertilizer," so he couldn't entirely condemn the white stuff.

Charly turned right on County Route 18. Another mile brought him to Ross Road, where he turned left, and drove past two fields to the old stone Dutch house belonging to retired Dr. William Ross.

It was a rough fieldstone one-story farmhouse surrounded by low stone walls, typical of the eighteenth-century Dutch houses built in the area, three miles from the Hudson River where Hendrick Hudson had sailed in 1609, looking for a passage to the Orient and the lucrative spice trade. Charly smiled. Spices and herbs were again being used as medicine. All the old peasant medications, the chamomile and valerian teas to help you sleep, the bearberry for urinary infections, the sage used as a blood purifier, the comfrey leaves to blanch and place on sprains and bruises. All coming back. Perhaps they'd never left, only pushed aside by the gluttonous drug companies that craved more and more money, so often at the expense of people's health.

The stones used to build old Doc's house were free building materials found in the fields, as opposed to the bricks of the gentry that had to be imported in those days. They were held together by a mixture of clay and horsehair, or chopped straw, whatever was available. The house was a sturdy rectangular box with additional boxes added over the years. It had been built by Doc's ancestors. The lintel stone was roughly inscribed *Jacob Ross 1793.*

Doc's wife Alma, active in the garden club, the historical society, and other local groups, had died some years before, not of cancer but of the radiation therapy that had seared and paralyzed her thorax so that she had to eat mush with a tube down her throat. It had been a horrible death and Doc, in consequence, had turned against the medical profession.

Alma, Doc claimed, could have gotten over her cancer. But the radiation burns, "worse than Hiroshima," were there for the rest of her life, which mercifully was a short one. After the funeral Dr. William Ross filled eighteen garbage bags and boxes with medical equipment and carried them to the dump. He practiced medicine no more.

Now Doc lived alone in his tidy, dusty house, eighty-eight years old, a clean, white-haired old man with his own teeth and most of his hair, who dined at Charly's once or twice a month. Lizzy Roland, Patty Perkins's mother, came over to "do a cleanup" every few months, to dust, polish the silver picture frames that held photographs from birth to young manhood of Will and Alma's only son Willy, who had died in Vietnam. "Two needless deaths, the result of so-called progress," Doc would often say bitterly.

Charly got his box of food from the van and brought it to the front door. He was about to knock when the door opened.

"Now, this is neighborly," Doc said, as always, as Charly carried the box to the kitchen. "Want a cup of tea?"

"No, no, Doc, thank you, I must hurry back." Doc's tea was as black as coffee, so strong it gave Charly indigestion and he'd have to take some Nux Vomica homeopathic pills, or perhaps some Carbo Vegetabilis. "But," Charly added, "there are one or two thing I would like to ask you. May I?"

"Of course, of course. I was just going through some of my old files. So many patients dead and buried. That's what happens when you're my age."

"Among your files," Charly asked, "is there the name Buonsarde?"

Will Ross chuckled. "Of course. I took care of the old people for years. Papa Buonsarde was a real, old-fashioned gangster. He catered to everyone's vices—gambling, prostitution, bootleg gin during Prohibition. He made a pile of money. Hogton was a wide-open town in those days. All the bad boys came up on the train, looking for wine and women and carousing."

"Do you know his sons?"

Doc led the way into the sitting room and he and Charly sat. "Papa Buonsarde had two sons, Ugo and Antonio. They both went to college, bright youngsters. Papa wanted to give them every opportunity to better themselves. But they didn't, they stayed in the business."

"Unlike me," Charly mused. "I often wonder what life would be like if I had stayed in Lons-le-Saunier and become a *charcutier,* like my father."

Doc smiled. "Who's to say, Charly? Well, anyway, those two boys . . . Ugo stayed up here and worked with his father, but Antonio, a sneaky lad as I recall, had words with his father, and went down to New Jersey, to work with another branch of the family. The Mafia, they call it now, or the mob, but whatever they call them, they were just gangsters. Then Antonio scooted off to Italy and that's the last I heard of him."

"The name Tony Fingers? Does it mean anything?"

"No, Charly, it doesn't. Well, Ugo stayed in the Catskills. I think he still runs the rackets, but I never hear a thing. It's all kept very quiet. Papa Buonsarde

63

was a good teacher: never have anything in your name, have everything run by other people, and if they get caught, your hands are clean. Or at least, seen to be clean."

Charly said, "I hear Antonio have a brokerage house in New York City. But tell me this, Doc: if the Buonsardes are gangsters, why would Antonio have the company in his name?"

Doc smiled. "Family pride, Charly. To many poor people, the Buonsardes were heroes. Like Robin Hood. They took money from rich gamblers, men who wanted booze and floozies, and helped poor people. I know a couple of Catholic churches that were kept going on Buonsarde money. They sent kids to college, helped widows. They made money from the world's gluttons, and spent it wisely. Good folks."

Charly nodded. "They sound *sympathique.*"

"Oh, they were. Old Papa Buonsarde sent me a big Smithfield ham every Christmas. He sent out hundreds of hams."

"So, Doc, you know little about the sons Ugo and Antonio."

"Very little, Charly. But the old folks . . . oh, my, I'd walk into their kitchen, and Mama would be standing at the stove, cooking. Veal knuckles simmering in white wine and tomato sauce all day, and pork that melted in your mouth, and white beans cooked with dandelions and garlic, it was grand. They were healthy, too. Mama had bursitis and weak ankles, and Papa had gallstones, but apart from that, they were fit. They used me because I never asked questions. Sometimes there were men with gunshot wounds to dress, they had what amounted to an army over there. They trusted me."

"But," Charly persisted, "you did not know the sons

very well."

"I didn't like Antonio, I can tell you that. Mr. Know-it-all, always knew best. And he was a snob, looked down his nose at me, at all country folk. He was just like your partner Maurice. A nasty piece of work. Ugo was just like his dad, quiet, probably tough, but outwardly a gentleman."

Charly told Doc about Buonsarde and Company, and what Julius had said.

"Done all the time, Charly. Why, I knew an old medico, used to summer on Block Island, where Alma and I used to go. An old politician had done the same thing to him. He'd saved the man's life, and the guy gave him a hot tip, to buy a certain stock. Well he did, and he lost his shirt. The politician got all his friends to buy, and then he sold out. What do you think about that? To do that to the doctor who saved his life?"

"Greed is wonderful, Doc," Charly said. "It keep us on our toes. Now, where would the medical profession be without greed? The drug companies sell medications which are so strong they have terrible side effect, so then the doctors have to treat all the side effect. Is a brilliant strategy. Of course sometime the strategy backfire, like Alma."

"I can't tell you how many people suffer from the ill effects of medications," Doc declared bitterly. "You're right. It's keeping the medical profession booming. And the medicos, they're well aware of it. Oh, yes."

Charly cleared his throat. "Now, Doc, another name. Matthew Kendell. Does that name mean anything to you?"

"No. Charly, it doesn't. But hang on a minute, I'll look through my files. I'm glad I saved them from the dump, I enjoy looking through them. He might have

65

come in once or twice and I forgot about him."

Doc shuffled into his little study. Charly sat in the comfortable living room and admired the furnishings: an old, cracked leather couch, but obviously of good quality. Two solid wing chairs on either side of the fireplace, with faded chintz slipcovers. A heavy walnut coffee table in front of the couch covered with newspapers, magazines, and medical journals. An elegant Federal mirror above an old four-drawer maple chest, also covered in medical magazines. Doc still kept up with his old profession. Three dark paintings on the walls, two of the Hudson River (in fall and spring) and one of cows in a pasture. Charly liked the one of the cows: they looked out from the painting, their eyes meeting yours, placidly chewing their cuds. They appeared to be at peace with their environment.

"Hah, found it." Doc shuffled back to the couch, holding an index card in his hand. "Let's see, now." He adjusted his glasses, held the card up to the light, at arm's length. "Card dated September seventeenth, 1977. Matthew Kendell. Came to me to treat cuts and scratches all over his arms. Said he was cutting brush and got scratched by thorns." Doc put the card on the coffee table and ran his hand over his face. "Now, isn't that funny. Looking at that card, I can see the man as if it were yesterday. Gave me the shivers, he did."

Charly leaned forward attentively. "Why, Doc?"

"Big man. Rough. Not a gentleman like Papa Buonsarde. Showed me his arms, all covered with scratches, looked horrible. Some were infected. And I remember thinking to myself, *You never got those scratches clearing brush, son.* I don't know why I thought that, but I did. At any rate, I could tell he was lying. Liars always have a funny way of looking at you, tryin' to see if you've bought their lies."

Charly chuckled. "Liars are wonderful, because they always believe the lies that others tell, they think they are the only ones who tell lies. I have had much practice with liars."

"Yes, well, I cleaned him up, gave him a shot of penicillin, told him to come back in a week if they hadn't cleared up. Never saw him again. But around about that time I read in the papers Kendell's wife had been found, drowned, been in the water a week or so. Papers said she must have fallen off his boat, they had a big motor launch moored in Hogton harbor. Now, you know what I thought then? And still think?"

Charly nodded. "Of course, of course. You think he push the wife in the water, and she scratch him trying to get away."

Old Doc put his finger aside his nose and wrinked. " 'Course I tolid the cops, for all the good it did. The old police chief, he'd accept money from anyone. This Kendell feller probably gave him a buck or two not to look into it. At any rate, I never heard another word about it. Now, Charly, why do you want to know all of this?"

Charly explained about the Buonsardes, and about Amanda Kendell.

"Wonderful." Doc slapped his thigh. "Who needs the movies? Well, I know this Amanda girl. At least, I think I do. Maiden name Winlove?"

Charly nodded. "You know everyone, Doc."

"Well, Charly, a doctor did in those days. Weren't that many doctors around. We didn't make much money, and the hours were long. Not at all like the medical profession today. Why, doctors are millionaires, today."

"Yes, yes, Doc," Charly agreed, hoping to forestall a

67

diatribe against the medical profession. He didn't like doctors either, but now he was after facts.

"Well, now, Amanda. Poor little mite, came from a rotten family. They lived down by the old dump, Trashtown, they called it, because the people used to pick through the trash. Can't do that now, of course. Why, one time, one of my patients gave me the most handsome rocking chair . . ."

"Amanda, Doc. If you please."

"Yes, Amanda. They had one of those unpronounceable Polish names, or maybe it was Ukrainian, you know, Wojiskolava, something like that. When the father died—of drink, I might add—the mother took up nursing again, she'd been a nurse before she married, and she changed their name to Winlove, hers and the two kids, Amanda and Gregory."

"Yes, yes, Doc. And the children? Do you remember about them?"

"Don't rush me, Charly. My memory is unfolding. Let's see. The girl, Amanda, she was kind of slow, I think she finally dropped out of school. Used to have a lot of colds, sinus trouble, that's what I treated her for. All nerves, I thought. And the boy?" Doc shook his head.

"Why do you shake your head, Doc?"

"Well, that boy. He was a strange one. Nowadays, everyone's big on giving names to things. He'd be described as a narcissist, I read an article about that just the other day. Narcissistic personality disorder. So self-important, the boy was. He was the king, and everything had to revolve around him."

"It sound like Maurice," Charly said.

"No, Maurice is an egotist. Greg was worse. One time, boy was just a little fella, about ten, I'd guess, his ma called me, scared to death. The child was hanging from a tree, cord around his neck, but also around his chest. He was passed out, blue. We got him down, revived him, he said he was trying to get into another psychic dimension, something he'd read about."

"Like the Eskimos," Charly said, and surprised Doc by adding, "the Danish explorer Peter Freuchen, he talk about that."

"I thought," Doc mused, "you only read stories about Frenchmen."

Charly shrugged. "Sometimes I read about others. The French are not the only interesting people on this earth."

"Hmmm," was all Doc said to that. "But to continue, Charly, there's a strange sexual practice where you hang yourself in order to have a really spectacular orgasm—or so it's said. Called autoerotic asphyxia. The old missionary position was always good enough for me, so I can't vouch for it. I wondered if that was what the boy was trying to do. I thought he was kind of young for sexual explorations."

"Maybe, maybe not," Charly said. "The young can surprise us. But what is this boy like now? He is a grown man."

"Don't know, Charly. Haven't seen the boy, or the girl, for that matter, in, oh, I'll bet twenty years. Greg's mother died when he was in high school. He used to visit her in the hospital, and he was caught stealing drugs. He'd gotten the keys of the drug room out of his mother's pocket. First they accused her, then she told them it must have been the boy. Well, sir, a few days later, the mother was found dead of an overdose of something. I always thought the boy had killed her, and so did the cops, but—no evidence."

"How could he get the keys without his mother's

knowing?" said Charly, the pragmatist.

"Oh, who knows, Charly. Maybe she put the keys in one of those lab coats with pockets, took it off, and forgot about the keys. I don't know. They sent him to reform school for stealing drugs, then, I suppose, he eventually got out, but I never saw him again."

Charly was disappointed. He'd hoped to learn more. "How did he get along with his sister, Doc?"

"Huh," Doc said. "There was something . . . Oh, yes, once the girl came to me, terrible attack, like asthma, couldn't breathe, but she'd had no history of asthma. She was wheezing something awful. Finally I got out of her that her brother had sprayed her in the face with insecticide. They were both in their teens, twelve, fourteen, like that, in other words, Gregory knew better. Well, he admitted it all right, said it was just a joke. Some joke. But I think he was trying to kill her."

Maurice Goes to the Big Apple

MAURICE BALEINE PARKED HIS MERCEDES IN AN underground garage just off Madison Avenue. The drive down to New York City had taken over three hours because of the snow, but he'd allowed for that. He walked up to Madison and Eighty-eighth, and smiled as he entered Count Antonio Buonsarde's stately apartment building.

"Your name, sir?" The old doorman consulted a list on a clipboard.

"Baleine, Maurice Baleine, Junior." Maurice hummed a little tune.

"Yes, sir, you're expected. Elevator's on your left, just inside."

"Of course, of course," Maurice said, implying he'd been here before.

A butler in a black suit opened the elevator door and Maurice walked directly into the penthouse foyer. The servant took Maurice's coat and scarf. The living room was crowded with perhaps twenty men, all dressed, as Maurice was, in dark, well-tailored suits. The air was heavy with cigar and cigarette smoke.

Beyond the room, wide glass doors opened onto a spotlit terrace massed with fir trees dripping snow and winking white lights. Maurice, who ignored such sights upstate, was struck by the beauty of this urban forest. In the living room the forest theme continued with tall urns holding boughs of pine and spruce covered in the same tiny white lights.

"A drink, sir?" A waiter offered cocktail franks with mustard.

"Perrier with lime, please."

Almost immediately, the drink materialized.

"Ah, Maurice, my dear friend. How good, how very, very kind of you to join us." Antonio Buonsarde, short and swarthy, his large head topped by a mane of white hair, clapped Maurice on the shoulder, since Maurice's two hands were engaged in holding his glass and manipulating the sausage, trying not to drop mustard on the silky oriental rug.

"You know I wouldn't miss it, Count." Maurice loved Buonsarde's accent, a rich brew of BBC English with the continental overlay of Italian, plus the plummy notes of the professional diplomat. Antonio sounded as if he were speaking through a mouthful of custard: a rich, cultured voice.

"So, you like my little pied-à-terre?" The count indicated the room and the mirrored dining room beyond with a sweep of his arm.

"Handsome," Maurice answered. "I especially admire the tapestry."

It was an elaborate hunting scene hung above one of the grey velour couches depicting short, squat dogs, teeth bared, cornering a profusely bleeding stag. The dogs bore a singular similarity to the count.

"Ah, you have excellent taste, my dear Maurice. A memento from my farm near Palermo. I have a matching tapestry in my apartment in Rome, and another, smaller one in my flat on Sloane Square in London."

Maurice nodded as if he, too, had pieds-à-terre dotted about the globe.

Buonsarde became brisk: "Well, my friend, you are the last to arrive, so we'd better get on with our little meeting." He clapped his hands for silence.

"If you will all be seated, gentlemen."

Since the two couches and the easy chairs were all taken, Maurice sat on a folding chair by the terrace door.

Buonsarde cleared his throat. "My dear colleagues and friends. It is a privilege for me to entertain you this evening, to offer you not only my hospitality but also my humble Wall Street expertise. Oh, yes"—the count held up his index finger in a pedagogic gesture—"I have been trading stocks for well over forty years, I will not tell you precisely how many as you might guess my age." There was appreciative laughter. "And I must tell you that Compu Class A, this stock which began so humbly, is climbing, climbing, climbing." There was a pause as Buonsarde let this fact sink in.

"You have read the financial reports. It is a most solid company. You have also read of the company's capabilities in the computer field, how it is not only holding its own but will soon surpass Microsoft. And this company, in which I have a few shares, is destined to make me—and you, if you are so agreeable—a modest amount of money." Buonsarde simpered at his understatement, and his audience chuckled.

For ten minutes Buonsarde spoke of the company's capabilities, its earning potential, its power. He ended with a prediction. A murmur went round the room. "Yes, yes," the count said, nodding. "This stock, which is selling for forty dollars a share, and was selling for ten dollars a share last year, will, I repeat, climb to eighty in the next four months and by the end of the year to one hundred and twenty dollars a share. This, I can almost promise."

A buzzing began in the room, as if bees were hiding in the greenery. It was silenced by Buonsarde's manicured fingers, held as a priest might hold his hands, fingers upright, while blessing the Host. "Next February," Buonsarde intoned solemnly, "we will congratulate ourselves on our good fortune." He lowered his hands. "I would be honored to answer questions."

"How can you be so sure, Antonio?" a man in his seventies, sitting on the couch, asked. "A lot of these computer stocks have plunged way down."

Buonsarde shook his leonine head. "Ah, my dear James Bessington the Third, I am neither infallible nor am I psychic. And, I must confess, I have been wrong, before. But"—here he drew himself up like a general— "I, personally, am so convinced that this stock will rise and rise, will, if I may be so bold, rocket to the moon, that Buonsarde and Company has bought one million dollars' worth of Compu Class A stock. One million."

The count shrugged his heavy shoulders and held his hands palms up, begging the murmuring to cease. Now his voice was sober, funereal: "Wall Street is the most treacherous street in the world. Stocks can plunge with enormous rapidity. One day you are a millionaire, and the next, a pauper. With Compu Class A, as with any stock, there are no guarantees. Together, we will be riding a wild horse. But it is a horse that I have faith in. A faith that I wish to share with my very good friends."

"Most impressive, damn good," said a deep voice. "Hear, hear."

Others took up the cry. Maurice's "hear, hear" was the loudest of all as the heady aroma of greed wafted through the room, and each man nodded to his neighbor. Yes, this was momentous. Financial history was being made.

Buonsarde bowed and concluded his remarks. "Three distinguished officers of Compu Class A have flown in from Ohio to be with us tonight. Tim Johnson, the president"—indicating a colorless young man sitting in an easy chair—"Harry Simms, vice president"—pointing out a plump gentleman in his sixties—"and Herman Erlich, the treasurer." Mr. Erlich adjusted his toupe, stood, and bowed.

"These gentlemen"—Buonsarde's voice held indulgent amusement—"own a few shares of Compu Class A stock, too." Everyone laughed.

"And during our meal," the count concluded, "if you have any questions, please don't hesitate to ask these members of the Compu Class A family. They are here to answer all of your queries, and to discuss the company's business strategy. And now, my esteemed colleagues, let us adjourn to the dining room for a simple meal. A meal for my very good friends."

Five white-draped tables of six places each stood around the dining room with centerpieces of fir branches and white orchids. The cutlery was solid, European silver. The plates were rimmed with gold. Maurice stood on line at the buffet and received portions of meat, potatoes, and vegetables of cafeteria caliber. He sniffed, recalling Charly's fussing over each little ingredient. This was solid men's food. Plain, unadorned, the food of financial titans who couldn't bother themselves with precious sauces and herbs with unpronounceable names.

Maurice nodded to a waiter offering San Pellegrino. (The other choices were Bordeaux and champagne.) He felt prosperous, manly, on the verge of untold riches— as, of course, the meeting had been designed to make him feel.

Maurice chatted with his five tablemates, they spoke with authority of Broadway shows they hadn't seen, of Lincoln Center concerts they hadn't attended. Maurice described New York's luxury restaurants with expertise, and its palatial hotels as if he'd personally inspected each room. In fact, he worked so hard at bluffing that it never occurred to him that his tablemates were as ignorant as he was of the city's current delights. Two men were from New Jersey, one from Connecticut, two from Pennsylvania. They were all as sharp as tacks. They were also a little bit drunk.

After the tables had been cleared, ice cream and brownies were served, then brandy. Cigars from a leather humidor were offered. It was nearly midnight when Maurice, feeling bonhomous and expansive, made his way out into the starry night.

As he set his cruise control to fifty and drifted north

through the snowy landscape, Maurice had already bought, in his mind, an apartment in Paris, one in London, and one in New York. And, yes, he'd made his decision: fifty thousand, not twenty-five. Every penny of his savings.

Dinner Guests

TABLE FIVE'S JUST COME IN; CHARLY, THE CROZIER party. You want to greet them?" Tommy Glade, the barman, stuck his head in the kitchen door.

It was half past six. The dining room of La Fermette was filling up. The snow had stopped in the late afternoon and there were no more cancellations. Waiters and customers chattered about the picture-postcard beauty of the night: the snow-laden fir trees, the feather-soft new snow covering the dirty slush underneath, the crisp cold. All of La Fermette's windows were aglow, and to hurry into the blazing warmth from the dry cold outside, to breathe in the tantalizing aromas of cooking wine and sizzling meat and burning applewood from the big fireplace in the barroom, was a tonic. Charly looked up at Tommy Glade and nodded. "Yes, yes, of course I must go and greet them. Thank you, Tommy."

Charly's white jacket was still clean, so he hurried into his office, plopped a tall white toque on his head, and bustled out to table five.

Charly hurried up to the four men, rubbing his hands together and smiling. "Ah, my friends, I hope you bring the appetite, for we have many good special tonight." And although the smile was still pasted on his face, Charly thought, *What is wrong with Win, he look terrible. And Morty, he look so angry.* But aloud, he

76

said, "Gentlemen, we are pleased to welcome you. May I offer a small aperitif on the house? And perhaps some Shrimps Charly?" Charly always cosseted his steady customers: the relations public.

Although Win appeared distracted, he remembered his duties as a host: introduced Charly to Howard Voss and Robbie Munro, antiques dealers from New York City and friends of long-standing. Howard Voss was small, plump, and pink, like a suckling pig. His grey hair was crinkly curly, and he wore little wire-rimmed glasses that slid up and down his nose as he nodded and smiled, sniffing at the good smells and clasping his hands together. Robbie Munro was a willowy, slightly-built man, who seemed to tilt sideways, pelvis thrust forward, back off-kilter, knees bent, like an adolescent girl's. *A chiropractor's nightmare,* Charly thought. Robbie had sallow skin and wavy black hair plastered down on his skull with some sort of pomade. *He look like a rumba dancer from the 1920s,* Charly mused, and then recognition hit.

"But, of course, of course." He told the table, "Voss & Munro, that very nice antiques shop in Greenwich Village, where I buy so many lovely thing. I have not seen you for many, many year."

It was the wrong thing to say. "Still enjoying your Lalique mistletoe vase?" Robbie hissed. "Not to mention the Biedemeier cupboard."

Too late, Charly recognized his error. Voss & Munro specialized in Americana. Because their knowledge of European antiques was scant, Charly had found there a Lalique mistletoe vase for twenty dollars and a Biedemeier pedestal cupboard for a hundred, knowing their value to be much greater. He had also found 1920s Baccarat lead crystal tumblers at a joke price and a

1920s set of Christofle cutlery for a negligible sum.

Charly coughed and tried to change the subject. "You are both looking *splendide*. The years, they do not touch you." Morty's anger and Win's discomfort were explained. Howard had always been an amiable, easygoing fellow, but Robbie Munro was a snake.

"We saw a Lalique mistletoe vase go for over three hundred dollars a few years ago," Munro stage-whispered in an angry voice. Charly pursed his lips and frowned, but said nothing.

Win cleared his throat. "Howard and Bob are upset," he explained, "because their house filled with antiques in Pennsylvania was robbed. Remember, Charly, I told you?"

Charly nodded, but remained silent, recalling that he had bought the antiques from Voss & Munro over twenty years ago. Wasn't that a long time to carry a grudge? And what should he have done? Overpaid? *Voyons*.

Win continued, "Charly, do you remember my telling you that I'd bought a Shaker washstand at Alwyn's in Hogton?"

Charly said, "I recall."

"Well," Win continued, "amazingly, it's one of Howard and Bob's pieces. Howard recognized it as soon as they arrived. We spent the entire afternoon at the police station, and then down in Hogton, identifying more stuff. Lord, I'm exhausted. What a nightmare."

Morty, still angry, tried to play the peacemaker. "We'll all feel better after some food, Charly. It's been a difficult afternoon."

"An understatement," Win sighed.

Robbie now turned on Win. "I can't believe you didn't recognize the piece, you've been to our house. I think you knew, and bought it anyway." From Robbie's tone of voice, he'd raised this objection before.

"Now, Robbie," Howard fussed, "we've been through all this . . ."

Morty turned to Robbie and said in a pleasant tone of voice: "Shut the fuck up, Robbie. You poisoned the afternoon with all your accusations, and now you're trying to poison the evening as well. I want to have a nice dinner without getting indigestion. Just keep quiet."

"You've never liked me," Robbie seethed.

"You're right, Robbie, I never have. You're the most abrasive person I've ever met. You'd find fault with a saint. But Howard and Win have been friends for many years, so I'm willing to put up with you. Why don't we at least try for some grown-up behavior, hmmm?"

"Oh, Morty," Win sighed. Win couldn't abide confrontations.

"Blaming Win is vicious and childish," Morty went on. "You got a lot of your stuff back and the insurance company will be very pleased."

Howard laughed delightedly. "Oh, the insurance company. Well, that's going to be a can of worms. Robbie overvalued everything. That supposedly Shaker washstand you bought, Win: Robbie had it valued at fifteen thousand, but the man in Alwyn's said it's a copy, not worth more than five, dealer price." His plump frame shook with giggles.

"I paid ten," Win admitted. "He said it was a Shaker copy, though a very good one, made by a real craftsman."

"You see, you see," Howard crowed. He seemed to be having a marvelous time. He, alone. Charly was frowning, Win looked done in, and Morty glistened with annoyance. Robbie drummed his fingers on the white tablecloth and looked off in the distance, his lips downturned.

"And where"—Charly kept his frown—"did the antiques dealer in Hogton get the stolen antiques?"

Win said calmly, "From a picker they've used for years. The man showed up in a truck, offered the entire load for a flat sum. The dealer's smart, though, he made the picker sign a statement saying that to the best of his knowledge the stuff was legit, that is to say, not stolen."

"And where did the picker get the antiques?" Charly persevered.

Morty smiled. "Ah, Charly, that's a job for the police. The picker got the stuff from a guy *he's* used for years, but when the cops called, the guy said he'd gotten it from someone else—it's going to be a job, tracing it. The crooks really covered their tracks."

Charly understood that his presence wasn't contributing anything helpful. "I see to the hors d'oeuvre," he muttered, and moved away, hearing Robbie's querulous voice following him sourly: "I'd no idea you'd moved to the country, *Monsieur* Poisson. You're the second familiar face I've seen up here . . ." Charly heard, but ignored the voice and stopped at the bar. "Take their order for drinks, Tommy, I offer their first one on the house."

As Charly moved past Win's table to the kitchen he heard Howard's high-pitched voice, "Oh, Robbie, I didn't know you'd seen someone else you knew, you didn't tell me . . ." Howard's voice got fainter and fainter as Charly moved away.

As he swung the kitchen door open and saw his crew hard at work, Julius garnishing a double order of Shrimps Charly with sprigs of marjoram, Benny preparing a rack of lamb for the oven, old Mick scrubbing a copper pot with a discarded lemon rind and salt, the way it was done in France, Charly again reflected on how lucky he was in his choice of help. What if he had a Robbie or a Howard in his kitchen? How had the two stayed together all these years? Perhaps, thought Charly, they were a pair from another incarnation, a past life. But a pair of what? It boggled the mind.

"What? What?" Charly jumped. Someone was standing at his elbow, saying something

"Oh, Tommy. Is anything wrong?"

Tommy Glade was grinning. "You'll never guess who just walked into the dining room."

The Course of Love

TOMMY COULDN'T STOP LAUGHING. "PATTY SAYS THEY didn't reserve, but she's showing them to table eleven. Bobby Matucci, dressed like a golfing dude from the country club, and a young lady."

"What is so funny?" Charly asked.

"She's the toughest little broad I've ever seen; and Bobby, he's acting like a lovesick sheep, mooning over her. It's a trip. Go out and see . . . "

Bobby Matucci was Mr. Wasp tonight: button-down yellow shirt, paisley tie, grey slacks, a tweed jacket of surprisingly good quality. He was freshly shaved and his black hair was slicked back. He exuded a powerful aroma of a woodsy aftershave. His companion was a young woman, barely five feet tall, wearing a clinging red knit dress and red spike heels. Her black shoulder-length hair was teased out into an old-style *Charlie's Angels* bouffante. She was plump and curvy, with high, round little breasts straining against the knitted material

81

of the dress, and little round buttocks, the cheeks like two rubber balls stuck onto her rear end. Her widely spaced eyes were huge with thickly applied mascara, eyeliner, glittery eye shadow, and a black silk beauty mark in the shape of a crescent moon was stuck just below her left eye. Patty Perkins, showing the couple to their table (after first taking their coats, a fake leopard for the girl, a shearling car coat for Bobby), did a doubletake when she saw the glittery spangles across the girl's lids. It must have taken her an hour just to do the eyes, Patty figured. The girl looked like a Mediterranean Barbie doll. "Enjoy your meal." Patty smiled briskly, and presented menus. *What if I had a daughter like that?* Patty wondered.

Elton Briggs, the waiter for table eleven, hurried up. "Sir, madame. Would you care for an aperitif?" Elton sensed that Bobby was out to impress the young bimbo, and if he could, he would have affected a French accent. But he couldn't. Using the word "aperitif" instead of "drink" was all that he could manage. Elton wondered who the little babe was. Mean little mouth, as tough as old boots. Bobby's problem, not his.

Bobby sat up in his chair. "You ever hear of a Singapore Sling?"

"No, sir," Elton said smoothly. "But I'm sure our barman knows. What's in it?"

"Beats hell outta me," Bobby said, "but I was watchin' one a them old movies the other night, and everyone's drinkin' Singapore Slings."

"No problem, sir, I'm sure. And for madame?"

There was a low-voiced conference. "Ginger ale with a maraschino cherry," Bobby told Elton.

"Very good, sir."

"It's cool," Tommy Glade told Elton. He reached

below the bar for his copy of *Practical Bar Management* by Harold J. Grossman: the barman's bible. There it was on page three-eighteen. You never knew what these suckers would ask for—Clover Club, a Bronx, a Pink Lady—all the old Prohibition cocktails were coming back into style. Okay, here we go: gin, cherry liqueur, lime juice. Tommy measured, shook the drink, then he added four drops each of Benedictine and brandy. He poured the mixture into a highball glass and garnished it with a slice of orange and—the suggested mint sprig being unavailable—two maraschino cherries on a long toothpick. Mmm, looked terrific. As long as he didn't have to drink it.

"Too bad you don't have one a' them little Chinese umbrellas," Elton said as Tommy presented the two drinks.

"Charly won't stock 'em, says they look chintzy, besides, he read somewhere people who order drinks with little umbrellas are lousy tippers."

"Fancy-drinks people are always lousy tippers," Elton said. "And if they order chicken breast, well-done meat, fish cooked to death, I'm lucky if I get ten percent. I don't know why the hell that is, but it's true."

A few minutes later Elton was again at the bar for table eleven. "Now they both want one. Lady says, tastes neat. Neat, I ask you."

Tommy winked. "Hey, man, that's what we're here for. But listen, Elt, warn 'em: it has a terrible kick. It's not lemonade. She looks kinda young."

Elton sighed. "She's tougher than poor old Bobby, that's for sure."

"We got to both order the Shrimps Charly," Bobby told Kimberly Calamare. "My Uncle Rex says they're terrific, but so fulla garlic, we both gotta eat 'em, else I'll kill you with my breath. God, Kimb, you're beautiful."

"Garlic's no big deal," Kimberly said, ignoring the compliment. When she picked up her glass, she kept her pinkie finger extended. "My mom, she loves the stuff. I sweartagod, she'd even put it in the ice cream if she could."

"And for your entree, sir, madame?" Elton, the pro.

Bobby guessed the steak, medium rare, au gratin potatoes, sautéed mushrooms on the side. House salad. The young lady (who, Elton guessed, would whine and stamp her foot if she didn't get her own way) wanted the chicken breast, really done, no sauce, french fries on the side.

"We don't serve french fries at night, madame. May I suggest the potatoes au gratin? You can have catsup on those, as well. " Elton had her number, all right. Probably chewed with her mouth open.

"Sure," Kimberly said. "What kinda dressing you got for the salad?"

"The house dressing goes on every salad, madame. Extra-virgin olive oil, balsamic vinegar, chopped shallots."

"Gee, I don't know . . . " Screwing up her mean little face.

"You'll love it, madame, it's cool." Elton bent down and whispered a lie in Kimberly's ear. "Sean Penn had it here last week, said it was the coolest salad he'd ever eaten."

"Hey, no shit," Kimberly said reverently. As Elton moved away, he heard Bobby ask, "What the guy say?"

At eight o'clock Charly again made his appearance in

the dining room. Glancing over at Win Crozier's table he saw they weren't done with their entrees, he'd stop by later. Not a visit he relished. He glided up to table eleven. "Monsieur Robert Mademoiselle. You enjoy your meal?"

"Hey, Charly," Bobby smiled proudly. "Like you to meet Kimberly Calamare."

"A pleasure to greet so beautiful a lady," Charly said, bending low to take Kimberly's outstretched hand and lift it to his lips. Kimberly didn't giggle. She took this as her due, like a queen. Charly was just about to compliment Kimberly on her chic appearance when he saw, out of the corner of his eye, a commotion at the front desk. A sun-tanned man, tall, thin, pencil mustache, in a sporty beige overcoat, was confronting Patty, peering into the gloom, waving his hands, motioning toward the rear.

Patty led the man to table eleven. "This is Mr. Calamare," Patty said in her "special" voice, reserved for VIPs and royalty, should either appear in Klover, New York.

Charly beamed and bowed. "Indeed an honor. Mr. Carlo Calamare, owner of the well-known Country Square."

"The Country *Squire*," Calamare said through clenched teeth.

Charly nodded. "Is what I say. Correct. An honor, sir, to receive you. May I offer a drink? A brandy, perhaps, or hot toddy?"

Calamare shook himself, realizing who he was and where he was: a restaurateur in another man's restaurant. Proprieties must be observed.

"No, no, thank you, sir. It's a family matter, if you don't mind."

Elton carried over a chair and pushed it against Calamare's legs, forcing him to sit. Charly backed away, moving sideways like a crab so that he could overhear. This was difficult, as Calamare's voice was low, so Charly stood at the bar, observing. Elton hurried over, after a bit.

"He ignores Bobby like he wasn't even there. Says to her, 'You little creep, sneakin' out, your mother's cryin' her eyes out, thinks you've been kidnapped.' Then I couldn't hear any more."

But they could see. Bobby shrugging, shaking his head, holding his hands palms up, as if he were powerless. Kimberly, lower lip stuck out, pouting. Then Calamare, gesturing, hands waving, then shrugging his shoulders in an "oh, what the hell" gesture. It was all done so silently that diners at adjacent tables didn't even turn around. A true restaurant family argument: don't do anything to alarm the other diners.

Elton moved from the bar to clear a table. He returned a few moments later to report: "She says to him, 'You should talk, you're nothin' but a crook yourself.' I think we should take over drinks, like, diffuse the situation. My guess is, parents grounded her, she snuck out."

"Good idea," Charly agreed. "Tommy, what do you think?"

"Three Singapore Slings coming up," Tommy said.

"And Elton," Charly went on, "take over a tray of dessert. If they eat, they do not fight. Say, compliment of the chef." Elton whipped off.

Charly moved around his restaurant, greeting patrons, smiling, bowing, complimenting the ladies on their appearance. His visit to the Crozier table passed without incident, as Robbie slumped, pouting, over his empty plate. When he passed by the bar, Tommy leaned over.

"It's like the movies, you know? Now she'll start crying, her dad'll try and shut her up. The worst is passed. They're drinking the drinks, eating the desserts."

About twenty minutes later Carlo Calamare and his daughter stood up, and the father took the daughter's unresisting arm and piloted her out of the room. With her mascara smeared from tears, she looked like a young, plump raccoon. Kimberly looked back at Bobby and gave him a forlorn little wave, with one finger. She didn't look very sad.

Bobby Matucci, alone at his table, raised his hand and male a scribbling motion to Elton, indicating that he wanted his check.

"All drinks and desserts compliments of the chef," Elton told Bobby.

"Gee, that's nice of Charly. Food was great. My date's up shit creek, she snuck out. Carlo don't like me too much, I guess."

"The course of love never runs smoothly," Elton murmured. "She's a beautiful young lady if I may say so, sir."

"Kimberly's the greatest," Bobby sighed. 'But her dad, well . . . "

"If it's meant to be, it'll happen," said Elton the philosopher. "Trust me."

"What would you do?" Bobby asked Elton.

Elton thought. "Maybe cool it for a few days? Don't call her, wait and see if she calls you."

"Yeah, I could do that, I guess." Bobby sounded undecided. He glanced at the check, pulled some crumpled twenty-dollar bills from his pocket, and counted them out. "Here, buddy, keep the change."

Even though it was late when the staff went home and

Charly locked up the restaurant, he drove over to Rex's place. Rex was sitting at his usual deuce, at the entrance to the Steak Heaven dining room, drinking his customary late-night anisette and soda. The bar was going full blast though the dining room had emptied out.

Charly, accepting a seltzer (Rex's red wine was too sour even to consider, tonight) told Rex about Bobby's visit. "And the papa Calamare, he look like so." Charly made a long face and frowned.

Rex brushed a fleck of dust from his dark blue sharkskin suit. "What a fuckin' mess," he said. "Bobby's moonin' around, in love with that mob guy's kid, it's gonna end bad, mark my words. He'll kill Bobby."

"Maybe not, Rex. The girl, she wrap her papa around her little finger. It is clear. And he love his daughter. That is also clear. So if the daughter love Bobby . . . maybe Carlo will leave Bobby alone."

"Dream on, Charly," Rex said heavily. 'This is real life, not some two-bit fuckin' movie."

Charly assumed a lordly stance, throwing his chest out, stabbing the air with his index finger. "Ah, *mon ami,* there you are wrong. Life itself, this life that we are living right now, it is the two-bit fucking movie. And not, if I may say so, worth the price of admission."

Sunday Morning

SUNDAY MORNING CHARLY WOKE RESTED AND cheerful, and later than usual—six o'clock instead of half past five. Last night had been busy, and today's reservations were substantial. It would be another profitable day.

La Fermette served dinner from noon to six on Sundays, though most customers arrived before three. By five, most of the food had run out, especially the popular prime rib. Individual roasted free-range chickens, roast stuffed pork, and roast lamb were also high on the list of favorites. Sundays were hearty-eating days, not fancy-eating days.

After dislodging a feline or two, Charly reached for his beret and clapped it on his head, then dropped some Bach flower remedies onto his tongue. As he walked downstairs, preceded by his four cats, he began making lists in his head: horseradish to grind, cumberland sauce to make from red currant jelly for the roast pork, mint sauce for the lamb, the stuffing for the pork, the marinade for the chickens, the onions to slice for the brandied onion soup, always a big Sunday seller.

As he spooned his Puerto Rican coffee into the Melita filter he wondered at the American predilection for sweet sauces to accompany meat. He couldn't understand it, and decided it was related to religion, in some arcane way.

Americans paid a lot of lip service to piety. The Puritans sounded like the Nazis, destroying and condemning everything that they, personally, didn't believe in. This was a strange country.

Opening the back door to call in his cats, Charly stepped out onto the little porch and took a deep breath, but only one. The frigid air rushing up his nostrils was a shock, and a sudden gust of wind shot through his flannel pajamas and his heavy woolen robe. He peered at the thermometer, not believing what he saw: nearly ten degrees below zero.

As he sipped the strong coffee Charly thought about Patty's friend Amanda Kendell, now deceased. He would like to meet this Mr. Kendell, the wife killer. He'd probably murdered his first wife, too, and Charly, who had a high opinion of his own assessments of people, felt that just by looking at the man he could determine his guilt. Or, of course, lack of guilt, though this was doubtful. One thing was certain. The joyful Amanda who had visited the restaurant had not killed herself. She was looking forward to a new life, she had plenty of money, and in the comfort of her sister's house she would begin rebuilding her existence. Ah, the poor woman. Charly brushed these thoughts from his head. There was too much to do, today. Tomorrow was his free day, and he could continue his thinking, then. But now . . . the Sunday show must begin.

To Charly's annoyance, the back door to the restaurant was unlocked. He occasionally forgot to lock up, and when this happened he envisioned thieves wrecking the place and stealing his valuable foodstuffs, as they would do in New York City. But Klover was still so casual that people left keys in cars, and didn't lock their houses when they went to the store. It was another world. Still, it was a careless thing to have done.

"I am filled with distractions," Charly muttered as he hurried from kitchen to dining room, then down to the cellar where extra supplies were kept. It couldn't be the cleaners, since they appeared at eight and it was only half past seven. But nothing appeared broken or stolen, padlocks were still on the liquor cage and the food cage, and no bottles had been taken from the bar. All was as he had left it last night. "But one of these fine days," Charly scolded himself, "I will be sorry." He went to his office and, with a thick felt-tipped pen, wrote *"Lock la Porte"* on a sheet of paper that he taped to the back door. The trouble was that he had so many notes to himself, taped here and there, that he simply forgot to look at them.

Next, Charly checked the reservations book in the dining room: twenty-four reservations, and on Sundays there were a fair number of walk-ins. He noted a lot of his old customers: Honoria Wells the heiress, Julius's aunt, was hosting a lunch for Peter and Dinah Vann, Emelie and Michael Crisp (from Crisp Combines in Albany, now retired), old Mrs. Collins, who drank straight bourbon, and Father Evangelista, the Catholic priest. The priest and Honoria shared a fascination for the assassination of John E Kennedy. Julius had told Charly that Father Evangelista would go over to Honoria's house and over drinks (many) and sandwiches (a few) they'd argue and speculate far into the night. They wouldn't stint on the booze at lunch. Peter Vann could put away the martinis, too. Charly smiled: the bill would be enormous. Honoria's father, a noted tippler, had made bathtub gin during Prohibition. Honoria had a tradition to maintain.

Old Doc would come with his doctor friend from Massachusetts, and Jimmy Houghton had reserved a table; he'd arrive as always with his office manager, old Evelyn Holmes, who was at least seventy but looked fifty.

Charly suddenly slapped at his forehead. The *choucroute*. His famous sauerkraut. Of course. The first thing that must be done—and it wasn't even on his list. Today's would be a spectacular *choucroute*, for he'd found some tasty sausages and he had plenty of duck fat, though goose fat would be better. Charly had helped his father make many *choucroutes* in the charcuterie in Lons-le-Saunier. The famous sauerkraut, sausage, and pork dish, *Choucroute Garnie,* was served at winter funerals in the Jura Mountains, and Jean Poisson's *choucroute* was the best in the Jura. Everyone said so.

Charly hurried to the kitchen and began assembling his *mise en place* for the *choucroute*: the sauerkraut, bacon slab, smoked pigs' knuckles, juniper berries, cloves, bouquet garni, white wine, chicken stock, duck fat, onions, coarse sea salt, pepper. The sausages and the pork chops would remain in the cold room, for the time being. They would be added at the last minute. There would be none of the traditional blood sausages, since Americans, who refused to eat so many French favorites (he thought with nostalgia of veal kidneys, calves' brains, sweetbreads, tripe), spurned this delicacy, too.

Benny appeared as Charly was soaking the sauerkraut in water. Unlike Charly, who dressed for an arctic expedition to walk the two hundred yards from his house to the restaurant, Benny wore a thin leather jacket, leather boots, and lined leather gloves. He came into the warm kitchen with his helmet under his arm. Charly, as always, said, "That is all you wear on your *moto*? You do not freeze? Turn into a *glaçon*? This morning it was ten degrees below zero. And the wind . . ." Mick Hitchens arrived, and Charly inspected his outerwear. "Like Mick, here, you should look. Nicely bundled up, like a sausage."

"Too cold to fool around," old Mick said. "I've got on layers on top of layers. Even Bruno, I let him out, he did his business, came straight in."

Said Benny, "I don't feel the cold that much. It's warmed up now, anyway, well above zero. Besides, if I was all trussed up my reaction time would be terrible. On a motorcycle, you have to move."

"Hum, hum," Charly muttered. He preferred to look like the Michelin tire man when facing the treacherous elements. For no amount of money would he drive a motorcycle. Even *le scooter*, a favorite French method of transportation was, Charly considered, dangerous. "You have lost more weight," he accused Benny. For Benny, once chubby, was becoming quite thin.

"It's not eating meat and sweets and drinking sodas. I still eat meat sometimes, but mainly, Mom cooks me rice and beans and vegetables and noodles and baked potatoes. And I only drink water, straight from the tap." Benny smiled. "It's sulfur water, so it really cleans you out."

"And all"—Charly frowned, curious—"for this Tae Kwon Do?" Benny was preparing for his black belt exam, and spent every moment in the gym.

"No, Charly, it's really for me. Like that book you lent me, remember? That guy, Van de Wetering, who spent time in a Zen Buddhist monastery? For him, it was a challenge. This is a challenge for me, too. It makes me feel clean to exercise, give up junk food, not eat meat. I don't know how to explain it, but it's a kind of purity. A lot of the guys at the gym live like that, especially the black belts. We're all trying to purify our bodies."

"It make you feel good about yourself," Charly said "More wise than the others, the crowd, the average man."

"Yep. That's right." Benny grinned. "You sure opened a can of worms when you offered me those lessons. It's opened up a whole new world."

"Not worms." Charly smiled. "They are meat, remember?"

"Oh, yeah, that's right. Oh, Mom was telling me, she talked to Amanda's sister Catherine yesterday, Catherine's arranged with Brad Greenpeace, you know, the undertaker, to have Amanda's body taken up to Worcester, for burial. As soon as the police release it.

Catherine talked to Matt Kendell, he didn't care. Said he'd just as soon have her cremated, throw the ashes in his backyard, but if she wanted the body, fine."

"The husband," Charly said in a sly tone, "does not want the body of the wife he murder to stay around and haunt him."

"Oh, Charly. Chief Stark thinks it's suicide. But, hey, maybe the brother killed her. One of the guys in Tae Kwon Do worked for Greg Winlove this past summer, refinishing furniture. He said he heard Greg on the phone, threatening to kill his sister. Greg bought something at an auction, assuming his sister'd lend him the money to pay for it as she'd done in the past, and this time she refused to pay. Greg was screaming, " 'I'll kill you, bitch.' "

"Hi, everyone, I heard that," Julius said. "Benny, let Charly do his thing, huh? It makes him so happy. Giving Chief Stark an ulcer. Oh, Charly, by the way, what's that car . . . "

But just then the telephone rang, and Charly snatched up the receiver. It was Win Crozier. Robbie Munro had disappeared.

"Disappeared, how?" Charly asked.

"Last night after we came home from the restaurant," Win explained, "Morty offered to make us all a mint infusion. Robbie wanted a scotch, and asked if he could make a phone call. So he went into the study with his drink and closed the door, and after a while he came out, all in a rush, said he had to meet someone, and he grabbed his coat, and the keys to their car, and rushed out. Howard kept saying he'd had too much to drink to drive safely."

"Yes, yes, that was evident," Charly interrupted. It had occurred to him that Robbie's hostility was caused by drink. And then the four men had consumed three bottles of wine, excessive even by Win's standards.

"But he rushed out anyway, and that's the last we saw of him." Win concluded, "I left the porch light on, and the inside hall light, but he never came in last night. Or this morning."

"Do you think he would come here? Why call me?" Charly asked.

"Well, I hate to say it," Win said, saying it, "but he was raving and ranting about you and how he wanted to go to your house and steal the Lalique vase back. So of course Howard and I wondered if he'd broken in."

"He did not come to my house," Charly said, "and though I leave the door to the restaurant open last night, by mistake, I check everything and all is correct. But I will look again. What kind of car was he driving?"

"It's a big black station wagon. A Chrysler Town and Country, Howard tells me. We've called the police, and we called the hospital, no one's been admitted who sounds like Robbie. I don't know what else to do."

"Who did he know up here? Remember, Win, he say at the restaurant, 'You are the second person I see that I knew before,' something like that."

"Oh, Charly, I don't know. I'd forgotten that. Howard and I, we'll put our heads together. If you hear anything, let me know?"

"Of course, Win, of course." Charly didn't mention that if Robbie crashed on a deserted side road and stayed in the car all night, he'd freeze.

"Howard's terribly worried," Win went on. "It seems Robbie's been acting very strange lately. And drinking more than he should."

After Charly hung up, Julius said, "I started to ask you, Charly, when the phone rang, what's that car doing

95

parked at the very end of your lot?"

"Car?" Charly said. "I did not see a car."

"It's right down at the end, by that clump of bushes, you couldn't see it if you walked from your house. But I saw it when I swung in from Route 65. It looks like a big black station wagon."

CHOUCROUTE GARNIE
YIELD: 4 SERVINGS

2 pounds sauerkraut

¼ cup goose, chicken, or duck fat

2 large onions, peeled and coarsely chopped

4 cloves garlic, peeled and coarsely chopped

1 large apple, cored, peeled, and coarsely chopped

½ pound slab bacon, blanched 10 minutes

4 smoked pigs' knuckles, blanched 10 minutes

6 juniper berries

4 cloves

1 bunch thyme, parsley, celery stalk, carrot, tied together

2 cups white wine

1 cup chicken stock

1 pound garlic sausage

4 smoked pork chops

1 pound smoked ham

8 potatoes, peeled and parboiled until nearly cooked through

Soak the sauerkraut in water for 1 hour. Drain well, then reserve in a dish towel to absorb remaining moisture. Meanwhile, on medium heat, melt fat and sauté onions and garlic until soft in a large, heavy, non-aluminum pot. Add sauerkraut and all remaining ingredients except sausages, pork chops, ham, and potatoes. Bring to a boil, lower heat and simmer 1 ½ hours, covered. Add remaining ingredients and cook 30 minutes longer. Serve with French mustard.

Charly Consults Authorities

"OOF," CHARLY SAID AS HE COLLAPSED INTO ONE OF the chairs at the big pine table in the corner of La Fermette's kitchen. It was nearly seven o'clock Sunday night. The last customer had departed an hour ago, the food had been put away, the kitchen cleaned, and Charly, Benny, Julius, and old Mick were ready to pack it in. Tomorrow the restaurant would be closed all day, and on Tuesday, open only for lunch. It was a nice break.

"What was Honoria's bill, if I might ask," said Julius.

"Four hundred and sixty dollar, and she leave a hundred-dollar tip," Charly answered. "They drink much wine, plus two bottles of Moët with the dessert, and I give everyone a digestif on the house. In New York City, it would have cost her over a thousand dollar. They eat, eat, eat."

Julius snorted. "She can afford it. By the way, what happened to Maurice? He didn't show his face all day."

Charly's lips tightened. "I do not know and I do not care. Why should he get half the profit, when he do none of the work?"

"We've been tellin' you that for years, Charly," Mick said. "I've got the bones for Bruno, I'm heading out now. Good night."

Benny said, "I wonder if the car's still out there? Can't see from here."

"We get so busy, I forget about the car," Charly said. "After you check this morning that there are no bodies, I call Win, and he say he will call the police. After that, I forget. *Entre nous,* between only us, I think Robbie, he

98

have the little friend and he drive here, meet the friend, they go off in the friend's car. Of course I do not say this to Win."

There was a knock at the back door and John Stark came in, stamping his feet. "I'm not staying, Charly, Ben, Julius; Betty's holding supper for me. I just wanted to tell you we checked out that car in your lot, doors were open but no bloodstains or anything suspicious, then Crozier and his friend got it, they had extra keys, brought it back to their place. Guy's still missing."

"Maybe is connected with the stolen antiques," said the great detective astutely. "This Munro is not a good man. I have experience with such men."

"Maybe he's selling kilos of cocaine," Stark answered. His heavy sarcasm implied, *maybe you should keep your nose out of my business.*

"Thank you, Chief Stark, for informing us," Charly said humbly as the back door slammed shut. He'd wanted to ask Stark about Amanda, but felt that this wasn't the right time. Besides, if there was news, the chief would tell him. Wouldn't he? "Come, we go home, now. Julius, have a good trip back to Albany, I call you during the week. We see you next Friday."

"You'd better hire me full time, Charly, to do the cooking while you run around catching the bad guys. I'm itching to leave the money business."

"Anytime you wish, Julius. I mean that with all my heart."

"Well, we'll see," Julius said, zipping up his yellow down jacket. "Get rid of Maurice, first. I won't work here full-time, knowing that man's getting half the profits and doing no work."

After Julius left, Benny put on his coat and helmet and went out to his motorcycle, and Charly began the

99

lengthy process of dressing for his return to his house. Finally bundled up, he twisted the little latch in the doorknob and slammed the back door shut. He rattled the knob and tried to turn it. It was firmly locked. Still, it might be a good idea to have Noah Van Gieson, the locksmith, take a look at the door. It might be easy for a thief to open. In *le cinéma*, the bad guys, *les mauvais types,* were always opening locks like this with credit cards. Now that he thought back, he was sure that he'd locked the back door last night. He saw himself jiggling the knob, exactly as he had just done it. Ah, well. He wasn't going to worry about it now.

Sunday nights were always pleasant for Charly. The restaurant closed early, so he had the entire evening to himself. Then tomorrow, Monday, the restaurant was closed all day. The fire was laid and Charly touched a match to the crunched-up newspapers. He went to his kitchen and fed the cats, then heated up a bowl of leek and potato soup. When the soup was bubbling, he poured it into a deep bowl and knifed in a knob of butter. He tore two slices of French bread into pieces and added them to the bowl. He carried the bowl to the little low blanket chest in front of his leather sofa.

At times like this, after a successful day at the restaurant, Charly would stare into the flames of his crackling fire and smile, thinking of all the good fortune that had come his way. Not bad for a little waiter from the Jura Mountains. He owned a fine restaurant, a comfortable house with lovely furniture, rugs knotted and stitched by hand in some far-off land, a bit of money for his old age stashed away in Switzerland and in three American brokerage firms: more than enough to pay Maurice off. He would call Jimmy Houghton tomorrow and discuss the matter. This time—for there had been discussions about Maurice in the past, which always fizzled out—Charly would follow through. Enough was enough.

After finishing his soup Charly made sure the screen was secure in front of the dying fire and climbed up to his all-white bathroom. He ran a bath in his six-foot tub, adding a generous amount of lavender-scented bubble bath. He got down the bottle of black dye that a friend sent him periodically from France, and set it by the side of the tub. When the bathwater was high, he lowered himself into the steaming tub.

He wet his hair, poured on the dye, let it set for five minutes, then rinsed. It was a wonderful product, he mused, the French really knew about hair dyes. No one would ever guess that his hair color wasn't natural.

When Charly had rinsed his hair he rose dripping from the tub, carrying the bottle of dye, and stood at the sink. With a very small brush he applied the dye to his mustache, peering in the mirror to make sure he covered all of the tiny hairs. He got into the tub again. When he judged that five minutes were up, he rinsed off his mustache, then soaped it with his olive oil soap from Marseille, rinsed it again, and sank back into the water.

Poor Amanda Kendell, no more hot baths for her. *I must meet with the husband,* Charly thought again as he dried himself with the fluffy towel. *I will think up a pretext for visiting him.*

The next order of business tonight was filling up his three bottles of Bach flower remedies: one for the kitchen, one for his bedroom, and one for his office at the restaurant. He went downstairs to the kitchen, got down his tin box of Bach remedies, washed out three small dropper bottles, got out a bottle of rum and a bottle of Evian water. He filled the dropper bottles three-quarters with pure water and added a drop of rum to each—the alcohol was a preservative. Then he took the tiny individual bottles of flowers, one by one, and added two drops to each of the three bottles: Aspen (for unknown fears), Beech (for criticism of other people, ever a failing of Charly's), Cerato (for those unsure of their own judgment), Chestnut Bud (for making the same mistakes over and over), Gentian (easily discouraged), Hornbeam (for those in need of an energy boost), Vervain (for those of strong convictions whose enthusiasms can go too far). There were thirty-eight remedies in all and Charly owned about thirty. The Bach flower consultant that he used, Mrs. Whaley, had told him he could add as many as a dozen to his bottle, but these seven were enough for now. Charly made sure that the bottles were screwed shut, then he put them away, along with the bottle of rum and the Evian water.

After making sure that all four cats were in the house (they were) he climbed upstairs, but at the head of the stairs he remembered he wanted to do the I Ching and so climbed down again, since his I Ching material was in the living room. "I do not have the orderly mind," Charly accused himself, but then, he reasoned, he liked running up and downstairs (a form of exercise) and enjoyed doing things in a certain order. Filling his Bach flower bottles (which he did every three weeks) always came *after* the hair dyeing and *before* the I Ching. That was the way it always had been.

In the living room Charly spread out his I Ching materials: his notebook for transcribing his messages, the Wilhelm/Baynes translation of the I Ching, the little leather bag with his three nickels. Opening up his notebook to a clean page, he threw the coins, inscribing the six broken and solid lines from the bottom up.

Broken, broken, solid, broken, solid, broken. He turned to the key at the back of the book. Ah-ah. *Chien. K'an* above, *Ken* below. Obstruction, number thirty-nine. Not good.

"The hexagram pictures a dangerous abyss lying before us and a steep, inaccessible mountain rising behind us. We are surrounded by obstacles . . ." Charly read on and on. It sounded like his situation, exactly. It was amazing, just how accurate the I Ching generally proved to be. However, *"This unswerving inner purpose brings good fortune in the end. An obstruction that lasts only for a time is useful for self-development. This is the value of adversity."* Obviously, he must find the murderer of Amanda Kendell.

Ah-ha, Charly said to himself, neglecting, or ignoring, the remainder of the message, *"Thus the superior man turns his attention to himself and molds his character."* Charly, like most people, only saw what he wanted to see. He closed the I Ching, believing that he had been instructed to expose Amanda's murderer and find the missing Robbie Munro. Wars are waged from blunders smaller than this one.

It was half past nine. The fire was out, though embers still glowed. Charly straightened the fire screen, made sure the doors were locked, and for the last time that evening, climbed the stairs followed by his four cats, who had known better, of course, than to follow him up the first time. He undressed, put on heavy flannel pajamas, and climbed into bed. He opened up an old Simenon murder mystery starring Inspector Maigret, but his eyes kept closing and he couldn't remember what he'd just read.

Charly arranged his pillows and snuggled into the soft down. Mrs. Barrol, he thought. The woman with the psychic powers in Hogton. Why not visit Mrs. Barrol? Perhaps it was a waste of time, but occasionally Mrs. Barrol hit the jackpot, and Charly received a true glimpse of future events. Too bad he wasn't psychic. His cats were, they always knew when a storm was coming, conveying this message to Charly by flicking their tails, staying close to home, and nervously scanning the horizon. Yes, yes, that's what he would do. Call Mrs. Barrol. And with that decision made, Charly slid into sleep.

Meeting Amanda's Men

CHARLY LEAPT OUT OF BED MONDAY MORNING bursting with energy and plans. He peered out into the darkness: little to be seen, though the howling wind might presage a storm. He turned on the light and looked at his cats: two on the bed, two in baskets. The two on the bed looked up at him, then looked toward the window and flattened their ears at the noise of the wind. They knew. A storm was coming.

Downstairs three brave cats, Frère, Marcelle, and Tin-Tin, padded outside, but the remaining one, Suzanne, looked at Charly in disgust. "*Eh bien,* you will have to use the cat litter," Charly told Suzanne.

Charly took up the cats' empty bowl of dry food and went to the pantry, where he kept the big dry food bag. He plunged in the clear plastic measuring cup and brought up, not only food pellets, but a long, thin tail. He set down the empty bowl and grasped the tail with thumb and forefinger. A tiny mouse struggled feebly. "*Ah, soyez la bienvenue, Madame Souris,*" Charly said, welcoming the mouse. He padded over to the

104

refrigerator and, stooping, laid the mouse on the linoleum, where it shook itself, then scampered under the appliance. *Imagine,* Charly thought, *with four cats in the house.* He reached for a plastic container and opened it, taking out one of Patty's shortbread cookies, which he slid under the refrigerator. The mouse must be sick of cat food.

He turned on his weather radio, which announced a blizzard due to hit Van Buren County between noon and three P.M. Charly turned his heat up to seventy-two degrees. When the wind blew from the northeast, it blew right through the inadequate insulation of the old house. What luck to have the blizzard arrive when the restaurant was closed. If the storm had hit on Saturday or Sunday, it would have blown away all of his profits.

After three cups of coffee and a bowl of cracked wheat cereal flavored with tamari sauce, a cut-up scallion, and some fresh coriander, Charly was ready for action. He would visit Matthew Kendell to inquire about some mythical shipping arrangements: nothing could be simpler. Then he'd return home and call Mrs. Barrol, see if he could get an appointment for today. He wouldn't, he decided craftily, call Kendell first. If the man didn't do the sort of haulage he was proposing, then there would be no reason for a visit and the entire point of the exercise would be lost.

Charly parked his van in front of a low grey building placed smack in the center of a parking lot filled with at least five sixteen-wheelers. Beyond the building at the back were loading bays, warehouses, and more trucks. Charly tried to imagine the financial outlay. Colossal. But perhaps some of the trucks were rented. *Appearance,* Charly thought, *can be deceiving.*

Charly knocked on the door of the big, ugly, cinder-block building. A decade ago, it would have been as incongruous as a UFO in the center of the countryside. But today, with so many small farms dying, these sprawling businesses were sprouting up more and more often.

Charly glanced at the buzzer to the left of the door frame. Underneath was a notice, RING BELL AND WALK IN. Charly rang the bell and walked in.

Intense heat hit Charly in the face. After the cold outside, it was a shock. Directly to the left in the entryway was a little window, and at the window was a receptionist with headphones clamped to her skull. She looked about twenty, with an acne-pitted face and stringy brown shoulder-length hair. She looked at Charly, cracked her gum, and said, "Kin I help ya?"

Charly looked at the soiled cream walls, the plywood doors. "Please tell Mr. Kendell that Mr. Charles Poisson would like to see him."

"You got an appointment, Mr. Porson?"

"No appointment."

The receptionist plugged in a line, rang, then waited. "Genman named Mr. Porson to see ya, Mr. K, no appointment."

"He says"—the girl cocked her head at Charly—"what's it about?"

"Moving merchandise from New York City to Klover," Charly said.

"Moving merchandise from New York to Klover," the girl repeated.

"He'll see you," the girl said "Go down that hallway"—she pointed with her finger—"and open the door at the end."

Charly opened the middle plywood door and found

himself in a long corridor with offices on either side. The doors were open and Charly could see men talking on the telephone, working at computers, studying spreadsheets. At the open door at the end Charly stopped. A big man, probably in his fifties, was sitting at a metal desk, working with a calculator. Charly cleared his throat. "Mr. Kendell?"

The man looked up and Charly stared at a wide, flat-nosed, craggy face. The man's greasy black hair (*not a grey hair in sight,* Charly thought enviously) grew straight back from his forehead. The face itself was a mass of wrinkles, an unhealthy yellow color, and out of the wrinkles peered two black eyes. Hung on the man's massive frame was a plaid flannel shirt. It looked like the man had lost weight recently. The shirt was far too big.

"Yeah? You the guy about the shipment from New York?"

If Charly had hoped for a moment of instant recognition ("He is the murderer, I can feel it") he hoped in vain. The man looked ill. His voice was soft and tired, not the harsh and grating voice that Charly expected to hear.

"My name is Charles Poisson. May I come in?"

"Yeah, sure."

Charly walked into the office, struggling out of his down jacket. The place was as hot as his restaurant kitchen. He stood facing the desk, there being no chair.

"I own a restaurant, Mr. Kendell, and I am expecting a shipment of pots and pans from France. They will come into port in New York. I need to have them shipped up here." Charly caught a whiff of sour body odor. Quite strong, like cumin powder rubbed on decomposing meat.

"How many?"

"How many pots and pans?" Charly tried not to breathe.

"No," Kendell said patiently. "How many lift vans?"

"Oh," Charly was confused. "Not even one lift van. Just a few crates, big wooden crates, about two hundred pounds per case, I do not know square footage, but each case would be about the size of your desk."

"I think you've been misinformed," the soft voice said. "Whoever told you we did small jobs? We do bulk, long distance haulage, like, you understand, ten, twenty lift vans. Big quantities, you understand?"

Charly nodded. "I see."

"You just need a guy with a pick-up truck."

"Yes," Charly said. "I understand. Forgive me for wasting your time, sir. I did not understand the nature of your business."

"No problem," Kendell said politely. "And thank you for stopping in." He bent to the papers on his desk, ignoring Charly who still stood at the desk, struggling to get his jacket back on. The telephone rang. Kendell picked up the receiver, listened, then said, "Yeah? Send him in."

Gregory Winlove stood at the receptionist's window, smoothing his hair, eyeing his reflection in the glass portion of the door. Greg loved to look at himself. He noted with approval the strong, virile face, the shoulder-length, curly hair, the straight nose, the full lips, the deep brown eyes. "Go on through, Greg," the receptionist told him. "He's 'spectin' ya."

"Thanks, Courtney." Gregory moved down the corridor, thinking of the money that came out of this big company. It was ridiculous that Matt was still asking for fifty percent of the profits from Greg's antiques business. Matt didn't need the money; Greg did.

Greg, his head down, crashed into someone. He looked over and saw a stranger, a short, compact man with hair and mustache so black they must be dyed. The stranger sputtered and waved his arms around, confused.

"Mon Dieu," Charly said, clawing at the wall to keep his balance. "My apologies, sir. Are you all right?" All of this in a heavy French accent, which Greg recognized, having been to the Paris antiques auctions.

Charly looked at the young man and thought he was seeing a ghost. Long brown curly hair, curious, vacant eyes, white skin. Looked just like Amanda Kendell. Charly stared, mouth open, and stammered, "You look like someone I have recently met. Someone who is now dead. Is a shock." He patted his chest, and breathed deeply. "Did I hurt you?"

Greg smiled, a sad, crooked smile just like the dead woman's. "I remind you of Amanda, don't I?" Even the voice was the same. "I'm Amanda's brother, Gregory Winlove."

"Ah, Gregory Winlove," Charly said, and thought, *A weak chin, too-soft lips for a man, not a handsome but a pretty face, a pederast without doubt, and the curious* sanpaku *eyes where white can be seen under the iris, indication of an unbalanced state.* Charly, a dabbler in Eastern philosophies, had read *You Are All Sanpaku* (by Sakurazawa Nyoiti, translated by William Dufty) which promoted a theory that such eyes indicated disorientation and proneness to accidents and criminal behavior. President Kennedy, Robert Kennedy, Marilyn Monroe, among others who had died violently, all had such eyes.

Charly bowed. "My deepest condolences, sir, on the death of your sister."

"Yes," Greg said in his sister's whispery voice. "Poor Amanda."

"But I must not keep you, sir. You are a busy man. With many funeral arrangements to discuss with Mr. Kendell."

Greg sniggered, an ugly sound. "Oh, not so many. And you are, sir?"

Charly bowed. "Monsieur Charles Poisson."

"Then I'll say good day, Monsieur Poisson." Greg continued down the hall, watched by Charly. He didn't know what to make of Gregory Winlove.

Mrs. Barrol on Seer Street

WHEN HE GOT HOME CHARLY HAD A BRACING CUP OF coffee and decided to call Mrs. Barrol, the psychic. No sign of snow, though the sky was grey and ominous. After four rings the receiver was picked up and a cracked old voice screeched, "Hilloo? Hilloo?" Mrs. Barrol sounded like a demented parrot.

Charly identified himself and asked when he could come for a reading.

"Mr. Pwasin?" the ancient voice croaked. " 'Course I remember you. You're the gentleman with the four men friends."

"No, Mrs. Barrol. I am the man from Klover, with the restaurant."

"The bawdy house? You Polish? No, Eyetalian, that's it; Eyetalian."

"No, Mrs. Barrol, I am French. I own La Fermette, a French restaurant. I consult with you a few months ago about one of my cats."

"Oh, that Mr. Pwasin," the tremulous old voice cackled. "One of your cats was lost. In a locked barn, she was. Suzanne was her name."

Amazing. "That is correct, Mrs. Barrol, you find her for me."

"I always find the pussies. They talk to me. I like the pussies, oh, yes. And you have four. Suzanne refused to go out this morning but the others went. Hated it, though."

"That is correct, Mrs. Barrol."

"I've had a cancellation, gentleman from Pittsfield, he's afraid of the blizzard. Want to come at one o'clock? Only do one reading a day, at my age."

"One o'clock would be fine, Mrs. Barrol. See you then." Perhaps she was ninety-four, as she claimed, though she didn't look it. Charly wondered who her other customers were—an Italian bawdy house owner and a gentleman with four men friends. He knew she had customers from Connecticut and Massachusetts, even Vermont. Mrs. Barrol, in her own way, was as well known as Charly's restaurant. She never asked for money, "lose me powers if I did that, dear," but clients left cash if they wished to return.

At five minutes to one Charly parked his van in front of a Victorian house at 112 Seer Street. Charly found the name curiously appropriate, until he found out that the Seer farm—Seer was an old Van Buren County name—had been located on the land. He hurried up the cracked cement walk, turned left, and followed another path. There was Mrs. Barrol's bright red door, which opened before Charly could knock.

"Come in, dear, don't let the cold air in, there's a good feller, hurry up now, cold outside, don't let the chill in with you."

She talk like I am one of her cats, Charly thought.

He walked past Mrs. Barrol into the hot house. It was dark in the front hall, with a feeble overhead light covered in a Japanese paper shade. To the left was the sitting room, where Mrs. Barrol gave her counselings, as she called them. Charly, with Mrs. Barrol at his heels, walked into the room.

It was a high-ceilinged room, painted white, with long yellowed lace curtains and faded deep red velvet draperies at the two long, narrow windows. The room had evidently been much larger, but plasterboard dividers halved the space so that it looked lopsided, too high for its small size. At the back were three dark wooden doors.

There was a horsehair settee, two straight-backed cracked leather chairs, a cocktail table of glass and wrought iron; a plant stand holding a large, luxurious fern, a muscular-looking rubber plant, and several pots of flowering geraniums. There were flowering African violets on the windowsill and pots of rosemary, sage, thyme. The lady certainly had a green thumb, whatever her psychic abilities. Mrs. Barrol's chair, where she communed with the givers of ultimate truths, was an upholstered red plastic lounge chair with rockers, pushed up to the cocktail table.

A glass-fronted bookcase was crammed with dusty-looking books (a set of Shakespeare's plays, the works of Mr. Dickens), and magazines and newspapers spilled out of a basket by a sealed fireplace with a marble mantel. Charly doubted if Mrs. Barrol read *Sports Illustrated* and *Woman's Day*, but the dentist on the

112

other side of the house gave her the old copies from his waiting room. In front of the fireplace was a kerosene stove that gave off heat and a mild odor. There were no pictures on the walls, though a silver, blue, and black Mardi Gras mask hung above the radiator.

"Take off your coat, you'll perish," Mrs. Barrol screeched. She still had the remains of an Irish brogue. "I'll go make the tea." Charly removed his coat and was about to throw it on a leather chair when he noticed an obese yellow cat sitting there, dozing. "Don't sit on the pussies," Mrs. Barrol called from the doorway, and Charly noticed another cat, white and black, asleep on a corner of the settee.

You always had a cup of tea at Mrs. Barrol's, and then she read the leaves. After the tea ceremony, she "did" the cards. Charly thought she merely used the tea and the cards as a vehicle for her own psychic flow—as she did her conversation at the beginning, to get your "feel," so to speak.

"Here you are, dear, a nice cup. Drink it all down, now, you remember, we have to read the leaves." Several objects that might have been tea leaves floated around in the cup.

Charly blew on the liquid and tried to sip it—it was boiling—while Mrs. Barrol babbled on about her two cats ("They don't like the cold, spend all the time in here") and the weather ("Frightful mess, isn't it, dear") and her groceries (the landlady did her shopping for her, potatoes and canned beans, Wheatena and oatmeal, never meat at her age, too hard to digest). Charly had once brought Mrs. Barrol one of Patty's cakes, but this had not been well received. "Fancy," she'd sniffed. "Now I prefer one of the pound cakes made by Sara Lee, though I appreciate the gesture." Charly, peering

113

into her old, wrinkled face, concluded that Mrs. Barrol still had all her teeth and, maybe, all of her wits. She peered at him out of intensely blue eyes—definitely not *sanpaku*—which looked as young as a child's. Her sparse grey hair was caught up in an untidy bun.

Mrs. Barrol, as tiny as an elf, was dressed in layers: Charly could see the hem of a flowered silk dress drooping beneath a black wool skirt. A grey woolen blouse was fastened at the neck with a cameo brooch. Next came a man's grey cardigan with leather patches at the elbows. She wore grey cotton stockings that wrinkled around her skinny legs, and ankle-high felt slippers. She smelled not unpleasantly of lavender, old sweat, kerosene, cinnamon, and rose water. It was a gentle odor, like Mrs. Barrol herself.

All the while, as Charly sipped his tea, Mrs. Barrol chattered on. "Not one to take offense, dear, but she does play the radio awful loud, and I do go to bed early you know, being of an age, and I'd have a word with her but I know she's going through troubled times, yes I do, you can't fool me, well, and that's that. And a young lady came last week, one of the airline stewardesses, going to get married, no you won't, I told her, he's going to declare himself for the priesthood, and she called me yesterday and it's so, there you are, dear, well, and that's that. Lady lost her diamond ring last month, calls me, 'Look in the wing chair in your living room under the cushion,' I told her and she did and there it was. Drink up, dear."

Finally Charly finished the scalding tea and Mrs. Barrol took the cup and swirled the dregs around. She turned the cup this way and that, muttering. "There it is, dear, an A, something sad you've heard about an A, a woman I think, she's sick or something bad." (Mrs.

Barrol never mentioned death.) "And an M, see that?"
Mrs. Barrol held the cup sideways but Charly could see
nothing. "It's an M, a man, close to you, there's a lesson
he must learn, oh, he's a handful, gives you lots of
aggravation, something bad cooking there, money, has
to do with money, doesn't everything. I see your money,
too, business going well but you must always control
the money, and I see new shoes," (Mrs. Barrol often
saw new shoes) "a nice brown pair, and I see
crookedness, you're an innocent, dear, always sticking
your nose where you shouldn't, and a woman you know
is going to fall out of love and a good thing too, the
man's using her, and you'll be facing a problem soon,
something's bothering you, and something will come of
that . . . "

"Something good?" Charly questioned, scribbling
furiously.

"I can't tell, dear, it's all muddled, it'll come out all
right but you'll go through some trying times. You think
you can cure the world and you can't, the world goes on
misbehaving, that's human nature. Now, dear, shuffle
the cards and pick out seven, lay them down and lay the
others on top."

Charly did as he was told. Mrs. Barrol picked the
cards up one by one. She saw a lot of crookedness, men
led by greed, a young man, very beautiful, but evil
through and through, someone Charly knew had
recently bought thing stolen (Ah-ha, thought Charly,
Win and his chest) and this would lead to a big
hanky-panky, especially since the thief was right in the
man's backyard, so to speak. And a youngster close to
Charly would have an accident, not a serious one—as
Charly clutched his chest, thinking of Benny and his
motorcycle. Charly would be signing some legal

115

documents (Mrs. Barrol always saw legal documents) and soon there would be a new era in Charly's life, "putting some bad people behind you."

"And," Mrs. Barrol concluded, "you're going to find something unpleasant soon and your heart is going to beat very fast." And all the while Charly was scribbling in his little Hermès leather notebook in a kind of shorthand. "Mrs. Barrol, if I mention the name Matthew Kendell to you, does that mean anything?"

Mrs. Barrol screwed up her face in thought, then wrinkled her nose. "Phew," she said, "he never bathes, does he? No, dear, can't see anything there, though I get the notion he's not a nice man."

Afterward, when he got home, Charly would go over his notes and write out the visit in longhand. He'd date it and go over it every now and again. A surprising number of things that Mrs. Barrol predicted actually came to pass, though the new shoes rarely did, and Charly signed so many documents that this was hardly a psychic revelation.

Mrs. Barrol gathered up the cards and fixed Charly with her piercing blue eyes. "You're one of the lucky ones, dear, an old soul. You're a kind man, know what's wrong and what's right. Most people don't. It's a gift and you've used it wisely. Some of the cards are terribly mixed up, but I see only good things for you, Mr. Saunders."

"Mr. Poisson," Charly murmured.

"Yes, yes, dear. Now you'll go, for my pussies will be wantin' their dinner and I must have my rest."

"Thank you, Mrs. Barrol, I leave an envelope on the table."

"That's fine, dear, you know I can't charge though everyone leaves me an envelope, yes they do. And

116

everything's of a price now, isn't it, shocking what they charge for fuel and even the potatoes and the cat food. You'll be all right, Mr. Pwasin, but watch out for the bad boys, they're all around you, I can feel it, a criminal element, but they won't do you harm in the end. They'll try, but they won't succeed. You'll be fine."

"Yes, yes, Mrs. Barrol, thank you so much. I call you in a few month if I may, I leave you fifty dollar." Charly struggled into his coat and clapped his beret on his head. He bowed to the old lady and backed out, as if facing royalty.

As Charly started to close the door Mrs. Barrol pulled it open and shrilled, "I think that nasty surprise will be in your refrigerator."

"Yes, yes, perhaps a bit of food has spoiled. I will check as soon as I get back to the restaurant."

Outside the sky had darkened considerably and snow was pelting down in a serious way. Charly got in his van and turned on the headlights. He always felt good after a visit with Mrs. Barrol. She made him feel that past, present, and future were swirling around like the snowflakes, all evanescent and due to melt, and that he was part of the swirling mass, caught up, beyond life and death, in the movement of the spheres.

Nothing Like a Good Chicken Stock

IT WAS AFTER TWO O'CLOCK WHEN CHARLY LEFT MRS. Barrol's, and the snow had begun to come down with such vigor that Charly knew the promised blizzard was here. Best to get home, and quickly.

Nevertheless if he took Short Street and then Route 32 for the three-mile trip to Klover, he would pass Win and Morty's shop, The Paint Barrel, and he could find out the latest news about Robbie Munro. "Mere curiosity," he assured himself, "I leave it all to the police as I promise John Stark."

"Howard's a basket case," Morty said in a bored voice. He was ready for an Abercrombie & Fitch storm in beige wide-wale corduroy trousers, lace-up tan rubber and leather boots, red turtleneck with matching red check Viyella shirt. "I told Win to stay home with Howard, I could handle the shop. Everyone's staying home today. Howard was driving me crazy, oozing around, wringing his hands and moaning, it's all his fault, ta-da, ta-da. He's devoted to the little rat, says it's his doing that Robbie skipped."

"His doing? Why?"

Morty made a face. "He says Robbie's been acting very cloak-and-dagger lately, running out to secret appointments, opening up a separate bank account, and Howard kept nagging him. He says Robbie starts the day, now, with scotch in his coffee. Howard's not a drinker, and he's appalled: thinks Robbie's turning into an alcoholic."

"Robbie is strange," Charly said diplomatically. "Paranoid, maybe?"

"No doubt," Morty said. "What brings you to town on this snowy day?"

"Oh, this and that," Charly said evasively. "Where does Howard think Robbie has gone?"

"He thinks Robbie met someone in your parking lot, went to the Amtrak station, and returned to New York. Howard was going to leave this morning but the

118

blizzard frightened him. He hates the snow."

"And who," Charly asked, "could that someone be?"

Morty made a dismissive gesture. "Oh, who knows? Robbie knows all sorts of strange creatures. We stopped into Rex's place yesterday afternoon and Robbie told us there was someone at the bar that he knew."

"Ah."

"I don't know who," Morty went on. "I recognized Tom Arnold, and that guy Kendell; and Greg Winlove, he's a good customer, here, and a couple of other people, but no one greeted Robbie that I could see."

"Greg Winlove," Charly pursued. "Now, he is a curious type, no?"

"Well, he's a customer, so I shouldn't speak ill," Morty said, "but he's so superior, he knows everything. He's always correcting me. The other day I called that grey over there 'moss grey,' and Greg said oh, no, it wasn't, it was 'dove grey.' Who cares?"

"So Howard will stay on?"

"Well"—Morty brushed a speck of dust from his trousers—"until the roads are cleared. I don't mind Howard, he's a good sort, always laughing and making jokes. Except now. Now, he's a wreck. Poor Win, he's known Howard for years."

"Ah, poor Howard," Charly said without much feeling. "Well, Morty, I go now. I wish you good luck. Robbie, I think, is foolish man. He is so upset about my Lalique vase, that he sell me for next to nothing."

Morty lowered his voice. "To tell the truth, Charly, we were sure he'd go gunning for you. He was raving about that damn vase. And when did it all happen, twenty years ago? Good Lord."

"Robbie is stupid," Charly said. "He and Howard, they sell me many fine and beautiful European antiques.

119

They think the pieces are worthless. They do not check. There are many books that tell you the value of such things. They are lazy."

"That's the fun of the antiques business," Morty said. "To find something wonderful for next-to-nothing. I've found lots. So has Win."

"Of course. A whole set of Christofle silver plate I buy from them," Charly continued, "for very little money. Robbie, he say to me, 'Oh, that is not sterling, only plate.' Ah, but what plate. Christofle is special."

Charly moved toward the door. "At least you're dressed for the weather," Morty said dryly. Charly was wearing heavy flannel trousers, a yellow woolen sweater with a navy flannel shirt peeking out, fleece-lined rubber boots, a down jacket, a thick scarf, a black wool cap with earflaps. Not one item could be called even remotely stylish.

"I dress to avoid the air currents."

"I think you've succeeded. Get a few snowflakes on you, you'll look like Frosty the Snowman."

"True, true," Charly agreed. "But I do not have a carrot for a nose."

Charly turned into Hubbard Road and noticed Benny's motorcycle parked by the restaurant kitchen door. A light was on in the kitchen. He walked into his restaurant. "Benny?" he called.

"In here," Benny shouted, coming out of the cold room. "Tae Kwon Do practice was cancelled this afternoon, so I thought I'd come here, get some more chicken stock going. If I use the big pot, I can turn it to low, it can simmer all night. Didn't you say you had a lot of carcasses in the upstairs freezer? I don't see them."

"They are in the basement freezer," Charly said. "Remember, when we make all the chicken roulade for cocktail parties before Christmas?"

"Oh, yeah," Benny said. "I'd forgotten."

"And you want to do all this on your free day?"

"Sure, Charly. I don't feel like reading, and Mom's still upset about Amanda. It's all she can talk about. This blizzard's gotten me all wound up, and I love to cook. It's restful. Lets me think about things."

"*Un philosophe,*" Charly mused. His beloved Benny was a philosopher of the kitchen. "Hokay. We go down to the basement, bring up the carcass of chicken. They are in a big plastic bag."

The big, upright freezer stood in a corner of the basement, rarely used, but Charly had bought it at an auction for a good price. As he and Benny climbed down the steps, he sniffed. Lemon. He'd bought a new citrus-scented cleaner recently, and it really made the place smell fresh. He imagined the cleaners had been down this morning. "We should use the big freezer more," he told Benny.

"You could buy all sorts of stuff, keep it down here," Benny said. "Cases of that good Plugra butter, it's hard to come by, and freeze sturgeon when those fishermen up the road bring back a big haul."

"Is idea," Charly said. "Now that we have a generator, even if we have power failure, the freezer will keep going. *Tiens,* that is curious." The padlock to the freezer was hanging open. "I do not unlock the padlock on the freezer. Did you, Benny?"

"No, but we probably didn't lock it. Nothing in it but the carcasses."

"True," Charly said, opening the freezer, then

jumping back with a grunt of surprise as a heavy object came tumbling out. It looked like a big oblong bag of clothing, a dark shape, frozen solid of course, and it spiraled out in a graceful, if rapid, arabesque. It landed with a thunk on the cement floor. Charly peered down. Benny looked over his shoulder.

Charly caught his breath. It was the body of a man. Thin and willowy, bent in the fetal position, with black hair plastered down on his skull like a 1920s rumba dancer's. It was Robbie Munro. He was very, very dead.

"Catastrophe," Charly screamed. Robbie stared at Charly and Benny with one glazed and frosted eye, his face mottled red and blue and purple. The other eye socket was dotted with blood, flesh, and bone. Robbie's mouth was pursed in an expression of dissatisfaction, as in life. He was frowning.

"Ai, ai, ai," Charly wailed and, backing off, knocked Benny over. Both sat down heavily on the concrete floor.

A New York Blizzard Doesn't Stop Charly

AS CHARLY FELL HE NOTICED A PIECE OF PAPER THAT had fluttered out of the freezer along with the body. He scooped it up and pocketed it, glancing furtively at Benny to see if he'd noticed.

"Here, Charly, get up, we'll go upstairs and call the police," Benny said. He scrambled to his feet. "You know this guy?"

"Yes, he is the missing guest of Win Crozier and Morty Cohen. It was his car—his and his friend's—that was in our parking lot. Mr. Robbie Munro. He dine here on Saturday. Not a nice man at all."

Benny pulled Charly to his feet and steered him toward the stairs. Together, they climbed up to the kitchen. "You are shaking, Benny."

"Well, it's a shock," Benny said. "I'm not as used to dead bodies as you are. And this one looks awful, doesn't he?"

"He look awfool," Charly agreed. He hurried to his office, got the dropper bottle of Rescue Remedy, and dropped four drops into each of two glasses. He added water from the tap. "Here, Benny, drink this down." Benny and Charly drank down their potions. Then Charly put some water in a saucepan. "I make us little hot toddy," he told Benny.

"Not for me, Charly. I feel fine, now." He grinned. "It's your Rescue Remedy. It works fast. Now, what's the lesson we must learn from this?"

"You do not believe in Dr. Bach, but that is hokay," Charly answered. "He will help you. The lesson? I think the lesson, here"—Charly pursed his lips and looked up at the ceiling—"is that we do not leave our freezer unlocked. I can think of no deep thought to attach to this horrible event."

"That's the spirit, Charly. Drink your booze. And call Chief Stark."

Maybe I shouldn't be a chef, thought Benny. *Maybe I should join the police. Of course, it wouldn't be as exciting as working at Charly's.*

"You call the police," Charly said. "My heart, it is beating too much." Charly drank a very large toddy. Then he had another.

John Stark and two of his officers, plus the forensic

123

team from the State Police, plus Dr. Bingham, who acted as coroner, plus Sam Higgins the photographer, had tramped a great deal of snow into the kitchen and basement. They had dusted for prints and made a big mess. Stark had questioned Charly and Benny. Did they know the victim? Did they have any idea how killer and victim had gotten in?

"He and his friend Howard Voss are guests of Win Crozier and Morty Cohen," Charly told the chief. "I go to their antiques shop years ago, in the city. I did not like him, he did not like me. A worm in another incarnation, no doubt. And he pout, like a little girl." Charly made a pouting face.

"You didn't care for the guy," Stark concluded.

"That is correct, Chief Stark. But I would never soil my hands by killing such—such canaille. He is a nothing, but a bad nothing."

Stark scratched his head. "Would you have killed him if he'd been—you know—a regular guy? Not a bad nothing?"

"Not even then," Charly said vehemently. He hiccuped quietly. "Killing is for the cow-ard. And I am not . . ."

"Right, Charly," Stark interrupted. "No one's accusing you. But I think we've got the picture. What did this guy do to you, exactly?"

"They sell me valuable antique very cheap. Only later do they find out the value. The other man, Howard, he laugh, say they should have known. But this man Robbie, he is furious—and with me! Can you imagine?"

"Nope, can't imagine it," Stark said dryly.

"The four men dine here Saturday night. After I close up, I think I lock the door, and I go over to Rex Cingale's. But on Sunday morning when I come, the kitchen door is open. I check dining room, I look down into basement, I look over kitchen, all is hokay."

"Come in tomorrow, Charly, sign a statement, okay? When you've—ah—calmed down. We'll go over everything then. You'll have a clearer head."

"Hokay, Chief Stark. My head, it is clear, now. My brain, not so clear."

"Don't go down into the cellar, okay? We've put a tape on the cellar door." Stark and the rest of the men left. Robbie, too, departed on a stretcher, bound for the autopsy room at the Van Buren County Hospital.

Charly, a bucket at his side, was mopping the kitchen floor. The cellar was where they kept their bar supplies, certain canned and bottled goods. How could they not go down into the cellar? But he wasn't going to argue with Stark. Benny was cleaning off surfaces.

Charly, wringing out his mop, said, "We will go home now, the cleaners can finish tomorrow, I give them a call. You want me to drive you home in the van? We put the *moto* in the back?"

"Nah, it's a short ride and I'm careful," Benny said. The chicken carcasses were now in a plastic bag in an outside garbage bin. They would be picked up tomorrow, weather permitting. Charly told Benny he couldn't bear the thought of cooking anything that had come into contact with that revolting specimen. Alive, Munro was bad; dead, he was frozen roadkill.

After Benny left, Charly put on his outerwear and locked the door behind him. He jiggled the knob. Even he could see that the lock was easy to pick. Dusk was falling, the snow was, too: beautiful yet treacherous.

Back at his house, Charly climbed up to his bedroom and removed his clothing. He felt contaminated. The

125

woolen garments went into a paper shopping bag, for the cleaner's. The washables went into the dirty clothes basket. Charly ran a bath, and as the tub was filling he remembered the slip of paper that had come fluttering down from the freezer, along with Robbie's body. He retrieved it from his trousers in the dry-cleaning bag.

On the slip of paper were scribbled two telephone numbers. One of them was his, the listed home telephone number that he let the machine answer. He also had an unlisted number for friends. The life of a restaurateur is like a politician's: odd people call, at all hours. The other telephone number looked like a local exchange, as well. He'd check, after his bath.

Lying in the bubbles Charly tried to reconstruct the crime. Robbie makes a telephone call (or two) from Win's house. Then he drives to La Fermette's deserted parking lot to meet someone. That person kills him, and carries his body to Charly's restaurant. Why the restaurant? It is the nearest place. Not another house, except for Charly's, for at least a quarter mile. And why the cellar freezer? Charly pondered. He rarely used his downstairs freezer, therefore the body could lie there for weeks and not be discovered. Now, who would know this? Well, Rex Cingale had an old freezer in his basement, and some of his other restaurateur friends did, too. Old freezers sometimes go for next to nothing at sales of defunct restaurants. What had Rex said? "Someday I'll find a use for it." Exactly. That's what he had thought, too, buying the appliance. So what did he know about the killer? The killer might have once worked in a restaurant. It wasn't much, but it was something.

Charly, almost sober by now, got out of the tub, dried himself, and put on his pajamas and robe. Downstairs, he checked his answering machine. The light was blinking. Charly pressed the PLAY button. "This is Robbie Munro, Mr. Poisson, of Voss & Munro Antiques. I'd like to meet with you to discuss getting back that Lalique vase you stole from us. Dark forces are at work. If you don't stop stealing my antiques I will be forced to use strong measures. Evildoers must be punished. I will call again." The machine clicked off.

The poor man is ga-ga, Charly thought. *I bought those antiques twenty years ago.* With great care he opened the machine and lifted off the tape. He put it in an envelope. He knew Stark would want to hear this.

Then he took out the piece of paper, smoothed it down, and peered at the other number. He dialed it and a message came on: "This is the Kendell house . . ." Charly hung up.

"Naw, the chief's gone home," said a voice at the police station. Charly then asked for Officer Matucci.

Officer Vincent Matucci was the brother of Bobby Matucci, gambler and bartender, though the similarity ended there. Vince was a huge man, at least six feet three, over two hundred pounds, almost as big as Stark. He was twenty-nine years old, a law-abiding man, marginally more intelligent than his brother Bobby and dedicated to his job. That he and Bobby were siblings was a genetic mystery. It was unthinkable that Mamma Matucci had produced one brother from another gene bank: both sons bore a striking resemblance to Papa Matucci. Bobby had inherited his father's weak chin, dreamy outlook, and slender build; Vince had inherited his father's brown, widely spaced eyes, his prominent nose, his mother's hefty peasant body, and her determination to get things done. In an honest way.

127

When Vince came on the line Charly was at his most deferential. "Officer Matucci, this is Charles Poisson, I found the body of Robbie Munro."

"Oh, yeah; Charly, what can we do for ya?"

Charly nervously cleared his throat. "Well, in cleaning out my pockets, I find a slip of paper with two telephone numbers on it, I think it fall out of the freezer. In the confusion of the moment, I pocket it, then I forget."

"Oh, yeah? In the confusion of the moment, uh?"

"That is correct, Officer." Charly's voice was very humble.

"So you, like, smoothed it out, wiped off any fingerprints, tryin' to see what it said. Am I right?"

"You are right." Charly's voice was weary.

"And what did it say?"

"It have two telephone numbers. Mine, and Mr. Matthew Kendell. I called. He is the man whose wife die. And there is something else. On my answering machine. The voice of Mr. Robbie Munro. A most strange message. I have removed the tape, being very careful about the fingerprint, and I have put it in an envelope for the police."

Vince Matucci shook his head. Whose fingerprints could possibly be on the tape, except for Charly's? He wasn't going to go into it, though. He merely said, "Thanks, Charly. I'm not comin' out now, though, and neither should you. Just hang on to them. You can bring them in the morning. Chief says you're comin' in, sign a statement."

"I will hang on to it, Officer, with my life," said the great detective.

"Allo, allo? Charles Poisson, 'ere." His other telephone,

128

the private line, had just rung. It was Maurice. He sounded sober and excited.

"Do you remember, Charly, you wanted to buy my shares a few months ago? Well, I think I'd like to get out of the restaurant business, sell you my shares. Is that agreeable? There's a big stock offering coming up, as I told you, and I want to put the money in that."

"Wonderful, Maurice," Charly said enthusiastically. "I will telephone Jimmy Houghton tomorrow, and ask that he sell some of my stock to pay you in cash, and also Jonathan Murray, my lawyer." Then, fearing that he sounded too happy about dumping his partner of many years, he added, "But of course, my heart, it is heavy."

"Yes, yes," Maurice said impatiently, "my heart is heavy, too. But time marches on, Charly, time marches on."

"Correct, Maurice. Time for you to march on your own."

"Exactly, Charly. I'm glad we see eye to eye."

Merveilleux, Charly thought as he hung up the telephone. Finally, he would be free of Maurice. A grand thought. The day was ending well, after all.

Charly Finds a Clue

CHARLY WAS AT THE KLOVER POLICE STATION EARLY Tuesday morning to dictate a statement, reread it, and sign it. This took a bit of time, but Charly wanted to get it right. Officer Matucci almost, but did not, lose his temper. Charly reminded him of his great-Uncle Mario, who never signed his name without first reading and rereading, changing, emending, editing, dissecting the document in question. "You sign somet'in wit'out readin', they'll get ya every time, the fuckers," Uncle Mario would say. So Officer Matucci bit his tongue as Charly dithered. Finally, both were satisfied with the report, and Charly signed his name with a flourish.

Charly also gave Officer Matucci the envelope containing Robbie's note, and the tape from the answering machine. Vince hurried him out of the station, not impolitely, but with a certain dispatch. It was, after all, a working day. The blizzard had stopped and the snowplows had cleared the roads.

Benny was slicing onions when Charly arrived at the kitchen. Mick was washing dishes. Based on past snowstorms, Charly decided to prepare for twenty customers: a quiet lunch, and no dinner to prepare since the restaurant was closed on Tuesday nights. The leek and potato soup was bubbling, as was a pot of pea soup, with ham hocks, celery, and carrots. They would form a dozen hamburgers, and prepare for eight or ten sandwiches. "I only make one egg pie," Charly decided, "very few will show up."

"I wouldn't count on that," old Mick said from the dishwashing station. "The minute folks hear that you find a body in your basement, they'll be here thick as thieves, snow or no snow."

"No one will know," Charly said confidently. "The police agreed not to tell the newspapers where the body was found. Think what it would do to our business, for customer to know a body was found here. Bad, bad."

"Hmpf," said Mick.

There was a knock on the door and Barbara Baleine, Maurice's wife and Charly's decorator, swept in. She was a big, imposing woman, almost as big as Charly's Tante Jeanne, taller than Charly and broader, too.

130

Covering her large frame was a fluffy beige down coat, tan gabardine slacks tucked into brown suede fur-lined boots, white cashmere sweater with matching shawl thrown over her short, curly, strawberry-blond hair. Charly liked her a lot.

"Hello, everyone," Barbara said. "Now, Charly, d'you have time to sit down for a minute? Maurice is driving me wild."

"Of course, my dear Barbara. Benny, bring over two coffee, would you?"

"You know," Barbara said as soon as they sat down, "Maurice and I are almost separated. I'll divorce him eventually. I can't take any more of his craziness. He's putting every cent he has into this awful stock, and he's going to lose his shirt. He asked me to lend him money, and I said no. He even called Mummy, but she just laughed."

"He call me last night," Charly said, "and he want me to buy his stock in La Fermette. I am happy, as I have wanted to get rid of Maurice for years."

"I know, Charly. But can you make sure he doesn't get the money for a while? I talked to Jimmy, he thinks the Compu stock's going to fall. Soon."

"Of course, my dear Barbara. You know"—here Charly lowered his voice—"that the stockbroker, Buonsarde, is supposed to be connected to the Mafia."

"Well," Barbara said, adjusting something in the vicinity of her big bosom, "I didn't know, but I'm not surprised. Maurice is a double Leo. All these wild enthusiasms for things that don't pan out."

"He is a triple-A donkey," Charly said. "If he lose his money, he will want you to support him. And he will spend until you have nothing left."

"Thank goodness Mummy made me sign a prenup,"

131

Barbara said. "I disagreed with her at the time, but see how wrong I was. No, Charly, it's time for Maurice to go. I think he's crazy."

"Yes, perhaps he is," Charly agreed. "Poor Maurice, with his fine education. He tells everyone he own the restaurant, that I am merely his cook. He lives in another world."

"That's what Dr. Metz said," Barbara agreed. "And it's not my world. I'll divorce him eventually, but for now, I'm not giving him one penny. Dr. Metz says, don't argue with him. Just say no."

"Is wise, my dear Barbara. Now, tell me, have you ever heard of an antiques shop in New York called Voss & Munro?"

Barbara frowned, running the name through her mental Rolodex. "I may have, Charly. I've never done business with them, but the name rings a bell. Not a nice bell. I don't think they have a good reputation."

"Ah-ha. They visit Win Crozier and . . ." Charly recounted the story of Win's washstand, and then of his and Benny's terrible discovery: Munro's body in his downstairs freezer. Barbara listened, openmouthed.

"Charly, that's horrible. Think of all the negative publicity if this gets out. A body in a restaurant? Oh, my. Why, if this gets into the papers . . ."

"It will not," Charly said. "The editor of the newspaper, he is a good customer. I call him last night."

Barbara took on a worldly air. She held up the fingers of her right hand and rubbed them together, the universal gesture for money changing hands.

"No, no, my dear Barbara, nothing as gauche as money." Charly acted affronted. "But he is an understanding man, he see that this kind of publicity would be bad for me. Besides"—Charly paused—"he has a few secrets, too, that he would not want known. And he knows that I know."

"I see." Barbara grinned. Charly had his own methods for dealing with "the relations public." A case of wine, a party at cost, a kilo tin of caviar, such things were not unknown. A bit of blackmail? That, too. "And dear Win and Morty, such sweeties," Barbara went on. Win and Morty had put a lot of business Barbara's way. "Have you told them? About the body, I mean."

"No," Charly said, "is not my business to do so. The police will have notified Win and Morty and Howard Voss yesterday, I am sure."

Barbara stood up. "Well, Charly, I'm off to Albany. The roads are plowed, and I'm meeting with a new client."

Right after Barbara left, John Stark stamped in, his face reddened from the wind. He accepted coffee and pound cake, then he pulled a piece of paper from his pocket. Although he disapproved of Charly's amateur meddling, this time, like it or not, Charly was part of the action.

"What d'you think of this, Charly. It's a copy of the suicide note found by Amanda Kendell's body."

Charly unfolded the paper and read:

"So oftin I've wanned to kill myself, just end the wole mess. And now it will be all taken careuf. I cannot take it any more and it will be so good to end it. I have been so depressed."

Charly read and reread the note, then frowned. "Hmmm, her *orthographe,* her spelling, is worse than mine. If I write a suicide note, it would not sound like that. Have you heard the result of the autopsy?"

"No, Charly, Doc Bingham's backed up. He's promised to get to it today. You know, we have so few homicides in Van Buren County we can't afford a full-time pathologist, so everything takes longer than it should. Amanda tried to kill herself twice before, I told you about that."

"Yes, Chief. But is it not convenient, her husband puts property in her name, then divorce, and the lawyer say the properties are legally hers. Then *eh, eh, hopla!* she kill herself. Is nice for Mr. Kendell, no?"

"All true, Charly."

"And when she come to our kitchen just the day before, she is so happy, she will begin the new life. Another slice of pound cake, Chief?"

Stark rose from his chair. "No, Charly, thanks. I gotta run. Vince says you signed the document. I'll let you know what Hy finds out, but I can almost promise you, no surprises from either Amanda or Munro. Him, they're thawing out. Good freezer you have. He's frozen solid."

"At least, he is not a suicide, eh, Chief?"

After Stark left, Charly decided to soak some more dried cepe mushrooms for the pasta with mushroom sauce that he always offered on Wednesday nights. He'd make the sauce this afternoon, sauté shallots and garlic, add flour, let the roux cook, add chicken stock and white wine, let it reduce, pour in Madeira, let it reduce some more. Meanwhile he'd sauté fresh white mushrooms and portobellos and add them and the drained cepes to the sauce. At this point, it would be cooled, then refrigerated and left to rest for a day, which would make it taste richer—an old chef's secret. Tomorrow, he'd add a spoonful of *glace de poulet* (chicken essence), heavy cream, and a big handful of chopped parsley.

Charly reached for the box of dried mushrooms. It

was on a shelf above the cutting area, a big red tin. He got down the box, lifted the top, reflecting that it must be quite empty, and he should fill it up again from the dried mushrooms that he kept in the upstairs freezer. There, on top of the plastic bag that preserved the mushrooms, was a piece of pale blue paper. He pulled out the paper and read, "*stek, oven frys, sandwich meat, visit Patty, get gas.*" He turned the paper over and read, "*So oftin I wanned to kill myself, just end the wole mess. I cannot take it any more and have been so dipresed.*"

"Mick! Benny!" Charly shouted. He held the paper out, and his hand was shaking. "Please come quick and see what I have found."

LEEK AND POTATO SOUP

YIELD: 8 SERVINGS

4 tablespoons butter

8 leeks, white and pale green part only, well washed to remove sand, sliced

4 large potatoes, peeled and chunked

8 cups chicken stock

Final enrichment: 4 tablespoons butter, salt and freshly ground white pepper to taste

Melt butter in large nonaluminum pot at medium-low heat and cook leeks and potatoes until they turn translucent, 6-8 minutes. Pour in stock, bring to a boil, lower heat and simmer, covered, one hour. Let cool. Either puree or leave vegetables whole. Taste for seasoning, adding salt, pepper, and butter as needed. Add more stock if too thick.

Gossip on the Menu at La Fermette

THERE WAS LITTLE TIME TO DISCUSS THE NOTE, however, since it was nearly noon and cars began pulling up outside. But Charly, Mick, and Benny at least had time to agree on one thing: that this paper proved that Amanda's message was part of a letter, and not a specifically written suicide note. Charly would call Stark after lunch.

Charly was surprised when Tommy Glade and Elton Briggs, the Tuesday lunch waiters, horned into the kitchen to announce that the barroom was already packed and more customers were arriving.

"They all want to know about that body you found yesterday," Elton said. "Place's mobbed, I hope you've got plenty of food."

"We made almost nothing. With the snow, we think no one will come. How could they know, when the papers have reported nothing, as yet?"

"Well," Elton said, "after I spoke with you last night, Charly, I told my Aunt Etta and she probably told a few ladies in her beauty parlor this morning: you know they all go there for the news as well as the wash-and-sets. And I saw the Richards' Produce truck driving away from here as I was driving up, so you probably told old Sam."

"Ah, yes," Charly sighed. "But I tell him not to tell anyone."

Elton snorted. "Sam's better than the newspapers. He reports all the news that isn't fit to print. And I talked to

Hubert Dupont last night, he's a waiter here tomorrow night, and he probably told a few people at the florist's where he works today. You didn't tell me it was a big secret."

"And they are all here," Charly concluded as he quickly sautéed more sausages and vegetables for two more egg pies, and Benny heated more chicken stock to make a quick batch of chicken noodle soup. Even Mick was working as a cook, washing and slicing more potatoes for french fries.

"Push the soups, Elton, and the sandwiches," Charly said. "We only have one egg pie until this next batch is done."

"Three egg pies with fries, two hot roast beef sandwiches, one pork sandwich down, hold the mayo, three pea soups, and two burgers." Tommy Glade slapped down the orders on the serving counter. More hamburger was defrosting in the microwave.

"They all want to talk to you, Charly," Elton said, putting down a fresh batch of orders.

"I go out when I can," Charly answered, dishing up soups and ladling gravy onto the hot sandwiches. Mick was now slicing the cold meat, while the dirty dishes piled up. They'd all pitch in after lunch. "No leftovers for Bruno today," Mick muttered to himself, but Charly heard.

"Plenty for Bruno, do not worry, Mick. And for you, too."

"I love that dog like a child," Mick said. "Don't forget, Charly, you promised to take Bruno if anything happens to me."

"Nothing happen to you, Mick, but if it does, then I will adopt Bruno and I will love him like a child. I promise. When you have cut the roast beef, cut the pork

138

and the ham."

The back door opened with a bang and a gust of icy wind, and Maurice Baleine sauntered into the frenzied kitchen. "Good afternoon, everybody," he called jauntily.

Charly looked up. "If you have come to work, Maurice, then take off your coat and start right now," he said coldly. "We have big crowd today, we did not expect. Do not stand around, Maurice, you are in the way."

"Touchy, aren't we?" Maurice sauntered over to the big pine table and sat down, not seeming to notice the kitchen's frantic air, Charly and Benny flipping burgers, cutting sandwiches, ladling soup, dishing up french fries.

"Benny, could you bring me a cup of soup? I don't care what kind." Maurice slouched down in his chair, making himself quite at home.

Benny affected not to hear. "You want me to check the egg pies, Charly?" Benny turned his back on Maurice and opened the oven. "Not done," he said.

"Ten more minute for the pies," Charly said. "If the egg is runny, no one will eat. Mick, we need more pork cut." Tommy Glade hurried into the kitchen and began loading a tray with food from the serving counter.

"Tommy," Charly said, "chicken noodle soup is ready now, be sure to push it." Charly turned to Maurice who was still sitting in an elegant camel-hair coat. "Maurice, take off your coat and begin to load the dishwasher. Be sure to scrape the dishes well. There is no time for sitting around."

Maurice looked amazed. "Scrape the dishes? What do you think I am?"

Charly put down his knife and walked over to the table, hands on hips. "I think you are a fool, Maurice.

139

So get out. We have no time for fools. If you cannot help, then leave. Out! Out!" And Charly, angry, pointed to the back door with a shaking finger.

Without a word, Maurice got up. But instead of heading for the back door, he sauntered toward the swinging doors of the dining room.

"Watch out, hot food behind you," Tommy shouted. Maurice turned abruptly, and in turning he collided with Tommy's tray. Tommy swung the tray sideways, trying to avoid Maurice's bulky body, but a bowl of steaming chicken noodle soup sailed off the tray and hit Maurice in the chest. His natty overcoat was drenched in chicken broth, noodles, and bits of chicken. The bowl crashed to the floor and broke. Tommy took one look at the mess and, shifting the tray on his shoulder, detoured around Maurice and pushed open the door to the barroom.

"Clean it up," Charly shouted, brushing past the counter to face Maurice. "Clean it up, now." Charly pointed to the mess.

Maurice took one look at Charly's face and did as he was told. He got a rag from the dishwashing area, wet it, and mopped up the soup. Then, without a word, he left the kitchen by the back door. Charly leaned against the counter and wiped his face with a corner of his apron. Idly, he picked up a noodle that Maurice had missed and flung it in the waste bin. It occurred to him that he hadn't called Jimmy Houghton, yet, to discuss Maurice's severance. Overcome with rage, Charly hurried into his office and with trembling fingers dropped four drops of Dr. Bach's Rescue Remedy onto his tongue. He could understand how murders occurred in restaurant kitchens. Cooks worked at fever pitch. Tension was high. Oh, yes, Maurice would have to go. He should have gone years ago.

"Well, we did it, Charly," old Mick said as he lifted a load of dishes from the dishwasher, then sat down at the table with a bowl of chicken noodle. Benny was slumped at the pine table, sipping pea soup. Charly had just returned from the dining room, where he'd been talking to the last of his lunch customers. He walked over to the stove, got a bowl of noodle soup, and sat at the table.

"Yes, Mick, thanks to you and Benny. And I learn something interesting, talking to the people. They know what happen, and they are not much interested. What they all want to do, why they all come today, is to give me their opinion. It is a homosexual murder and homosexuals love dining out in restaurant, so that is why body is here; it is a local who has murdered a stranger and brought him to my kitchen because I am not a local; it is the police who are jealous because I treat Chief Stark and his family to dinner once or twice a year, and do not treat the rest of the force; the murdered man is a woman in disguise, a lesbian murder, and they choose my kitchen because I only have male help; which is not true, since Patty work here. Ah, I have never heard so many stories. Now I see what poor Chief Stark go through." Charly shook his head in disgust.

"And why he doesn't like your buttin' in," Mick pointed out.

Charly shrugged this off. "But my advice is good advice, the advice I hear in my dining room is kre-zee."

Benny nudged Mick with his elbow, but neither man said a word. All you could hear was slurping.

"And," Charly continued. "There are even leftover for you, Mick, and Bruno. You see what good planning can do?"

CHARLY HANDLED AMANDA'S NOTE CAREFULLY. HE picked it up by a corner and dropped it in a manila envelope. This time, Charly vowed, the police would have no cause for complaint.

"Good afternoon, Officer. Is Chief Stark in?" Stark, hearing Charly's voice, came out of his office and beckoned Charly in.

"Well, Charly, I take back everything I said. We've had some surprising news from Hy Bingham, he just called. He hasn't written up the autopsy report yet, but he wanted me to know. Amanda's hyoid bone was fractured on both sides and there are bruises around her neck, indicating that she was strangled to death. Her eyes were filled with petechiae, you know, little red hemorrhages, plus there was skin lividity around her throat. The gunshot came after she was dead."

"Ah." Charly wasn't surprised. "I am shocked."

"Right," Stark said and thought, *good thing he doesn't make a living at being an actor.* "Yep, after she was dead, someone stuck a gun in her mouth and pulled the trigger. There was no gunshot residue on her hands, but that doesn't mean much. Nobody bagged her hands, we were sure we were dealing with suicide."

"So now it is murder," Charly said.

"Yep."

"And, Chief, look at what I find this morning." Charly explained to Stark that after Amanda had left the restaurant Friday afternoon, she told Patty she'd lost her list. They'd looked around the kitchen, but the list had not been found. He remembered that particularly, since both he and Patty had joked about making lists, and how they then lost the lists.

"Now I see what happen. Amanda dropped the list in the mushroom box when she put down her purse. This is the first time since Friday that I open the box."

"I wonder who she was writing to?" Stark mused.

"She was going to visit her sister in Massachusetts," Charly reminded Stark. "She probably write to a friend who live nearby. I do that when I visit my family. I write to my friends, asking if maybe we can have lunch."

"So do I," Stark agreed. "Or I call. I called several people last summer when Betsy and the girls and I went to Maine. Just to alert them."

"And," Charly continued, "she is not pleased with what she say, so she throw away the page. Then, being of a frugal nature, again something that I do, she use the other side for list. She write badly, Chief. So she probably ruin several sheet of paper."

"I did check the wastebaskets in the house," Stark said, "just out of habit. There was one in Amanda's office, and it was empty. The one upstairs in their bathroom had normal stuff, and there was none in their bedroom."

"So there were at least two page that she throw away," Charly mused. "The one found near her body, and the one in the mushroom box. Probably more thrown away by the killer."

Stark got up, indicating that his interview with Charly was over. Enough was enough. Now, Charly wanted to waste time on theorizing. "Don't waste too much time on theories, Charly," Stark said, but he knew that he was talking to the air.

When Charly walked in the back door of his house, the

telephone (his private one) was ringing. It was Rex Cingale.

"We all set for tonight, Charly?"

"Tonight? Oh, *mon Dieu.* Tuesday, I forgot. Of course, Rex."

Several times a month Rex and Charly would dine at local restaurants, to measure the competition. Tonight, they had planned to visit The Country Squire across the Hudson River. Charly enjoyed Rex's company. Rex was a walking encyclopedia of Van Buren County gossip, and though Patty, Benny, Julius, indeed most of Charly's friends, turned up their noses at Steak Heaven, it was a successful operation, of its kind. The steaks were first class; the bar was jammed from opening to closing.

Rex enjoyed Charly's company, too. He admitted that Charly's place was "a fuckin' class act," and Charly, with his constant fussing, his homeopathy, his eating fads, and his flower essences, was the image of Rex's Uncle Mario, who drank artichoke water as a diuretic, put garlic slivers in his shoes to stimulate the circulation, nibbled on mulberry leaves to firm up his gums, and spent his winter evenings cracking apricot pits to get at the kernels, which he preserved in sugared vodka and used as a rejuvenating tonic. Neither Uncle Mario nor Charly would divulge their ages, either.

"I'll bring the pickup, it's got four-wheel drive," Rex said. He wasn't crazy about Charly's driving. "That fuckin' Lincoln, I love it, but it don't do well in the snow. Fishtails goin' around corners. You call and reserve?"

"No, Rex, I forgot. After what happened with Bobby, do you think it wise to go there? They may think we are snooping. Perhaps it would be better just to show up,

144

not make a reservation."

"Not professional," Rex said. "Besides, Carlo's the general manager of the whole shebang, he probably won't even be in the dining room. And, in any case, so what? I told you what Angie Vongola said. There's no legal way Bobby could offer his shares in my restaurant as collateral."

"True, Rex." Charly wondered if he'd see Ugo Buonsarde, his newest customer. Ugo reputedly owned The Country Squire. But he didn't mention this to Rex. "So you pick me up, eh? Five o'clock?"

"Let's make it half past, Charly. Place like that, probably don't even open until six, and it won't take us a half hour."

"Hokay, Rex. I dress with care. Like the man who has many thousands to spend on pleasure. Too bad I do not own a diamond ring."

"I'll wear enough diamonds for both of us, Charly."

The Country Squire restaurant was part of a big complex designed for weekend guests: nightclub, coffee shop, luxury motel, hotel and restaurant, gym, mini golf course, tennis courts, swimming pools both indoor and outdoor. Rex drove up to the red-canopied restaurant entrance, where a valet stood ready to take his pickup. The valet was dressed for the weather in a sensible down jacket, though he wore an elaborate hat, a wide-brimmed felt number like an old-time riverboat gambler's. There was a pheasant feather in its crown. Rex pocketed the valet chit, and he and Charly entered the restaurant.

The maître d' greeted them like old friends. Ushered them to a corner table overlooking the snowy golf course. Rex and Charly, in a professional capacity, noted the effusiveness of his welcome.

"Makes ya feel good," Rex said. "Like it's okay to spend money."

"Yes," Charly agreed. "But perhaps too friendly. A courteous welcome is one thing; this guy, he pretend I am the most wonderful person in the world. It make me suspicious."

Rex was delighted. "My Uncle Mario woulda said the exact same thing. You go up to Mario, you say, 'Uncle Mario, I am so happy to see you, you look terrific, I never seen you looking so good,' and you know what the old geezer says? He says, 'Whaddaya want, kid, cut the bullshit.' "

Another waiter appeared, this time a very young man. "Can I get you gentlemen a drink? My name's Julian, I'm going to be your server, tonight."

"Julian, huh?" Rex said. True to his word, Rex had worn a diamond ring, diamond tie tack, and a gold bracelet studded with diamonds.

"That's correct, sir."

Rex ordered a Campari soda, Charly a Dubonnet.

"I don't like this 'I'm gonna be your server' business," Rex said. "Too phony. I did that at my store, my dining-room customers would shit."

"Is the fashion, Rex. But I agree. Not for me, either. And of course, most of my customers know all the waiters, anyway."

"That's right. My waiters been with me for years, too. Fancy place," Rex said, looking around, admiring the large crystal chandelier, the red velvet banquettes, the pine wainscotting, the red flocked-velvet wallpaper.

To Charly, it looked hideous. He merely nodded. "Money has been spent," he agreed. That, at least, was true.

146

The large leather-backed menus held no surprises as far as Charly was concerned. Almost everything was a "value added" product, cooked and frozen by the manufacturer: the battered jalapeño peppers, potato skins, fried shrimp, spring rolls, cream soups, escargots, stuffed mushrooms, guacamole platter. The entrees, too, aroused suspicion: shrimp stuffed with crabmeat, sole stuffed with seafood, marinated steak, breaded veal cutlet, barbecued pork chops, chicken breast stuffed with various fillings, the fisherman's platter, the roast half duckling. All the products advertised in the food-trade publications under headlines like "We do the work, you reap the profits."

"All that high-priced shit my distributor carries," Rex said.

"You right, Rex. High food cost. And not tasty."

"Man," Rex continued, "their kitchen must be wall-to-wall freezers. You remember when I was buyin' all that frozen garbage?"

"I remember, Rex. And you say Angelo and Ricky, your broilermen, they cannot make the potato, the vegetable."

"We're makin' our own baked potatoes, mashed potatoes, zucchini with garlic. My Aunt Philomena's helping the guys. We're saving money and, the best thing, people eat the stuff. Before, I was throwin' half the stuff away."

Julian glided up. "Gentlemen, may I present the wine list?"

Charly accepted the gold-tasseled folder and began to thumb through the pages. He knew that Rex wasn't much of a wine drinker, but he was curious. Some fine-sounding wines, here, at suspiciously low prices. "They don't have a watchamacallit, a wine waiter," Rex

147

commented.

"A sommelier," Charly said. "No, I imagine most of their customers drink Coca-Cola or blended whiskey. I bet you, less than five percent order wine. Is big list, but . . . not a good list." He looked around the dining room, which was less than half full. The customers were, for the most part, middle-aged, with a lot of polyester and rhinestones in evidence.

When Julian again appeared to take their dinner order, Charly and Rex both ordered steak, stuffed baked potato, and something which the menu referred to coyly as "vegetable medley supreme." Charly ordered the 1992 Barolo, and salad with house dressing.

"I do not think that this will be a memorable meal," Charly said.

"Neither do I," Rex said, then coughed significantly as Carlo Calamare glided up to their table. Tonight, Carlo was a study in black, an outfit that, Charly figured, a Texas funeral director would be proud of: black sharkskin suit, black and silver cowboy boots, a silver and rhinestone bolo tie clasp, silver belt buckle shaped like a saguaro cactus, which was digging into Carlo's middle. His black hair was slicked back with brilliantine and his sallow skin shone in the dim light. Woodsy cologne had been lavishly applied.

"An honor to have you with us tonight, Mr. Cingale, Mr. Poisson," Calamare said politely. "May I offer you a drink?"

"No more for me," Rex said. "I gotta drive, and we ordered wine."

"We thank you, sir," Charly said, annoyed at Rex for mentioning the wine. If Calamare was smart, he'd find out they'd ordered the 1992 Barolo and substitute a good brand for the—no doubt—inferior wine on the list.

148

"Then your first drinks will be on the house," Calamare said. "Please let us know if there's anything we can do for you. And enjoy your dinner."

Calamare started to bow himself away, but Charly said, "You have some very beautiful thing in this room. The crystal chandelier, the grandfather clock in the entrance, the painting of the woods and deer above the bar. Did you find the antiques locally?"

Calamare smiled. "All of our rooms are furnished with antiques," he told them. "And you'd be surprised at how many we sell. We hire an antiques expert to find the furniture, and to tell us how much it's worth. He buys much of it at auction and estate sales. What we don't use ourselves, we store in a big barn at the back of the building. Why, just this past weekend, a couple liked the furnishings in their suite so much, they bought every bit of it." Calamare chuckled. "And it's not cheap, either."

"The painting above the bar is particularly fine," Charly said.

"New this week. We sold the one hanging there last week. Now, you're sure there's nothing we can do for you gentlemen?"

Charly and Rex both shook their heads and Calamare glided away. "You can quit buggin' Bobby," Rex muttered as soon as Carlo was out of earshot.

Julian arrived with the Barolo, which he opened expertly. He poured a small amount into Charly's glass. Charly sipped, then nodded to the waiter.

Before Charly could stop him, Rex picked up his glass and took a big gulp. He made a face. "This stuff," he told Charly, coughing, "would take the varnish off my bar. And my varnish is thick."

Charly sniffed at his glass, then took another cautious

149

swallow. No wonder Ugo Buonsarde told Charly his Barolo was the best. But that was what the French call *"un compliment de la main gauche,"* a left-handed compliment, since this was the worst wine Charly had ever drunk. Anything compared to this was ambrosia. "It is certainly a terrible wine," Charly agreed. "It is not a Barolo from Italy. In fact, it is doubtful that it is even wine."

The remainder of the meal showed little improvement on the wine. The steak had been in its marinade a long time, and Rex pronounced it "fuckin' mush." The baked stuffed potatoes were freezer-burned and still frozen in the center, and the "vegetable medley supreme" turned out to be frozen mixed vegetables topped with a trio of canned artichoke hearts, which were, in turn, covered with a hollandaise sauce that, Charly decided, had come from a dry mix, since it tasted bitter and too salty. Neither real butter, nor real egg yolks, nor real lemon juice, had ever come near it. The salad, which arrived with the main courses, was shredded iceberg lettuce topped with a gelatinous orange lava that tasted mainly of sugar, vinegar, and something metallic.

"A remarkable meal," Charly said truthfully to Carlo Calamare, who glided up to offer desserts and coffee on the house, "remembering the delicious desserts you offered me, Mr. Poisson."

At least he got my name right, Charly thought. He told Carlo that he would love a rich dessert, and what did Mr. Calamare suggest? Both Rex and Charly settled on Calamare's choice, "The Country Squire Extravaganza," which was billed as a mound of macadamia brittle ice cream covered in chocolate and butterscotch sauces, with shaved chocolate, strawberries, and almond wafers. When it arrived, a mammoth portion sizzling with Fourth of July sparklers, the entire dining room turned to look. Charly smiled at Rex.

"See, Rex, we do learn something after all."

"What, Charly?" Rex asked, his mouth full.

"We learn that people who will eat the worst food will still demand a serious dessert. And pay for it. I look at the menu. This dessert is ten dollar. Each serving meant for two people."

Both Charly and Rex ate every drop of their dessert.

As Rex and Charly prepared to drive home Charly said, "Rex, could you drive around, we see the entire complex?"

The white brick buildings were joined together by a series of glass-enclosed breezeways, and the ficus trees inside and the fir trees outside were garlanded with winking white lights. It was a handsome layout.

Beyond the lighted areas were a series of barns, which looked ghostly silhouetted against the blue-white snow. Rex stopped by one of the barns and Charly, flashlight in hand, walked to the window and peered inside. Then he turned and reentered the car. "Is filled with furniture," he told Rex. "Hundreds of pieces of furniture, from top to bottom. The Country Squire's antiques furniture business must be profitable, indeed."

Charly Fights for Independence

IT WAS NINE O'CLOCK WEDNESDAY MORNING WHEN Charly pulled up in front of Jimmy Houghton's small grey clapboard office—actually a house—on Court

Street in Hogton. The building had been a Quaker Meeting House and Charly found it amusing that today, thousands of dollars changed hands daily in a former house of worship.

Jimmy was Charly's investment adviser, and apart from modest sums in Swiss and Luxembourg banks—of which Jimmy was not aware, nor was the IRS—Jimmy handled Charly's savings. And since Charly had the peasant's aversion to spending money frivolously, these savings had accrued, over the years, into a handsome pile. Buying Maurice's shares was a small price to pay for the luxury of not having that arrogant man around.

"Charly, how lovely to see you," said Evelyn Holmes, Jimmy's office manager. Evelyn, a retired schoolteacher, had the figure of a praying mantis, tall, thin, and stooped. She favored well-cut tweed suits and silk blouses in shades of green and blue. She was dressed today in pale green. Charly imagined Evelyn bending over the brussels sprouts in his garden, like a benevolent insect. Like Charly, Evelyn loved cats and now she asked, "How do your cats like this weather?"

"Tairrible," Charly said. "They do not go out, they scratch their cat litter all over the floor, they blame me for the snow. They look at me like so." And Charly looked down his nose, imitating a cat's look of disdain.

Evelyn gave a good belly laugh. "So do mine. So I give them little treats, a can of tuna fish, a few bits of chicken, they love that. Jimmy's on the phone, he'll be out in just a few minutes. You're right on time."

Although the little brass plaque outside the office door said HOUGHTON AND HOUGHTON the elder Houghton, Jimmy's uncle, had been dead for many years. A few months ago Jimmy, a fussy, slightly built man not given to aggressive behavior (but given to frequent dyspepsia), had shot and killed Walter Maxwell, Charly's once-best customer, who was just about to shoot Charly. Walter had killed Jimmy's father years before, and Jimmy, biding his time, gave new meaning to the word "patience." It was like the investments Jimmy suggested: they never produced immediate results, but if you waited, you realized a tidy profit. Jimmy Houghton was a cautious and patient man.

But now even Jimmy's legendary patience, and Charly's not-so-legendary patience, had come to an end. "You've waited far too long in my opinion," Jimmy said, frowning. They were sitting in Jimmy's white-painted office, a plain room, though the Hokusai prints on the wall were genuine and so was the wine-colored Kazak rug on the floor. Like Charly, Jimmy lived simply, but surrounded himself with quality. "Maurice is going to get worse, not better. He's not a well man, Charly, either physically or mentally. He's too fat, drinks too much, and he has delusions of grandeur."

Charly sighed. "Yes, I know. But, I promise his father . . ."

"That's beside the point, Charly. You've given him chance after chance. And now, he doesn't come into the restaurant at all, you tell me. But this time he's the one who wants out, so you're in the clear."

"He does not even come in to greet the customers in the evening. Our Maurice is too grand for that. And of course he still want half the profit."

"'There you are, Charly. We'll offer him the money, sign the papers in a couple of days at Jonathan's office. I'll delay so that he won't have the money to put into that awful Compu stock; it's shot up in the last few days and I have a feeling Buonsarde's going to sell out soon. Maurice will lose everything. Now, with your little sum for a nest egg, he can start over doing something else. Look, I'll call him, and so will Jonathan. You needn't."

"I speak with Jonathan too, Jimmy," Charly said. "He say since our contract call for equal pay for equal work, we can hold that over his head."

"We'll offer him a generous settlement, I'll go over the papers this afternoon," Jimmy fussed. "No need for you to feel guilty. If it wasn't for you, there wouldn't be a restaurant. Didn't you bail out Maurice's father?"

Charly nodded, and sighed. "I hate to see the end of anything."

Jimmy smiled. "So do I, Charly. I'll be dealing with Maxwell's death for years. For thirty years I planned my vengeance and when it happened—it was a big nothing. He was going to shoot, I shot first. Bang. Done. It had become my life, getting even with Walter. Now, what?"

"Who knows?" Charly shrugged. "You still have your *indigestions?*"

"Why, no, Charly, come to think of it, I haven't had an upset stomach since—well, for months. Maybe since Walter."

Charly smiled and stroked his mustache. "Life without Walter and life without an upset tummy. You will have to find another agony."

In La Fermette's kitchen, Benny was preparing lunch and Mick was cleaning the outside of the deep fat fryer.

"I changed the oil this morning first thing, Charly," Mick said. "And now it's heating. Those fried spuds are your best item."

"How are you feeling, Mick? Still catty-wumpus?" It had taken Charly a while to learn old Mick's expressions. Catty-wumpus meant poorly.

"Hunky-dory, Charly." Hunky-dory, Charly knew,

154

was good.

"I'm preparing for an average lunch, Charly," Benny said. "If more people come, well, we have enough food. Chief Stark called, and Julius. I told 'em both you'd call back."

"Let me get my egg pie in the oven, then I call. After lunch, Benny, we can mix the meat loaf and boil the chickens and start the short rib."

Wednesday dinners were never crowded, but to entice the locals Charly offered homey, inexpensive specials: tonight there was the now-famous meat loaf, a chicken and dumpling stew, short ribs in a wine and tomato sauce, pasta with woodland mushrooms. "American favorites with a French accent," the menu boasted. It seemed to work. The locals didn't come in droves, but they came in larger numbers than before.

Charly called Stark. After Charly had annoyed the Klover Police Department in his efforts to help an ongoing investigation some months back, he vowed he'd never call Stark again. This seemed to work. Now, Stark stopped in more often, and appeared to have forgiven Charly's bumbling. He certainly hadn't forgotten, because Stark never forgot anything.

"Funny thing, Charly," Stark now said. "I just got the report from Hy Bingham. Robbie Munro was strangled, too, hyoid bones fractured, leaving marks. Shot in the eye probably after death."

"Just like Amanda."

"Yeah, just like Amanda. And I tried to call Kendell, you know, his is the telephone number on your piece of paper that came from Robby's pocket, and guess what? He's out of town, the girl didn't, or wouldn't, tell me where. And she says she doesn't know when he'll be back."

155

"*Tiens*, imagine that. It gives one food for thought, does it not, Chief?"

"Does indeed, Charly, it does indeed."

Charly then called Julius and gave him a progress report on the murders. "Way to go, Charly." Julius thought Charly's investigations into criminal activities a foolish hobby. Why risk getting yourself killed? But he also knew that Charly would ignore his advice.

"Oh, by the way," Julius continued. "The word is that Compu Class A, which was rising, is going to drop. I'll bet you Buonsarde will sell, soon. The SEC's really breathing down his neck, he'll want to take the money and run."

"Run where?"

"Back to Italy, probably, if he can sneak out without being stopped."

Lunch, as Benny predicted, was served to about thirty customers, and after lunch some simple preparations were made for tonight's dinner. Mick left with a bag for Bruno, and Benny went off to his martial-arts practice. This left Charly with a good two hours to get into trouble. Which he immediately did.

BRAISED SHORT RIBS

YIELD: 4 SERVINGS

4-5 pounds beef short ribs
1 cup flour, or as needed
¼ cup oil
2 large onions, peeled and chopped
4 cloves garlic, peeled and chopped
4 leek whites, chopped
4 carrots, scrubbed and chopped
1 cup tomato puree
1 cup red wine, heated to boiling
2 cups beef stock, heated to boiling
Pinches of thyme and basil $^1/16$ teaspoon each) and 2 bay leaves
To thicken, at end: 1 scant tablespoon cornstarch dissolved in a
   bit of water
Salt and freshly ground pepper and chopped flat-leaf parsley to
   taste

Roll short ribs in flour and sauté in heated oil at medium heat
with onion, garlic, leek whites, and carrots in heavy pot until
brown. Lift out ribs and vegetables and discard oil. Replace
ribs and vegetables in pot with remaining ingredients except
for thickener and final seasoning. Bring to a boil on top of
stove, then bake 4 hours in a 300° oven. Skim fat off the top
and discard. Mix cornstarch with water and pour into pot.
Bake 15 minutes longer, then taste for seasoning, adding salt
and pepper as needed. Serve sprinkled with chopped parsley
and mashed or boiled potatoes.

Charly Snoops

A BAD ANGEL WAS CERTAINLY LURKING AS CHARLY set off in his red van Wednesday afternoon. His plan was to visit Matthew Kendell's house, simply to look around. Kendell was out of town. What harm could there be? Perhaps at the man's house, Charly could get a "feel" for this murderous individual.

Charly drove out to Weber Road. It was a pleasant area, high on a hill overlooking the Hudson River. The houses were set back from the road with long driveways, and the landscaping and buildings had an affluent air: 1920s shingled palaces, or "bungalows" as they were called in Newport, and clapboard pseudo-colonials probably built in the fifties, and sprawling one-story ranch houses of newer vintage. According to the telephone book, the Kendell house was number 136—and there it was with "136" right on the mailbox, and "Kendell" stenciled in black.

If he met someone at the house, Charly decided, it would be an easy matter to introduce himself and say he was looking for another number, and must have made a mistake. A mistake is not a crime. He pulled over to the side of the road and peered down the driveway.

He could barely see the big, low ranch house. The sky was dark, and other houses had lights on, but this place looked deserted. Dark clouds scudded overhead, and from the Hudson River he could hear a mournful clang, possibly from a bell buoy near one of the tiny, ancient lighthouses.

Charly turned into the driveway and parked in front of a two-car garage, now shut. He got out of his van and sniffed the air. Metallic. Sooty. Smelled like more snow.

He walked up a neatly shoveled path to the back door and peered in a window.

There was a grimy entrance, which opened into a large room. It was a kitchen, built in the fifties, wall-to-wall cupboards. Hard to see, very dark. What looked like an opened plastic package of cheap bread was on a counter. The sink was filled with dirty dishes. The kitchen had a desolate look, and even in the dim light Charly could make out smudges and dirty finger marks on cupboards and walls. The linoleum floor needed sweeping—dust balls, scraps of paper littered the sink area.

Charly backed away from the window and began a tour of the outside, which looked unfinished and raw, with no bushes or other landscaping to hinder him as he stepped through the snow, peering in casement windows. How could anyone live in such an ugly place? Yet it had the makings of a handsome house. Barbara Baleine could turn it into a showplace.

Now, this must be the dining room—a big dark table, four high-backed chairs with wooden backs, nothing else. Did anyone ever dine in this room? Charly doubted it. He turned a corner, peered in the next window. This must be the living room, a cheap-looking couch and two upholstered chairs clustered around a glass-topped cocktail table. A nearly empty bookcase in one corner. No paintings or ornaments on the walls. Did these people ever do any entertaining? Probably not.

By now Charly was at the front of the house. Two more living-room windows, then the front door, then another room that must be a study. This room, at least, looked lived in. There was a cracked leather couch, magazines and newspapers strewn on a low table, a big television set. A glass ashtray overflowed with cigarette butts. An empty, torn pizza carton and several half-filled glasses rested atop newspapers. Nothing on the walls here, either. Four more windows. Charly stepped past two rooms, one empty of furniture but filled with boxes, another containing a double bed, stripped, more boxes, a bureau, and a dressing table. Another bedroom, this one large, with a wide bed, unmade, a bureau with a drawer open, spilling out socks. A mirror, and a wall of closets, folding doors open, clothing on the floor.

Perhaps Kendell was moving out, Charly thought, getting settled in a new house that wouldn't remind him of the wife he'd murdered. Charly high-stepped through the snow, ending up at the back door. Automatically, his hand snaked out to the doorknob. He grasped it in his gloved hand, and turned. The door opened.

Charly took a deep breath and stepped into the little foyer leading to the kitchen. He breathed stale air, spoiled food, cigarette smoke.

He was about to move into the rest of the house when headlights flashed on the walls and Charly realized that a car was moving up the driveway. He backed out, shutting the kitchen door behind him, as the headlights pinned him, silhouetted against the now-closed kitchen door.

A dark red car, a sports utility vehicle, braked and stopped abreast of Charly's van. Shaking, his heart thumping, Charly walked down the path and approached the car. *Mon Dieu,* that was a close one.

The driver's door opened and a man got out. Charly recognized him at once: it was Gregory Winlove, Amanda's brother, the man he'd met in the corridor of Kendell Transports.

"Allo, allo, Mr. Winlove," Charly called. "I come to see Mr. Kendell, but he is not here." That's it, pretend he didn't know Kendell was away.

"And you are? Oh, I recognize you, you're the man who bumped into me at Matt's offce. I can't recall your name." Winlove smiled down at Charly, not a friendly smile. It was the grimace of a shark who smells blood.

"Poisson, Charles Poisson," Charly said. "I try to call Mr. Kendell at his office, but he is never there. So I think he is home. There must be much to do when a wife die, funeral preparations and such."

"No, he's out of town," Winlove told Charly. "We're not sure when he's coming back. But perhaps I can help you? I'm staying here for a few days, until they fix my furnace."

"Ah. You have been here long?" Charly thought of the telephone number that Robbie Munro had jotted down.

"Since my sister died."

"A sad time," Charly said, adopting a funereal tone. "Again, my condolences, sir. I will see Mr. Kendell at another time."

Gregory persisted. "But maybe I can help you? I do work with Matt, you know. What did you want to see him about?"

Charly took a deep breath. Should he upstage the police, flush the killer out into the open? *Oui.* It was a moment of madness. "We find a paper left by your sister when she visit our restaurant the day before her death. On one side is a list, on the other, part of a letter, like the suicide note. This," Charly improvised rapidly, "is what I wanted to tell Mr. Kendell. I think it would put his mind at rest."

"Why? Why tell him that?"

"The Mrs. Amanda, your sister, sir, she was so happy when she visit us at the kitchen," Charly babbled, "and

161

my employees and I, we wish her well. That is what I wanted to tell Mr. Kendell, how happy she was."

And, head lowered, Charly moved quickly to his van and got in, slamming the door. Nothing he'd said made much sense, Charly realized, but Winlove frightened him. He'd simply talked for the sake of talking and if Kendell had killed his wife, this would put the man on the defensive. Charly turned the key in the ignition, and the engine roared. He backed out of Kendell's driveway as fast as he could.

Despite the cold, sweat was pouring down Charly's face. Why had Winlove frightened him so? Charly's armpits were sticky, and his knees were trembling. And why was it suddenly so dark? Had he gone blind? Oh, the lights. He'd forgotten to turn on the headlights. It wasn't even four o'clock, but darkness was closing in. He looked back at the house. One by one, lights began appearing in the windows.

Charly drove back to his house, fed his cats, let them out, turned up the thermostat so the house would be warm when he came in tonight.

He went to his study and found the telephone book. Winlove. There it was. Charly dialed the number and after three rings an answering machine came on. He recognized Winlove's voice, telling callers that he could be reached at such and such a number, the same number that had been on the note in Robbie Munro's pocket. This put a different light on matters. Perhaps Munro had been calling Winlove, not Kendell. Digesting this information, Charly called the cats in and left the house. A full moon was rising.

The restaurant kitchen was dark. *Benny must be having a good time at his practice,* Charly thought as he turned on the lights, turned on the ovens, lit the fire under the big pot of chicken stock. He went to his office and hung up his coat, sat down at his desk and removed his boots, putting on his stout leather kitchen shoes.

The answering machine was blinking. Charly pressed the button, and heard Patty's voice, dry and brittle and strange, and what she said frightened him more than all the Matt Kendells and Greg Winloves in the world:

"Charly, it's Patty. Benny's had an accident at Tae Kwon Do. They say he can't see. They've called an ambulance to take him to the hospital. I'm going over there now."

Another message came on right after Patty's. "Charly, it's Fred Deering. Benny had a little accident at Tae Kwon Do this afternoon, it's nothing serious so don't worry. He was hit in the head and his eyesight's fuzzy, so they're taking him to the hospital to have a neurologist look at him. He won't be able to help you tonight, so Max and I will be over around four."

Charly sat at his desk and put his face in his hands. Not serious? Benny can't see, and it's not serious? He could be dead by now, or blind. Perhaps the blow had affected his brain. Oh, Benny, Benny, the son he'd never had. Feeling the bile rise in his throat Charly rushed to the little employees' toilet off the back hall, where he vomited until his stomach cramped.

A Close Call

"HELLO, CHARLY? YO, CHARLY, YOU HERE? IT'S MAX and Fred."

Charly stumbled out of the toilet, his face still wet from the cold water he'd sloshed on it. He breathed in shallow gasps, and his face was grey.

"Hey, *Charly,* it's okay, man. He's gonna be fine, man. Jeez, you look terrible. Don't worry. It's okay. Not to worry." Max Helder—short, squat, built like a bull—put his big hands on Charly's shoulders and clasped him to his chest.

Fred, standing behind Max, said, "Yeah, Charly, Ben's gonna be okay. I promise you. He's not hurt bad." Fred clapped Charly on the shoulder.

"Is hokay? Is really hokay? Benny is not dead?"

"He got punched on the side of the head," Max said matter-of-factly. "He passed out for a second or two. When he came round, he said he couldn't see. Then he was seeing double. Pretty typical with head blows. I've had 'em, so has Fred. Not a big deal. It goes away."

Fred continued, "So the master, you know, he called 911, got an ambulance. I don't think it's serious, honest I don't. Ben was joking with us while we waited. He said, 'Wow, kid, you got some punch' to the guy who hit him. It was an accident. We all had our helmets on, we were sparring. This isn't the first time the master's had to call an ambulance. He does it so the insurance won't bug him, lawsuits, you know. But Benny's fine, Charly, really he is. Here, sit down." And Fred and Max, each holding one of Charly's elbows, guided him to a chair. Max reached up for the cooking brandy and poured a slug into a coffee mug. He handed it to Charly. Charly gulped it down, then held out his mug for another slug. Already, he was beginning to feel a little better.

"Pee-you, Charly, you spill brandy all over yourself?"

Benny was sitting up in bed at the hospital. Charly was standing near the bed. Patty was slouched in a chair, dressed in her cooking clothes: elastic-waisted

164

jeans, plaid shirt. She didn't have any makeup on. She looked like she'd been crying, and there was a smudge of flour near one eye.

"Max and Fred, they give me little brandy," Charly said. He sighed. "Ah, la la, what a business." Now that he could see that Benny was not only alive but cheerful, with eyes alert and pink cheeks, Charly felt exhausted. He looked over at Patty. She looked like Charly felt— completely done in. Her usually tidy hair hung in limp tendrils around her forehead and ears.

"When the master called me," she said, "I panicked. I ate three brownies and rushed in here with my apron still on. It's in my purse. I think I'm in sugar shock." Patty smiled, which made her look, Charly thought, like a Raphael Madonna. "But I'll make you both laugh. Just as I was leaving Wes Hinkley drove up, and when I told him about you, Benny, he said, 'It's a communist conspiracy, all those orientals ganging up on us.' "

Benny giggled. "Ma, you gotta kick him out. Town Board or not."

Patty smiled. "Well, son, you'd have been proud of me. 'That does it, Wes,' I said. 'Don't come by here ever again. I'm sick of you and Esme, the two of you. Get someone else to mix up Esme's horrible, junky recipes.' "

"*Ma!*"

Charly laughed out loud. Suddenly he felt wonderful.

Patty grinned. "Well, the man's a jerk. Why did it take me so long to find out? Come on, Charly, let's let this child get some rest. The doctor says he'll be out tomorrow morning; they want to keep him in for observation tonight, take advantage of that pricey medical insurance you got for us."

"I'll be in tomorrow," Benny called.

Charly hugged Patty in the parking lot. Patty hugged Charly back. Charly was so relieved at Benny's condition that he felt exhilarated, and not even the steadily falling snow bothered him. And to top off the good news, Patty had dumped Wes Hinkley. If there were cancellations, so what? It didn't matter. He also wasn't accustomed to two big slugs of brandy in the afternoon.

As he drove along, first down Route 56, then down Game Club Road, he sang a little tune, a drinking song from the days when he and his fellow waiters got together after work at the café on the Rue de la Pompe in Paris. "*Boire un petit coup c'est agree-a-ble, boire un petit coup, c'est doux.*" (Drinking a little shot is agreeable, drinking a little shot is nice.) Charly drove slowly, now, for the road twisted and turned and the snowflakes were pounding down on his windshield. "*Mais il ne faut pas rouler dessous la table . . .*" (But one mustn't roll under the table . . .)

Perhaps the two brandies actually helped, because when Charly saw two big headlights piercing the snowflakes and coming straight at him on his side of the road, he didn't panic. He was on a small overpass with the Klover Creek just below, with spindly guardrails separating the road from thin air. Had Charly been entirely sober, no doubt he would have braked and skidded, or swerved and lost control of the bulky van and plunged down through the rails to the creek below. But, "Ha, how dare he?" Charly muttered as he headed, without thought, straight for the oncoming car, leaning on his horn.

It was over in a breath. The other car, a big maroon sports utility vehicle, swerved back into its own lane and continued at top speed. Charly heard brakes screeching in the distance, then nothing.

His stomach heaving, he pulled the van over to the side of the road, got out, and for the second time that afternoon vomited. He remained bent over a long time. *Where does it all come from,* Charly thought as he got back into the van.

"Who do you think it was?" Max asked Charly as he sat at the big pine table in the restaurant kitchen sipping a chamomile tea. ("No, Fred, no more brandy.") Charly could smell meat loaf, and chicken stew, and short ribs braising in the oven. The two young men had done everything.

"Who knows?" Charly said. "The car, I have seen it before. And the driver? Drunk? He was not driving like a sober man. Later, after he pass me, I hear brakes making a screech."

"You could have been killed, Charly. That's a dangerous little road," Max said. "A deep red sports vehicle, um?"

"You know, I just remember, Gregory Winlove, the brother of the woman who was killed on Saturday, he have a car like that." Charly visualized Greg Winlove's car, parked at Kendell's. Yes, it could have been the same car. But with the snow falling, maybe he was mistaken. Maybe the car wasn't maroon. Hard to say. And there were lots of sports utility vehicles around, they were the stylish car of the moment.

"It's a bad business," old Mick said, shaking his head. "You think someone's out to get you, Charly? You been up to mischief? Where'd you go this afternoon? You got that look in your eye, like you was up to no good."

"I go to Kendell's house, just to look around, and I meet Gregory Winlove there. He say that he is staying

167

in the house while his furnace is being repaired."

"Sounds all catty-wumpus," Mick said, just as Tommy Glade burst through the swinging doors into the kitchen.

"That Buonsarde guy's here with his two bodyguards, askin' for you, Charly. Says he didn't reserve, but hopes you've got room. Elton seated him at table five."

Tommy was filling in for Patty as host for the evening, Patty being too exhausted to come in. Charly checked his white jacket. Yes, it was still clean. He put on his tall white toque and hurried into the dining room, where guests were being seated. The Buonsarde party, he noted, had been given water, bread, butter, and mushroom spread. Charly rubbed his hands together and bowed. "An honor, Signor Buonsarde."

"The honor is entirely mine, Chef Poisson. Had I known that my business on this side of the river would take so long, I would have telephoned for a reservation. But I did not."

"Ah, bizzy, bizzy," Charly murmured, wondering if Buonsarde's business had anything to do with Bobby Matucci.

"I had to visit the hospital," Buonsarde continued. "A man I have known for many years had a heart attack, and I wanted to visit with him. I stayed much longer than I had planned, as tragedy has recently struck his house, and we talked for a long time."

"Ah, *quelle coincidence,* I, too, have just returned from the hospital, my sous-chef Benny Perkins, he injure himself in Tae Kwon Do. But the injury is a slight one, I am happy to say."

"That is good," Buonsarde said. "All forms of judo are dangerous, yet they help a young man achieve self-confidence, as well as a certain fearlessness."

168

Buonsarde sat up straight in his chair. Charly assumed the respectfully attentive attitude so beloved by his customers, the attitude that told them Charly was absorbing their pearls of wisdom. Charly was well aware that listening is an art.

"You see, Chef Poisson, so much in life is bluff. People try to threaten us, they pretend they are better than us because of their physical strength, or a weapon in their hands, or because they have money, or a name respected in society. For all of these things, they affect superiority."

Charly nodded, but said nothing.

"But," Buonsarde continued, "by a simple movement of our bodies, a twist of the shoulder, or the manner in which we hold our heads, the man well versed in the ancient oriental arts can deflect that superiority. He can indicate, by one simple movement, that he is impervious to his adversary."

Buonsarde had spoken. He grasped a piece of still-warm bread, and pointed. Francesco passed him the mushroom spread and the butter.

"The wisdom of the Tao Te Ching," Charly agreed, "the subtlety of the I Ching, the hu-mi-li-ty of the superior man." Charly bowed, indicating his own humility.

Buonsarde smiled. "I see that we understand each other perfectly, Chef. We will drink some of your good Barolo to that. Now, what do you suggest for dinner? Seeing my old friend has made me very hungry."

"It is the relief," Charly said, hand on heart. "You are well, your friend may be dying. It could happen to you, but so far, it has not. You are grateful to the fates for having spared you. And this causes hunger."

Buonsarde nodded thoughtfully.

Charly continued, "I would recommend the short ribs of beef, a simple yet hearty meal. Braised in red wine with leeks and garlic and beautiful carrots, with tomato puree and thyme and bay leaf. With that, horseradish mashed potato nice and buttery, and, perhaps, a salad of fresh chicory and escarole hearts. To begin, a platter of shrimps in garlic . . . "

Other items were discussed, but Buonsarde had been seduced by the short ribs. Charly bustled off to the kitchen to oversee their meal, reflecting that while shoulder and head movements were all very good, Buonsarde and his bodyguards did rely on something more. He had caught a metallic glint near Francesco's armpit when the man passed the mushroom spread, and seen the bulge in Gianni's jacket.

Idly, Charly wondered who Buonsarde had been seeing at the hospital. Someone who had just had a heart attack and who had recently suffered a tragedy in his life. And how could Charly find out the identity of this person?

Charly Is Warned

CHIEF OF POLICE JOHN STARK HAD RETURNED TO HIS old habit of stopping by Charly's for coffee. Charly made excellent coffee, but besides that, Charly always had his ear to the ground. In his job, he heard a lot of news. Stark passed along snippets, and Charly would know other bits gleaned from his customers, and together, the bits would occasionally yield certain answers. This morning was a case in point.

"Had an incident on Game Club Road yesterday afternoon, Charly, you hear about it? Car turned over,

170

caught fire, guy got out but barely."

"It was a deep red sports vehicle, going very fast?"

"Yeah, how'd you know?" Stark forked in apple pie. There you go.

"The car, it try to run me down."

"You don't say. Tell me."

"I am driving along, and a big dark red car, it come at me on my side of the road. I lean on my horn, and it move back. Then, as I continue on my way, I hear brakes going 'eek, eek'."

"Bet it was the same car. You see who was driving?"

"No. Who was driving?"

"Guy called Greg Winlove. Lucky he wasn't belted in. Car rolled over, he crawled out, gas tank exploded. If he'd been belted in, he'd a' been fried."

"The brother of Amanda Kendell."

"Yeah, you know him?"

"I have met him," Charly said. "When the car come at me, I think the person has fallen asleep, or perhaps had too much to drink."

"Winlove *wanted* us to do a Breathalyzer, because of the insurance. He was clean. He told us an animal crossed the road, he braked, then skidded, car turned over. Those big, boxy cars do have a tendency, you know. They're not made for speed, despite what everyone thinks."

Old Mick appeared at the table. "Excuse me, Chief, but Charly wanted me to tell him when it was nine-thirty. He's going over to the hospital, pick up our Benny. You hear about Benny?"

Charly and Mick told Stark about Benny.

"Well, I'm glad it wasn't serious," Stark said. As always, he thought of his son Johnny, killed in a car crash after his senior prom a few years back. It never went away, the hurt, the pain.

"He'll be more careful next time, Charly. Sad to say, we seem to learn more from the bad times, not the good ones. Gotta run, Charly, Mick, thanks for the coffee and the pie."

"Mr. Benjamin Perkins?"

The grey-haired volunteer receptionist consulted a list. "Here, I've got his room number, I'll call."

The number didn't pick up. But just then an elevator opened down the hall and Charly saw Benny emerging with three other people, one of them Matthew Kendell. Kendell was carrying a big plastic bag. He looked white and haggard. Patient or visitor, Charly wondered as Kendell, unseeing, walked slowly past.

"Thanks, Charly, for picking me up. You ready to roll?" Benny was carrying his motorcycle helmet.

Charly held up a cautionary finger. *"Une minute,"* he whispered.

As they watched, a man in a white coat with a stethoscope came up to Kendell. The two men spoke in low tones, both laughed, and the doctor made a show of punching Kendell's arm. "You'll be fine, big fella," the doctor called as he moved away, "just keep on taking that Lanoxin." Kendell walked slowly toward the hospital entrance, where a taxi waited.

"The police have been looking for Kendell, but his office say he is out of town," Charly told Benny. "And last night Signor Buonsarde come to dine, he say he is over here visiting a friend in hospital, a friend who has had a tragedy in his family. Might be Kendell, eh?"

"Yeah, Charly. Can we stop by the gym? My motorcycle's still there."

Charly and Benny dusted off snow and got the vehicle into the van.

"I feel terrific, Charly. I could ride my machine to the restaurant, but I know it'd drive you crazy."

"One skid in snow, you hit head, you dead," Charly said

Benny gave a snort. "Come on, Charly. If anyone's gonna get killed, it's you with your snooping. Listen. You got a starving sous-chef on your hands. You wouldn't believe the garbage they feed you in there."

"Yes, we feed you, Benny. Then you can make some more potato and leek soup. Elmo Richard, he send over wonderful leek, big and fat but not woody in center. Not like the small thin thing I grow in my garden. We have plenty of chicken stock, though you know that in France, my Tante Jeanne, she never use chicken stock. Where would she get chicken, which is so costly? No, water only, but at the end, a big *noix* of butter."

"As big as a walnut," Benny said. He'd heard the story many times, about how the French used water, not stock, to flavor their soups, then used butter, salt, and pepper as enrichment.

"I must call Stark," Charly said. "And tell him Kendell was in hospital. He will be interested. And delicious meat loaf you must make too."

"Charly, you're gonna get yourself in trouble, sticking your nose in. Chief Stark's gonna blow his stack. What's the point of all this?"

"Justice, my dear Benny, I am after justice. That man Kendell kill his wife, I am convince. He kill his wife and make it look like suicide." Charly pronounced it in the French manner, "swee-ceed."

"Life is tough enough, Charly, stop trying to turn it

into a movie."

"You sound like Rex Cingale, Benny. Now, I am convince that Ugo Buonsarde, he visit Kendell in hospital. I must meet with Buonsarde on some pretext, and get him to talk about Kendell. *Tiens,* did I not tell Buonsarde the next time I make tripe, I let him know? *Eh bien,* I make a big pot of Tripes à la Mode de Caen, and I invite Buonsarde. And we drink wine, and we talk." Charly turned into his parking lot giving little grunts of satisfaction: "Ah, ah, ah."

A vintage black Ford coupe, so clean it must have just come from the car wash, stood near the back door. "I think the good Dr. Ross has come to pay us a visit," Charly said as he and Benny walked in the back door.

Doc Ross and Mick Hitchens were sitting at the pine table, drinking coffee and talking about the blizzard of '87.

"I stopped in, Charly, because I ran into John Stark and he told me you were nearly run down by Gregory Winlove. I wanted to warn you," old Doc said. "I told you Greg's a narcissist, and they can't bear to be crossed. Now, Mick tells me you're snooping over at that Kendell man's, and you've got Winlove's bowels all in an uproar. I'm warning you, Charly, stay away. I just read an article about a man with a narcissistic personality disorder, went around killing folks simply because they got in his way. And now look what happened. Winlove tries to force you off the road. Does Stark know you'd been snooping over at Kendell's?"

"Well . . ."

"And now," Doc went on, "Winlove will blame you for the loss of his car. That's the way their minds work, those fellers. He'll think that it was your fault that his car turned over. And he'll try to punish you."

"I think Charly should tell Chief Stark," Mick said.

"Of course he should. But will you?" Doc looked stern. "Tell the truth, Charly, and shame the devil."

Mick said, "You was snooping over to Kendell's, right?"

Charly nodded.

"And Winlove caught you over there, didn't he?"

Charly nodded again.

"Were you actually in the house, or outside? I know you, Charly. If the door was open, you'd walk in, wouldn't you?"

"Well . . . actually, Mick, Doc, I open the kitchen door, just to test it, you understand, and it swing open. And I step inside, but then I see headlights coming up the driveway, Gregory's car it turn out, so I go outside, fast."

"Greg has something to hide, what, I don't know," Doc pointed out. "He's out to get you, my boy. If I were you, I'd go right over to Stark's."

"Ah, perhaps." He hated telling Stark he'd been snooping. It had taken him months to reestablish good relations with the Chief of Police.

"I think about it, Doc, hokay?" Charly turned his attention to the *mise en place* for the meat loaf. For the moment, this was far more important.

CHARLY'S MEAT LOAF

YIELD: 6-8 SERVINGS

3 pounds fatty ground beef
1 cup white mushrooms, finely chopped
1 clove garlic, finely chopped
2 shallots, finely chopped
½ cup parsley, finely chopped
Pinches of basil and marjoram and sea salt (⅛ teaspoon, each)
1 cup bread crumbs
1 egg, beaten
½ cup strong beef stock

Combine all ingredients, mixing well with your (very clean) hands. Pat into a greased loaf pan. Bake in a preheated 350° oven 1½ hours. Let sit 15 minutes before unmolding. Drain off liquids and serve.

Winlove Wages War

FOR SOMEONE WHO'D JUST HAD HIS CAR FLIP OVER AND then burn up, Gregory Winlove felt remarkably fit. He'd probably cracked a couple of ribs and he'd bound his rib cage with an Ace bandage, refusing to go to the hospital. He'd asked the cops to drive him to Matt Kendell's house, after all Matt was his brother-in-law. There, he'd borrowed Amanda's Oldsmobile, He'd found her keys on the board in the kitchen.

Next, Greg drove over to his house: he wanted to check the thermostat. He'd told Matt his furnace was broken, because he wanted to stay at Matt's for a few days and keep an eye on him. Matt had a bad heart, and with luck, Greg could make it a lot worse. This heart attack was his third. The next one would finish the man off, for sure. And then, Greg would have full control of the antiques business that he now shared with Matt.

"Nobody messes with me, do they?" Greg smiled at himself in the front hall mirror. "Bye, bye, Mandy, not wanting to let me have that money; bye, bye, Matt, you're off to the happy hunting ground, too." Greg stared at the mirror. Was that a pimple on the side of his chin? Oh, God, it looked awful.

Greg sprinted upstairs to his bathroom, washed his hands with almond-glycerine soap, dried them, and squirted some beige gel onto his fingers, then massaged the gel into his face. Much better. You could hardly see the pimple now. He inspected his face, then smiled seductively. You handsome devil.

He stuck his head in his bedroom—beautiful, the George III four-poster, the Chippendale slant-front desk,

177

the Queen Anne fruitwood side chair: those three pieces alone would get him to Paris for a six months' stay, not at the Crillon, of course, but to that very nice little pension on the Rue du Bac. Maybe he'd stay a year, wait for things to cool down over here. He smiled at himself again, this time in the early Georgian walnut mirror in the upstairs hall. "You're a genius, Gregory darling," he said with a smile.

He checked the main guest room—more big-bucks furniture—and glanced in the closet, at those lovely chiffon and lace and silk ball gowns, each one hand-tailored and hand-sewn, every sequin, every paillette. "A fortune in frocks"—he imitated the clipped British accent of one of his New York clients. Well, now, he couldn't complain. But, oh, God, why did his white-trash brother-in-law, who had all that money, have to live like that? Just to walk in that filthy, ugly house made Greg feel queasy.

"The perfect lunch crowd," old Mick said as he mopped the kitchen floor around Benny and Charly. "Come early, leave early. Now, if you two fellers will just move over there for a minute . . . "

Charly and Benny were standing by the chopping block, and Charly had a big knob of celeriac, or root celery, in his hands. "Now, Benny, you see what I mean by matchstick?" Charly demonstrated with his ten-inch chef's knife. "Like julienne, only a bit bigger. We cannot use the machine, it make them too big or too small. Hokay, now this is the real Celeri Remoulade, very simple. You see what I do? Peel the celeriac, *céleri-rave* in French, slice, put in vinegar water to keep it nice and white, and . . ."

Charly's knife flashed, and mound after mound of

celeriac matchsticks were cut and scooped into the pan of acidulated water. "Meanwhile, your water on the stove is boiling nicely, no? So we drain the celeriac in a colander, throw it into the boiling water, *et, hop!* Quickly drain, we want crunchy. It blanch not even a minute. Now the dressing. Nothing but our nice homemade mayonnaise and some of our good Maille mustard." Charly plopped the mustard into the mayonnaise bowl and stirred, then dipped in a finger to taste. He poured in a few drops of water, stirred, then poured the sauce over the still-steaming celeriac sticks. "You see?"

"That's it? It's so simple." Benny took a matchstick and chewed.

"That's it," Charly agreed. "Everything is simple in professional cooking, Benny. The chefs keep it so. It is only the housewife who make the complicated recipe with twenty-five ingredients."

"Keep your life as simple as your recipes, Charly," old Mick called from the sink. "Don't you go mixin' with the bad boys. We just get that Maxwell feller out of our hair, and along comes that gangster from across the river."

"In principle you are correct, Mick," Charly said. "But in practice, these are the customers who spend the money."

"Hmpf. Well then, Charly, I got nothing else to say."

Charly couldn't stop himself. "Are you sure, Mick, that you do not know the Winlove man? You have lived here all your life."

"Well, I told you I didn't know him before, but now that I think on it, he might a' worked over at the chair factory with me, some youngster was always stealing stuff . . . I got to wonderin' the other night, after you'd asked. I have a suspicion that boy's name was Winlove."

Charly raised an eyebrow. "So Mr. Gregory Winlove, he has always liked to steal things, eh? Can you ask the foreman?"

Mick chuckled. "You can if you know one of them spiritualists who talk to the dead, Charly."

"And the other employees?"

"Long gone, Charly."

There were only a few men at the Steak Heaven bar that afternoon, watching a soap on the big television screen. Rex Cingale was sitting in the far corner, sipping espresso and talking to Vinnie, behind the bar, and Charly.

"Ya know, I miss the little squirt?" Rex said. "Never thought I'd say that about Bobby, but it's the truth."

"He'll be back, Uncle Rex," Vinnie said. "You ready for another, Charly

"Only if Rex is having one."

"Two doubles, Vinnie," Rex said. "So, Charly, that's the story. Bobby's gonna work off the money by tending bar over at The Country Squire. "

"But only two, three days a week," Charly said. "It give him new, how you say, perspective on life."

"Some perspective," Vinnie sniggered. "Two big tits and a watermelon ass, that girl he's so crazy 'bout's gonna look just like her mom—a barrel—in about five years."

Rex said, "You hear what happened, Charly? Whatshername, Kimberly Calamare, went on a hunger strike after her father dragged her home from that dinner with Bobby at your place. She refused to eat her mother's cooking, and the mom goes ape-shit."

"She's a cagey little bitch, I'll give her that," Vinnie went on. "She's got those two wrapped around her little finger. So Mama's hysterical, and drives Carlo crazy, and someone comes up with this cockamamie scheme . . . "

" . . . to have Bobby work over there, payin' off his debt," Rex finished. "Gonna be barman three days or nights a week. A' course, Bobby thinks it's great. He thinks he's in love." Rex snorted.

"It's Carlo, has his eye on Bobby," Vinnie said wisely. "I gotta suspicion not too many men are courtin' Ms. Kimberly, she's as spoiled as they come, and she's gettin' fatter by the day. Her ass is going south, fast. See, if Carlo could get Bobby to many her, he'd get Bobby in the mob. Bobby's a yes-man."

"Cut the shit, Vinnie." Rex frowned. "No nephew of mine . . ."

"Here's your espresso, Uncle Rex, Charly," Vinnie interrupted. "And so, Charly, now we got us a new barman . . . " Changing the subject, fast.

"Which works out good," Rex continued. "He's Angie Vongola's cousin's kid, Vinnie's showin' him the ropes. He's got a nice way about him, uh, Vinnie?"

"Very nice, Uncle Rex. Doesn't drink, doesn't gamble."

"To change the subject," Charly said, "What do you know, either of you, about Matthew Kendell and Gregory Winlove?"

Rex shrugged "Not much. They come in, Kendell's a big Canadian Club drinker, or rather he was, now he's takin' it easy, he's had a couple of heart attacks recently. And the other one you mentioned, Winlove, never drinks the hard stuff at all, drinks a seltzer or a ginger ale."

"They come in together?"

"Oh, sometimes. I get the feeling that though they do some work together, they're not good friends. Winlove's a snotty bastard."

"What sort of work do they do together?" Charly asked.

"Vinnie, you know? Something to do with trucking. I think Kendell lends Winlove trucks for his antiques. Refinishes old stuff he buys at junk shops. I heard he makes furniture, too. Win Crozier says it's good stuff."

Vinnie hissed, "Shhh, you guys. Knock it off."

Charly smelled Kendell before he saw him, standing at the bar.

"Yes, Mr. Kendell," Vinnie said respectfully. "What can I get you?"

"Two coffees to go, white, with sugar. Real coffee, not that Guinea shit."

As he stood at the bar Kendell reached into his pocket and brought out a small bottle. He shook two tablets into his hand, threw them into his mouth, and chewed. Charly was close enough to read the label: CALCIUM.

"Yessir, coming right up."

Vinnie placed the two containers of coffee on the counter. Kendell paid and left.

"Well, I go too, now," Charly said, glancing at the clock. "Thank you for the coffee, Rex, Vinnie. And for the information."

"They're not regular customers, you know, Kendell and Winlove. I see 'em, what, once a week?"

In the Steak Heaven parking lot Charly noticed, as he trudged over to his van, Kendell's big Jaguar parked near the front steps. Kendell was in the driver's seat, and the windows were cracked open. Gregory Winlove sat in the passenger seat. Both men were sipping coffee and smoking. Charly could smell the sweet odor of marijuana drifting out of the car.

That night at dinner at La Fermette, the name Winlove came up again, with Win Crozier, Morty Cohen, and Howard Voss.

"The cops traced Howard's and Robbie's stolen antiques back to Greg Winlove," Win told Charly. "What do you think of that?"

"And here's what's so horrible," Howard said. "Winlove told the cops he got a call from Robbie, saying Robbie had some antiques to dispose of. Greg went down to our Pennsylvania house and gave Robbie cash for about twenty pieces. The whole robbery scheme was a fake. Thieves never stole our antiques. Robbie sold them."

"Haw," Charly asked, "does Greg know it was Robbie who sold him the antiques? Did he know Robbie before?"

"The cops," Howard said. "They showed Greg a picture of Robbie's body, he identified Robbie as being the man he met at our house."

"Of course," Charly mused, "you have only the word of Greg Winlove. Robbie is not here to defend himself."

"The insurance company," Howard said, "is not very amused."

Later that night, at home, Charly looked up Lanoxin in one of his favorite reference books, the *Guide to Prescription Drugs.* Charly was terrified of prescription drugs because of their toxic side effects. When a customer told Charly about a drug he was taking, Charly would frequently check in his book.

Lanoxin, said the book, was a brand name for digoxin, made from digitalis, or foxglove. It was a heart medication. He scanned the section entitled "How This Drug Works"—"By increasing the availability of calcium within the heart muscle." The side effects included hallucinations, neuralgia, blindness (very rare), disorientation (most common in the elderly), heart rhythm disturbances. He scanned the "Caution" paragraph. "Narrow margin of safe use; consult physician if you are taking calcium supplements and avoid large doses; avoid dairy two hours before and after taking drug; avoid caffeine; marijuana can cause possible accentuation of heart failure; effects may be increased by Librium, Valium, and other tranquilizers. Most diuretics are dangerous . . ." The list of cautions went on and on. Charly sighed as he recalled Kendell chewing on calcium tablets, drinking coffee with cream, and smoking marijuana outside Steak Heaven.

Tripe Preparations

WHEN CHARLY'S EYES FLEW OPEN ON FRIDAY morning at five-thirty-two, a dream was fading: he and Ugo Buonsarde and old Mrs. Barrol were sitting in a gondola on a smelly Venice canal eating purple sorbet, and Ugo was saying, "This is the first time I've ever eaten tripe sorbet." Mrs. Barrol answered, "Oh, no, dear, all the bad boys eat tripe sorbet." It was summer in the dream and Charly was sweating.

Ridicule, Charly thought as he stuck his nose out from under the down comforter. He was sweating, the bed smelled rank, and he wondered if he was catching a cold, it being one of his beliefs that when your excretions—urine, feces, sweat—smelled bad, it was a sure sign of illness.

The room was hot, and Charly, padding over to the thermostat, saw that he'd forgotten to lower it last night. *Merde,* he muttered. Money wasted, and to sleep in a too-hot room was as bad as sleeping with an open window, most unhealthy. He hadn't noticed last night, too preoccupied with his theories. *This is what came of meddling . . . Mick Hitchens was right. I should stop immediately,* Charly thought, knowing that he wouldn't.

Nonetheless, as he performed his morning rituals, feeding the cats and letting them out, making his Puerto Rican coffee, taking his Bach flower remedies, eating a big bowl of hot cracked wheat cereal, lying in his bath, he thought about the dream. Tripe sorbet was sinister. Purple? Like eggplant, one of the nightshade vegetables that caused arthritis pain. Not a good sign.

"First," Charly instructed Benny, "I will make up two bouquets garnis." He gathered thyme sprigs, parsley, bay leaves, and wrapped them with thread, making two bundles. "And as you can see, my carrots and onions and garlic are already cut, and so is my tripe, *bien entendu.*"

Benny observed. Even old Mick wandered over to watch what was clearly a ceremonial procedure. Charly made Tripes à la Mode de Caen only once or twice a winter for a few hearty souls. Most Americans ate tripe in bologna and frankfurters, camouflaged with MSG and sodium nitrite, but a dish of tripe made Charly's customers shudder. Innards, which the French loved, were not popular in Klover, New York.

"Now," Charly continued, "I lay some tripe at the bottom of my earthenware casserole, I sprinkle on some sea salt and pepper, I add a layer of vegetables, some of my blanched calves' foot, a bouquet garni, then another

185

layer of tripe, and one of vegetables . . ." When he finished, the casserole was almost full. Charly poured over white wine, chicken stock, and apple brandy. Then he mixed up a paste of flour and water, to seal the edges of the casserole lid, to prevent the escape of steam.

"I have heated up the old oven in the corner, since the tripe must cook at least ten hours in a low oven," Charly told them. "Here, Benny, help me carry it over. In the old days, in my father's village, when the women make dishes that need long, slow cooking, they take them to the baker's where they cook all night, for the baker's oven is always lit."

"It sounds complicated but it isn't," Benny commented. "I bet I could cook beans like that."

"Soak them first," Charly cautioned. "They would be delicious. Always make the oven do the work. Long, slow cooking is the secret to many food."

Charly closed the oven door and wiped his hands on his apron. "I salivate," he told the two men, "at the thought of that tripe."

Benny did not salivate, but didn't give Charly the benefit of this thought. He'd already tasted brains, kidneys, tongue, pigs' feet, urged by Charly, and none had lifted his spirits. In fact, they had intensified his desire to eschew animal protein altogether.

The back door opened and Julius hurried into the warmth, shivering in his bright yellow down jacket.

"Hello, everyone. Snow flurries coming, I heard it on the radio. Charly, that Compu stock dropped late yesterday afternoon, just as we thought. Stock rose to seventy, then a big block of shares was sold and panic set in. Now the stock's worth almost nothing. Compu Class A is dead. I didn't call you last night, didn't want to upset you. Maurice will know soon enough."

"Ah. *Mon Dieu.* Poor Maurice."

"You haven't given Maurice the restaurant money, have you?"

"No, no, the papers have not even been signed."

"Good. Soon Maurice'll be free to make another big mistake. Here, Charly, I brought you something to amuse you." Julius, unconcerned with Maurice's tragedy, held out an ornate menu. "It will make you laugh."

Charly opened the menu, which was held together with a gold ribbon.

"*Tiens,*" he said. "Is from new restaurant across the river."

"That's right," Julius agreed. "Kid's millionaire dad's bankrolling the operation. Very elegant place. I ate there with some customers a couple of nights ago. Suede banquettes, mirrors, looks like a Bloomingdale's showroom. New York decorator. Villeroy & Boch china, crystal glassware, I tell you, it's nuts." Julius grinned. "Food stinks, though."

"Navet," Charly read. "A curious name for a restaurant. In France, when someone is stupid, we call him a *navet,* a turnip. It is not a compliment. When someone is sick, all thin and white, we say he has the *sang de navet,* the blood of a turnip. I wonder why he call it that?"

"He's a foodie," Julius said. "He's young and he wants to impress. People love French names, even if they don't know what they mean. They think they're stylish. You do know what a foodie is, don't you?"

"Not really," Charly said. He didn't have the remotest idea.

"It's someone who looks on food as theater," Julius explained. "Food as fashion, food as—oh, hell, I don't

187

know, food as something to show off with. See"—Julius took the menu from Charly's hands—"all the fancy names and phrases? A *pavé* of salmon, a *flan* of salsify, *tapenade* vinaigrette, *jus* of chicken, *ponzu* vinaigrette, whatever the hell that is. I call it the foodie fuck, ninety cents' worth of ingredients, a pretentious description, and a menu price of $24.95. I've also heard it called tweezer food because it's so artfully arranged on the plate, it looks like it's been placed there with tweezers."

Charly smiled. "I remember, once, speaking to an Italian restaurateur. He is the owner of a famous restaurant in New York. It has moved since I dined there. He tell me about young chefs who charge twenty-five dollars for a plate of spaghetti with tomato sauce. He is talking about the foodie chef, no?"

"Precisely," Julius agreed. "Foodie chefs may not know how to cook, but they all know foodie-speak. You know, 'a chayote tian with warm, sesame-crusted, house-smoked crayfish, caramelized Vidalia onions, lobster jus, field greens, pincholine olives, and a risotto of millet.' It's fashion food."

"You cannot have a risotto of millet, my dear Julius," said Charly pedantically, "since riso means rice and a risotto is a stew of rice."

"You're right, Charly. Meaningless. Just trying to impress."

Benny wandered over. He took the menu and scrutinized it. "Nothing sounds like food," he complained. "It's like the guys in Tae Kwon Do who yell really loud even though they can't deliver the kicks."

"Charly delivers the kicks," Julius said.

"*Mais oui*," Benny said. He and Julius grinned at each other. "Thanks for calling me in the hospital, Julius."

"Hey," Julius said, "you're our superstar, Benny."

"You three are so wrapped up in your tomfoolery you didn't see what I just seen," old Mick said, shuffling over. "That damn fool Maurice, drivin' down Hubbard Road 'bout sixty miles an hour. Least, I suppose it's him, it's his car. Didn't even stop when he got to Route 65, just roared on. Some fine day a truck's gonna get him."

"And then we'll have pâté de Maurice on toast," Julius joked. "Which way did he turn?"

"Left toward Hogton," Mick said.

"And toward the Taconic," Julius mused. "Bet he's roaring into New York, going to tear Count Buonsarde, aka Tony Fingers, limb from limb."

"Ah." Charly shook his head. "The count is long gone. No doubt on Alitalia first class, on his way to Palermo."

Charly and Julius were both partially right. Maurice was on his way to New York City. Count Buonsarde, however, was not on his way to Sicily. He was less than ten miles away, hiding out at his brother Ugo's house in the Catskill Mountains. He'd arrived last night, and the brothers had eaten a nice *risotto coi funghi,* rice with mushrooms, prepared by Gianni.

Maurice had received the news this morning about the Compu stock, and he'd been on the telephone ever since: to Buonsarde and Company, where an answering machine told him to please leave his name; to Buonsarde's apartment, where the manservant said the count was out of town; to Compu Class A in Ohio where all the principals were in a meeting.

Maurice was out of the house before Barbara could question him. He was convinced that a mistake had been

189

made, that the count would chuckle at his fears. To get to New York as quickly as possible was his only aim.

Maurice switched on the radio as he sped toward the Taconic Parkway.

"The Securities and Exchange Commission is looking into allegations of fraud by Buonsarde and Company, a Wall Street firm that is alleged to have bought ten-dollar shares in an Ohio-based company, Compu Class A, pumped them up, and sold them in a front-running scheme when the stock reached seventy dollars. Antonio Buonsarde, the president, cannot be reached. Early this morning investigators from the SEC entered the offices of Buonsarde's company with a search warrant and are packing up files pertaining to the Ohio firm. An SEC spokesperson, who spoke on condition of anonymity, said, 'A lot of little people got burned on this one, especially retirees who appear to make up the bulk of Buonsarde's client list.'"

Maurice pulled his Mercedes over to the side of the road. So it was true. His fifty thousand had vanished. He'd been tricked, like a rube. He, a Princeton man, had been seduced by a lowly crook. *I'm as bad as Daddy,* he thought in a rare moment of introspection. He put his head down on the steering wheel and cried like a baby.

Julius Prendergast had warned him; even that prissy Jimmy Houghton had told Charly not to invest in the Ohio company. And Maurice had pooh-poohed them, insisting that Buonsarde was a financial genius and that Compu Class A was a rising star. Maurice felt momentarily betrayed. But not for long. He wasn't a double Leo for nothing. He'd recoup his losses, never fear. Let's see now. There was that snuffbox of Daddy's, he'd been offered $40,000 by a collector years ago; there was a Chagall lithograph—$25,000; and that eighteenth-century chair made by a noted French cabinetmaker; and what about the Picasso print? He was far from destitute.

Maurice turned around and drove slowly home. He thought of Charly's money, he'd be getting that next week. His spirits rose.

"Hello, I'm back," he called to his wife.

"I'm in my office," Barbara called. "What happened?"

"It's snowing too hard to drive to the city, I'll reschedule," Maurice lied.

"Hear about that Compu stock?" Barbara called. "It dropped to nothing."

"I thought it would, so I only bought a few shares."

Barbara didn't believe this for a minute. Maurice spoke in his "funny" voice. She always knew when he was lying.

At his desk, Maurice rummaged around for his old address book. What was the guy's name? Lester Pingry. He'd run into Lester in the city. Lester said he'd recently sold his grandmother's furniture through an antiques broker in upstate New York. Maurice had noted the name, just in case. Oh, here it was. Under Lester's name, Gregory Winlove, with the same area code.

Winlove, Winlove, had a familiar ring, but he couldn't place it. Maurice dialed. Gregory Winlove, eh? An aristocratic name. Maurice had a feeling that he and this Mr. Winlove would get along splendidly.

Dubious Relations

"THIS NUMBER HAS BEEN TEMPORARILY CHANGED TO . . ." The recording gave a new number, same prefix. This time a man answered the telephone.

"Hello? I would like to speak with Mr. Gregory Winlove."

"Speaking."

"Mr. Winlove, this is Maurice Baleine, a friend of Lester Pingry's. He was a Princeton classmate of mine." Maurice always managed to insert the name Princeton when he spoke to strangers. It impressed them to no end.

Gregory Winlove smiled. He remembered Lester, a drunk and a snob, whose grandmother had left him same beautiful furniture. Lester always mentioned Princeton, too. Assholes did that, trying to impress. Ergo, this guy was an asshole, too. Good. Very easy guys to deal with, snobs and assholes.

"I live in a little town called Klover, New York. And you? I thought I recognized the prefix. It's Van Buren County too, isn't it?"

"What can I help you with, Mr. Baleine," Gregory said, ignoring Maurice's question about his whereabouts.

Maurice gave a braying laugh ("har, har,") to indicate that his call was of a trifling nature. "Mr. Winlove, I gather you're an expert on antiques. Lester told me you helped him dispose of some family pieces. Is that correct?"

"Yes, I helped Mr. Pingry. It's the sort of thing I do."

"I have an objet d'art I'd like to sell." Maurice gave it

192

the full French pronunciation. "It's a snuffbox, eighteenth century, gold and enamel, in my family for generations," he lied. His father had taken the piece in payment of a restaurant debt. He wouldn't mention his other treasures, yet.

"I have to be in the vicinity of Klover this afternoon, Mr. Baleine. Would you like me to stop by your house, have a look?"

"No!" barked Maurice. "I mean, it's in a safety deposit box at the bank. I don't want to go out in the snow, and it's, ah, a private matter. Perhaps we could meet in some neutral spot?"

Gregory smiled. Better and better. Guy was desperate and didn't want his family to know. "Call me, Mr. Baleine, when you get the piece. We could meet at, say, The Country Squire near Gaitskill. Tomorrow afternoon?"

"Perfect," Maurice said. "I'll, ah, get it from the bank, then call to confirm tomorrow morning and we can set a time."

"Excellent," Gregory said "We'll talk tomorrow. Oh, by the way, Mr. Baleine, if I'm not being indiscreet, what is your occupation?"

"I'm a restaurateur," Maurice said importantly. "I own La Fermette, the finest French restaurant in Van Buren County."

"A wonderful place, I've dined there many times," Gregory lied. He rarely dined out, and though he knew of a French restaurant on Route 65, it was owned, he'd heard, by a man with a heavy French accent. "So you're the owner of La Fermette. The sole owner?"

Maurice laughed merrily, as if being the sole owner of such a restaurant were an impossibility. Also, he suspected that Winlove might have met Charly. "Good

193

heavens, of course not. One of my cooks has a share in the place and, oh, others do too. We do a lot of catering, we're famous."

"I'm sure you are," Winlove said. Something was wrong here. If the guy's restaurant was so successful, why was he selling his snuffbox? Had he been caught with his pants down, had to pay someone off? Or maybe he was a gambler? Something smelled.

The following morning The Country Squire was quiet, so Bobby Matucci, the newest barman, spent his time cleaning the bar well, making espresso, cleaning the espresso machines, and replenishing the bar supplies.

Carlo Calamare had discovered that Bobby could take apart, clean, and, most important, put back together the espresso machines that Carlo bought at the distress sales of failed restaurants. People saw the gleaming brass and copper machines at restaurant shows and bought them without a thought to their upkeep. They were never cleaned and a few hundred espresso cups later, the machines broke down. Bobby would take the machines apart, soak parts encrusted with coffee oil and grease, and put the machines back together, machines that Carlo sold at a nice profit. Carlo's antiques buyer, Gregory Winlove, had suggested selling the machines to antiques shops as well as restaurants, since espresso had become such a craze.

"I've just gotten in three more espresso machines, beauties but filthy," Carlo told his newest barman. "Maybe you could take a look at them?"

"Of course, Mr. C."

"They're in the grey barn. Right at the front, in wooden crates."

At this point in time Carlo was feeling quite kindly

disposed toward Bobby. Bobby had been working at The Country Squire just two days, but already Kimberly was a reformed character. She'd quit her hunger strike, quit lolling around the house in her bathrobe, and again looked the little beauty that Carlo adored, eating and talking and laughing in her charming manner.

Carlo's wife Silvana, who had been the image of Kimberly at nineteen but now, at thirty-eight, looked like a beach ball on short, fat legs, had correspondingly cheered up and gone back to cooking the *polpo alla Napoli,* the *vitello arrosto*, the *pollo alla diavolo* that Carlo loved to eat. (He'd never eaten in his own restaurant, for good reason.)

Peace was restored. Silvana Calamare was singing as she sweated her garlic in the big cast-iron pots, and Kimberly had even offered to tidy up her father's office, going through the vendor files that were gathering dust, and throwing out all the literature on restaurant equipment that Carlo never intended to buy, but couldn't bear to throw away.

Of course, Carlo realized, his office was next to the bar (and to Bobby Matucci), but, hey, so what? The guy was an airhead, but he looked good and Carlo knew he could scare the shit out of him, if necessary. He was not tough. What better qualities could you want in a son-in-law.

Who knew what Kimberly got up to when she squeezed into her little red Ford and roared off, ostensibly seeing girlfriends. Now, at least, Carlo knew where his daughter was, and if, God forbid, she were to find herself in an interesting condition, at least Carlo knew where to pin the blame.

The gaze of adoration, like a shepherd bedazzled by the madonna, that illuminated Bobby's handsome face when he looked at Kimberly made Carlo almost—but not quite—forgive the young man his sins. Carlo had already decided that if Bobby and Kimberly were to marry, part of Carlo's wedding present would be the erasing of Bobby's debt. With proper supervision, Bobby could be a dutiful, if not brilliant, soldier in the Buonsarde army's fight against law and order.

"Bobby?"

"Yessir, Mr. Calamare?"

"Mr. Buonsarde is coming in at eleven o'clock for a meeting in the Thomas Jefferson Room. Kimberly's checking it over, now. Could we have espresso and pastries for seven twenty minutes after everyone's gone in?"

"Yessir, Mr. Calamare. Consider it done."

"That's what I like to hear," Carlo said, not quite smiling. "Respect from a young man."

"Yes, Mr. C." Bobby smiled, showing his beautiful white teeth. "I was brung up right, Mr. C, my grandparents, from the old country, ya know, they laid down the law. And my mom and pop still follow that law. Respect. For. Your. Elders."

A fine young man, thought Carlo Calamare as he walked toward the James Monroe Room where Gregory Winlove would soon be meeting with a client, he'd just called. Couldn't get here earlier to pick up his payment because of car trouble, so he said. Lotta excuses, that guy had.

Carlo looked at his watch. Half past ten. Just time to run through the local papers that he'd neglected all week. They rarely contained news, but it had become a habit. The newspapers were so thin, he'd save them up, then whip through three, four, five. It rarely took more than fifteen minutes.

Bobby decided not to go into the Thomas Jefferson Room. If he saw Kimberly, he'd want to envelop her in his arms, breathe in her perfume, and feel her voluptuous body straining against his. This was not a smart idea with Mr. C roaming around.

He glanced at his watch. Time to run over to the barn, check out the newly acquired espresso machines. He loved the ornate coffeemakers. Fucking glitz. He slipped on his shearling jacket and ran outside.

Bobby skipped into the grey barn behind the nightclub and flipped on the light switch. He immediately spied a big wooden crate, with a smaller one next to it, right where Mr. C said they would be. Two machines in the big crate, one in the smaller. He squatted down beside them. Oh, they were beauties. He ran his hand over the smooth chrome, the copper and brass decorations. Real showpieces. He'd have fun cleaning these babies.

Something in the big crate caught his eye. A money clip, wedged into the corner, with a wad of bills rolled up. He grasped the wad, undid the clip, counted the money. Hundred-dollar bills, ten of them. His heart gave a lurch, and so did his bowels.

Bobby grinned, thinking of what he could do with a grand. Start to pay off his debt, for one thing. Or grab Kimberly and whisk her off to Miami Beach. He was shaking with excitement. But then another thought flashed into his mind. This was a setup. Bobby would bet the farm on it. Mr. C was testing him, he'd put the money there deliberate.

Carlo sat on the uncomfortable Victorian couch in the James Monroe Room and glanced at the papers. His eye caught the headlines, but as usual there was nothing of interest. NiMo was upping their rates; the Livingston school board was in a quandary about computers; the Hogton politicians were squabbling again. What a yawn. He scanned the obituaries and the police blotter, and here a very small paragraph in the Wednesday newspaper grabbed at his gut:

"The body of Robert Munro, a New York City and Pennsylvania antiques dealer, was found in a local cellar on Monday afternoon. The cause of death is undetermined. Mr. Munro was on heart medication and under the care of a New York physician."

"Jesus Key-rist!" Carlo screamed. He threw down the newspaper and rushed for his office.

Being of Italian peasant stock, which is exactly like French peasant stock, suspicious of everything, Bobby looked at the bills and they screamed "setup, setup." Bobby's intellect might not be of the highest, but he had the instincts of a feral animal. He checked his watch. Nearly eleven. He hurried back to the main building, the money in his pocket, and sure enough, there was Mr. Calamare standing in the doorway waiting for the Buonsarde party. He looked upset about something and Bobby hoped he wasn't the cause. He was doubly glad that he hadn't dallied in the Thomas Jefferson Room with the most beautiful woman in the world.

Bobby, looking serious, faced his boss. He reached into his pocket and withdrew the bills. "I think you dropped this, Mr. Calamare, sir?" he said in his most urbane voice.

Just then a black Rolls-Royce pulled up in front of the building. Bobby stood next to Calamare like a soldier, head high, as the *capo di tutti capi* and another man with a mane of white hair emerged from the car and walked up the path to The Country Squire.

A Conference
Across the River

CARLO CALAMARE *HAD* PUT THE THOUSAND DOLLARS in the crate, but he hadn't done it to test Bobby. It was payment to Gregory Winlove for a job.

"Just do it, but don't tell me nothing about it afterward," Carlo told Winlove. "A grand will be in the barn, in a crate up front."

Carlo had asked Gregory to threaten the shit out of a certain party, Robbie Munro, who had overstepped his bounds. Munro was running an insurance scam, he'd gotten Greg to steal antiques from his own house in Pennsylvania and was sure to be caught, thus endangering the entire Buonsarde antiques-theft operation.

"I hear he's a houseguest of that Crozier guy where Mr. B buys all his paints and stuff," Carlo said. Carlo had ways of knowing things like that. Greg wondered how to secretly meet Munro, a houseguest of Mr. Winthrop Crozier, without the others in the house knowing, then Munro actually called Greg late one night to set up his own meeting (drunk as usual) but unfortunately things got out of hand.

It was the first time Gregory had been asked to perform a service of this nature, these jobs being the province of Gianni and Francesco, Buonsarde's legbreakers. But this time, Carlo didn't want his boss to know. He'd taken Winlove into his confidence. Big mistake. Mr. B didn't look kindly on mistakes. No wonder Winlove hadn't picked up the money.

"Scare the shit outta him," Carlo had told Winlove. You never went for the final solution if it could be avoided. Corpses had a way of interesting the fuzz in a very unhealthy way. Beatings, no one took seriously. But a dead body? Ai, ai, ai, what stupidity. And on the other side of the river? With an honest, unbribable head cop to deal with? What did Gregory, that fucking nut, *do* to the guy? And why was the newspaper article so cagey—"in a local cellar?" Maybe Gregory pushed Munro around, guy had a seizure and croaked. But if that was the case, why hadn't Gregory told him? Now the shit was really going to hit the fan.

When Bobby Matucci handed Carlo the bills, Carlo kept his thoughts to himself and merely said, "Thanks, Bobby, I'll remember this. Musta fallen out of my pocket. You count it?"

"Of course, Mr. C. A thousand."

"That's correct. Now don't forget, espresso and pastries for us and Mr. B, for the two Mr. B's I should say, the other guy's Anthony, his brother. But he don't want nobody to know he's here, so don't mention it, all right?"

"My lips are sealed, Mr. Calamare, sir."

The green and gold Thomas Jefferson Room was furnished with the ponderous Victorian furniture that The Country Squire's customers loved. Heavy curtains of green taffeta hung at the windows, and the couches and chairs were of the period—upright and scratchy. A solid mahogany table in the center of the room could seat twenty.

Ugo Buonsarde sat at the head of the table, with his brother Anthony to his left. Ranged around the table were Francesco and Gianni; Carlo, the general manager of The Country Squire hotel, motel, and restaurant complex; Sergio Frascati, the food and beverage manager; and Gino Teresa, the manager of the hotel-motel operation.

Gino Teresa had a complex job. Local businessmen often brought in ladies for the afternoon, and Gino's job was to keep this part of the business discreet. Mr. Livingston, a local banker, must not know that Mr. Ranieri, a car dealer, was on the premises at the same time. When Mrs. Livingston was there with Dr. Soames, and Mrs. Ranieri was there with Hector Stratton, things really got tricky. The Country Squire could be a busy place on a snowy afternoon. Timing—entrances and exits—was vital. Not a hint of impropriety, not a taint of lewdness, must be associated with The Country Squire and its patrons. Gino was a diplomat of Machiavellian stature. And even more important, blackmail was beneath his dignity. Everyone's secrets were safe with Gino, and everyone knew it. Luckily the complex had a lot of exits.

Ugo and his brother were respectfully greeted. The employees—Carlo, Sergio, and Gino—presented their weekly written reports, their profits and expenses. Nothing was put in writing that could incriminate the operation. Ugo collected the reports in a pile. "Anything to add?"

"No, Mr. Buonsarde," the men said. Bobby now appeared with a huge tray, followed by a waiter with another huge tray. Espresso, cream, sugar, lemon peels, spoons, demitasse cups, plates of *cannoli, sfogliatelle, crostata* of damson plum.

While the men stood, drank, and ate, Ugo questioned them about their work: Which dishes were the best sellers? How could they increase wine usage? Should they think about converting more single rooms to junior suites? Which singers and bands attracted the most people in the nightclub? Any employee complaints? Were the local police happy? As was the custom, not a word was spoken about the illegal gambling, or the rooms rented by the hour for quite astonishing sums. These were private matters that would be addressed to the individual managers.

The men sat down again for the final summing up. "My brother Anthony will be with us for a few days," Ugo told them. "I'd rather you didn't mention this to anyone. Any reporters, law officers, people like that come around, you've never seen my brother. Carlo, I'm a bit concerned about an antiques situation. A man I know, Winthrop Crozier, bought a hot washstand. An embarrassment. All of our plumbing fixtures are from Crozier Plumbing."

Carlo felt sick. Ugo continued, "The antiques expert who helps us with our furniture operation, Gregory Winlove, is not, I feel, entirely trustworthy. He's not one of us, nor is Kendell of Kendell Transports. We must break with both. But until that time, we'll maintain a closer watch on these men."

Carlo shifted uneasily in his seat. "I think I gotta talk to you in private, Mr. B. Something's come up."

Ugo, Antonio, Gianni, Francesco, and Carlo stood in the parking lot. Carlo had decided to tell his boss the truth, or almost the truth: that he'd hired Winlove to intimidate Munro, and Munro, according to the local paper, appeared to have suffered a heart attack. Winlove must have panicked and left the guy in someone's cellar.

Ugo was not pleased. "You know, it's bad to bring in locals. We have our own ways of doing business."

"I know that, Ugo," Carlo said. "But when I figured

out Munro called Winlove to lift his own antiques for the insurance, I didn't want to involve us. If I used an outsider, we could never be associated with the operation."

Ugo nodded. "You've got a point, Carlo. A good point."

"It's important that my part be undetected, too, Ugo," Anthony said. "Many of the antiques came from my clients. So it's a tricky business. Carlo was right to use an outsider. He just chose the wrong outsider, that's all."

Not only did Anthony give Carlo a list of houses filled with antiques, he also knew when his customers would be away—Mustique in January, Florida in February, St. Croix in March. Carlo would give the list to Winlove, and Winlove would hire some of Kendell's men and trucks, trucks that were small, unobtrusive, with no lettering on the outside. The antiques would be brought directly to The Country Squire's barns.

It was an insane thing for Robbie to rob himself. Worse, for Winthrop Crozier to buy one of the hot items. For Winthrop to actually know Voss and Munro was the worst kind of coincidence.

"The best thing to do," Ugo concluded, "is to say nothing. Maybe Winlove should have an accident, I'll have to weigh the issues. Let's find out, first, what really happened to Munro. I don't trust newspaper accounts and I don't trust Winlove. Now, how could we find out?"

"The perfect person." Carlo had an inspiration. "Bobby Matucci has a brother who's a cop in the Klover Police."

"Let's go to the bar," Ugo said.

❖❖❖

Bobby realized he was being honored. To actually meet Ugo Buonsarde, the big chief, was a very big deal. He stood at attention.

"I'm saddened by the death of a man vacationing in Klover," Ugo told Bobby. "I want to send his partner a condolence letter, but I don't know how the man died. Can you find out?"

Bobby thought for a bit. "Gee, Mr. Buonsarde, I'm sure I can. Brad Greenpeace, the undertaker, often drinks at my uncle's place."

Ugo said, "According to the newspaper, the police were involved."

"Then I'll call my brother Vince, he's a cop," Bobby said.

"Excellent. Could you please call now? The deceased man's name is Mr. Robert Munro. I think he died sometime this week."

Bobby dialed the police station in Klover, and was put through to Vince. "Vince, I gotta have some information. Guy croaked, name's Robert Munro, I'd like to find out the details. You workin' the case? No, no, my lips are sealed. *Jeez*, you kiddin' me? In Poisson's freezer? Guy was strangled, then shot? Poisson's a suspect? You really think he killed the guy, huh? Oh, I see. Only Officer Hughes thinks that. Munro made a threatening phone call to Charly? Hey, Vince, talkin' to me? Like talkin' to the fuckin' grave."

Bobby told Ugo the surprising story. Officers Reynolds and Hughes were handling the investigation, and Clem Hughes, who hated foreigners, wanted to nail Charly for the crime. Stark had told the papers very little, but they'd gotten the story anyway.

"Thank you, Bobby, that will be all," Ugo said. Bobby bowed and backed away, feeling like he'd had an audience with the pope.

As the men walked toward the exit Ugo said, "He appears to be a capable young man, this Bobby."

"He shows promise," Carlo said, carefully not reminding Ugo this was the same Bobby who owed the gambling operation ten Gs. "He's courting my daughter Kimberly."

"She could do worse," Ugo said. He wasn't fond of Carlo's fat, spoiled daughter. "Now, this amazing story of Robbie Munro being stuffed in Charly Poisson's freezer. Could Winlove really be that stupid?"

"Yes," Carlo said immediately. "Guy's nuts. I told him to threaten the little twerp, he offs him. He's coming in, couple hours. I'll make him talk."

"No, no," Ugo said. "Don't say a word to Winlove. I'll speak to Gianni and Francesco. Winlove's a loose cannon. I'll deal with it. Up here in the winter, road accidents are a dime a dozen. As for Munro's death, once Winlove's—ah—departed, we'll spread the word it's just another homosexual murder, Winlove killed his lover, and the police won't pursue it too heavily."

"Winlove's meeting someone here this afternoon, I don't know who. Guy wants to sell him something," Carlo said. "Should we allow that?"

"Yes," Ugo said. "Don't do anything out of the ordinary. And don't say a word to Winlove about Munro. Just pay him, that's all."

The men, who were standing just outside the main door, looked around as the door inched open. Bobby cleared his throat.

"Telephone call for Mr. Buonsarde, sir. It's Mr. Poisson from across the river. You know, the French restaurant." The men hurried inside.

"Ah, Monsieur Poisson, comment ça va?" said Ugo

in very passable French. "You, what? Tripes à la Mode de Caen? Splendid, splendid. They will cook all day, of course. And then? Ah, just a moment. I must confer. A relative is visiting."

Ugo covered the mouthpiece and said to his brother, "Monsieur Poisson wants us to dine with him tomorrow night, Saturday, or perhaps Sunday as his guests. He's making tripe."

Anthony shook his head. Too risky. One of the clients he had encouraged to buy Compu stock lived in Klover and claimed—obviously a lie, the man was a nitwit—that he owned a French restaurant. Perhaps he worked there as a greeter, whatever, but it was too much of a risk.

Ugo was disappointed. "I am heartbroken, Monsieur Poisson, both Saturday and Sunday are out of the question because of family matters. But, a thought. Is there any way you could come here on Monday, your day off as I recall? Could you bring the tripe for lunch?"

Ugo smiled. This was agreeable. Lunch on Monday. They would sit down in Ugo's kitchen to a meal of tripe. Charly was to bring nothing else, Ugo insisted. He would provide the remainder of the meal, plenty of bread of course, and wine, and perhaps a salad and cheese. Ugo gave Charly the directions and hung up, rubbing his hands in anticipation.

"He's a marvelous chef," Ugo told Anthony. "He cooks just like Mama. Perhaps, *perhaps* better than Mama. His tripe will be superb. It's always better when it sits a few days, the flavors intensify."

Perilous Pacts

GREGORY WINLOVE SAT AT HIS DESK REVIEWING, ONCE again, *The Essential Guide to Prescription Drugs*, over a thousand pages listing most of the drugs on the U.S. market, their side effects, prohibitions and precautions for use.

With a little bit of luck poor Matt Kendell would soon have another heart attack. He was already depressed, his skin was yellow, and his wife's death had really knocked him out. Guy wasn't in good shape at all.

Gregory had high hopes for the antiques-theft ring. It could be turned into an international venture, with outposts in London, Paris, South America, perhaps even the Orient. But Matt had vetoed any further enlargement of the business. He said he didn't want to mess with the Buonsardes, and this was their thing. And what did he need it for? He made plenty of money with his trucking business.

Greg had smiled at Matt, agreed with him, praised his wisdom, meanwhile making plans with a few of the truckers who didn't share their boss's conservatism. Greg, with his oversized ego, was convinced that with Matt out of the picture, he could seize the trucking business and start a worldwide antiques-theft operation.

Yep, he was doing all the right (that is to say, wrong) things according to the drug book: urging Matt to take calcium for his aging bones (calcium was proscribed when taking Lanoxin); feeding Matt marijuana ("possible accentuation of heart failure"); slipping a potent diuretic into Matt's morning coffee, thereby causing a potentially dangerous loss of potassium;

dissolving a Valium into his food, which, the book said, caused a further imbalance in his heartbeats. Sooner or later, Greg was certain, one or all of these measures would activate another heart attack.

This was why Greg had to be living with Matt. He also had Matt taking two Lanoxins a day instead of one, persuading him at night that he hadn't taken his morning pill. It paid to plan ahead.

Charly Poisson sat in Stark's cramped office. He clasped and unclasped his hands. He cleared his throat. He was nervous.

"It has come to my attention, Chief Stark . . ." Charly coughed. "I have heard . . ." He cleared his throat again. "People have told me that you think that I—ah—killed Robbie Munro."

Stark shook his head. "I don't think you killed Munro, Charly. Only Officer Hughes thinks you killed Munro."

"Why does Officer Hughes think I kill Munro?"

Stark shrugged. "Maybe he thinks you're snooping around. Munro did leave that threatening message on your machine. What if he had turned up, you killed him, then hid his body in your freezer, thinking to get rid of it at a later date? That's the way Clem's mind works."

"I see."

"And you did call the antiques dealers' association to ask questions about Voss & Munro. Hughes knows that because when he called the association, they told him someone else had just called from Klover. He figured it had to be you. And I know you called the newspaper, asking the owner to keep La Fermette's name out, because he and I had a little chat after the article appeared."

Charly shrugged "I did not call the antiques dealers' association. I ask Barbara Baleine to call. I am not even a member, so they would not tell me anything. I did call the newspaper owner, he is a good customer, and he agree with me that it would do no good to mention my place of business."

"Well, there you are, Charly"

"Of course I have an interest. Is natural. The body was found in my freezer. I did not put it there. Which means that someone came into my restaurant, opened a locked door, carried the body down to the cellar. I have many chicken carcasses down there to make broth, and all of these must be thrown out. It is lucky I do not have hundreds of dollars' worth of food in that freezer, for that too would have to be thrown out."

"Charly."

"Yes, Chief Stark?"

"Please don't interfere."

"Hokay, Chief."

"Let me tell you how things are going. I've put Hughes and Reynolds on the case. Hughes is retiring soon, he wants to go out with a good record. He's never forgotten how you messed around in the Maxwell case, wiping the prints off that pen."

Charly assumed a dejected pose. Sighed loudly. Which Stark ignored.

"He'd love to solve this thing, and he'd love it to be an outsider, not a local. He'll be looking for a part-time job when he retires, and he doesn't want people saying, 'He put a local boy in jail.' "

"Is normal, I suppose," Charly said.

"I'll tell you this," Stark continued "We ran Munro's name through the NCIC, the National Crime Information Center, and he had a sheet. He was involved in stolen antiques some years ago. We ran his partner's name through too, came up negative. We're working with the state police on this." Stark stood up. "Now, don't you have meals to get ready? No one thinks you killed Robbie, Charly, put your mind to rest."

"No one except Officer Hughes."

"Well, yeah. But I wouldn't let that worry you." Stark winked at Charly, which made him feel better. Clem Hughes was a fussy old woman. Stark, without a word of criticism toward his officer, had let Charly know just what he thought of Officer Hughes.

Maurice hummed a carefree tune as he wheeled his Mercedes into a parking space at The Country Squire. In his pocket was the snuffbox and in his head was the price dear Daddy had been offered: forty thousand dollars. His father was such a hoarder. An uneducated know-nothing. Whereas Maurice was a Princeton man. (He ignored the fact that his father, that uneducated know-nothing, had paid for his education.) Maurice would have sold the piece and spent the money immediately on something grand. Anyway, he wouldn't sell the box to Winlove yet. He'd hear Winlove's price, then drive down to the city and compare it with the auction houses.

Maurice felt surprisingly cheerful for a man who had just lost his savings. He'd made many bad investments, though never one quite so big. He'd learned the art at his father's knee, though this never occurred to him, either. Maurice had always patronized his father—his dad's friendship with that nobody, the peasant Charly Poisson, showed what a simpleton he was.

"I have an appointment with Gregory Winlove," Maurice said haughtily to the young woman behind the desk. He looked around the lobby with its wood-paneled walls, velour furniture, crystal sconces, oil paintings of woodland scenes: a handsome place, he thought. "Lots of money, here," he said to no one in particular. He wondered if Winlove was part owner.

"Right this way, sir," the woman said, and escorted Maurice down the hall to the James Monroe Room. She opened the door with a flourish, then left, her high heels soundless in the thick carpeting.

Maurice stood in the doorway and admired the ornate Victorian room. It looked like a grand salon in Paris at the turn of the century, or at least, like the pictures Maurice had seen of such rooms, with the ponderous furniture, the heavy curtains and swags, the crystal chandelier. *Much nicer than Barbara's plain rooms,* he thought. He spied an astonishingly handsome man sitting at the head of the big mahogany table.

"Mr. Winlove?" Maurice asked from the doorway.

"Come in, come in, it's Mr. Baleine, is it not?" Gregory stood up, tall and slender. *He looks like a movie star,* Maurice thought, impressed with Gregory's glossy brown hair tied in a ponytail, wool plaid shirt with beige cashmere turtleneck underneath, tan gabardine trousers tucked into soft leather boots.

Maurice assumed an imperious stance, feet together, head up, and looked across at the man. Then, right hand outstretched, he approached the table. "A pleasure, sir, a pleasure," he said in a condescending voice, implying that he, Maurice, was doing the man a favor, not the other way around. This kind of snobbery worked well in the New York City world of expense-account restaurants.

After offering Winlove his hand, Maurice sat down at the table. He reached into his pocket for the snuffbox.

211

He unfolded the tissue paper and placed the three-inch box on the table. "It's a little beauty, isn't it?" he said.

Gregory looked at the box, then picked it up, turned it this way and that, got out a jeweler's magnifying glass, and examined the underside, the inside, the corners, the sides, the top. "It's a beauty all right," he told Maurice. "No markings, but that doesn't mean anything. Many eighteenth-century pieces were unmarked, and this was made in the late 1700s, I'd guess. A heavy grade of gold, and this is fine enamel work." Painted with a fine brush on the enameled top was a shepherdess and shepherd in a field. The shepherd was gazing into the woman's eyes while coyly lifting her skirt. There were trees in the background, and a vivid blue sky. Without perfect eyesight, you would need a magnifying glass to pick out the details.

Maurice, forgetting his vow, blurted out, "My father was offered forty thousand for this twenty years ago. I expect it's worth much more, now."

Gregory affected well-bred disappointment. He knew that a similar box had sold for well over a hundred thousand at an auction in Paris not long ago. He subscribed to many magazines on the antiques business.

"Ah, Mr. Baleine, I'm sure that's true. Twenty years ago there was a positive mania for snuffboxes such as these. People paid the earth, in many cases much more than the piece was worth. Then, as with all crazes, the snuffbox mania peaked, and prices dropped drastically."

Maurice's disappointment was genuine. His shoulders drooped, he forgot to act haughty. The corners of his mouth turned down. "Ah."

"Still," Gregory went on soothingly, "this is a beauty, well worth twenty or thirty thousand." He straightened his shoulders and looked Maurice in the eye. He could see that Maurice was desperate to sell. "Frankly, Mr. Baleine, I think it would be a pity to sell this now, when the market's so low. Hang on to it for five, ten years, the market's bound to pick up."

"Well . . . that's a possibility, of course . . ."

"Or else"—Gregory's voice became brisk—"Take it into New York. Or better yet, Paris. That's where the money is today. Walk into Hédiard, or Fauchon on the Place de la Madeleine, and it's wall-to-wall Arabs. Or try a specialized shop in New York like À La Vieille Russie on Fifth Avenue. Or, of course, Parkeby's, though they have a reputation for undervaluing, and of course they take a hefty surcharge. Whatever you get from one of the big auction houses, you'll actually walk away with less than half that sum after commission and taxes. Whatever you decide to do, Mr. Baleine"—Gregory smiled warmly at this fat asshole with his Princeton diploma and his Ph.D. in naiveté—"don't make a quick decision. That's a valuable piece. Now's just a bad time to sell."

Maurice forgot his previous decision, that this visit was simply an inquiry into the box's value. He could tell that this man, urging him not to sell, was honest in his desire for him to get the best price possible.

"On the other hand," Maurice said, "a bird in the hand is worth two in the bush, eh?" He laughed jovially, as if he had coined this quaint phrase.

"Well . . . " This time it was Gregory's turn to hesitate. "You could say that, of course. And thirty thousand is thirty thousand, eh?" Gregory lowered his head, then lifted his eyes and smiled seductively at Maurice. "And, ahem, I wouldn't say this to just anyone, Mr. Baleine, but you are so obviously a man of the world, I think we could forgo the formalities of a bill

213

of sale and simply deal in cash. Then we wouldn't report the sales tax to the Internal Revenue." He chuckled, man-to-man. "Then your thirty thousand really would be thirty thousand. Not a bad deal, actually."

"Right," Maurice said. "I'll do it."

"Of course, Mr. Baleine," Gregory said smoothly. "It's your decision. Shall we shake on it?"

Maurice told Gregory that it was a pleasure doing business with a professional and Gregory told Maurice that it was a pleasure doing business with such a knowledgeable collector of objets d'art. Gregory said that if Maurice would be pleased to wait, he'd ring for coffee to be served while he went and got the money. He indicated a small side table covered with magazines and newspapers dealing with financial matters: *Fortune, The Wall Street Journal*, the *London Financial Times*. "Make yourself comfortable, Mr. Baleine. How do you take your coffee?"

"Cream and sugar, please, Mr. Winlove. And please call me Maurice."

"Certainly, Maurice, with pleasure. And I'm Gregory, or Greg if you prefer. I'll be about five, ten minutes. Make yourself at home."

While Maurice sat smiling, hands clasped, Gregory left the room and walked down the hall. He spoke to a waiter, then knocked on Carlo Calamare's office door. He was told to come in.

"I've got a live one, Carlo." Greg told about the snuffbox, and about Maurice, a friend of Lester Pingry, whom both men remembered with pleasure. They'd made a fortune from Lester's grandmother's furniture.

"You couldn't have got it for less?" Carlo asked. "I mean, thirty Gs . . . "

214

"Listen, Carlo, this is the tip of the iceberg. We'll make it up on the other stuff. I can tell; the sucker's hard up for cash, I know he's got a few more pieces to unload. Trust me. Says he owns a French restaurant—not true. He's not a businessman. He's a real gaff, just like Lester."

"French restaurant, huh?" said Carlo. "Mr. B's all gung ho about a French restaurant near Klover, I'll ask him. What's the name of his place?"

"Here," Gregory said. "I'll write it down for you."

Carlo, meanwhile, turned to his safe. He withdrew a shopping bag, and began counting out packets of hundred-dollar bills. He took three large Post Office Priority Mail envelopes from his desk (the post office gave them to you free) and put ten thousand dollars' worth of bills in each one. He piled the envelopes one atop the other and slid a large rubber band around the trio.

"Here you are, Gregory."

"Thanks, Carlo. As soon as I see this dummy off, I'll bring the box to you, put it in the safe. It's a real beauty."

As soon as Gregory left, Carlo slipped on his overcoat and hurried to his car. He wanted to show Ugo the name of the restaurant. In the parking lot, he saw Gianni and Francesco walking away from a nondescript car, but he didn't think anything of it. He waved, the men waved back.

"Here you are, Mr., er, Maurice," Greg said, entering the James Monroe Room where Maurice was sitting at the table drinking coffee and reading *Fortune*. He was afraid that *The Wall Street Journal* would mention Buonsarde and Co., a subject that made him uncomfortable.

"Why don't you count it in front of me, Maurice, that's what Lester always did. This way, there's no misunderstanding."

"Of course, of course." The money was exact. Maurice shrugged into his overcoat and, with the envelopes tucked tightly under his arm, headed for the back door and the parking lot.

"Just let me get my coat, Maurice, I'll see you to your car."

"No, no, Gregory, I wouldn't think of it. I'll call you about some other pieces I have, maybe they would interest you."

Maurice hurried to the parking lot. Christ, it was cold. He opened the car door and put the three envelopes on the backseat. As soon as he started the motor he turned the heat to HIGH and turned on the fan, even though the car would take several minutes to heat up.

As Maurice prepared to drive away, he noticed a familiar figure hurrying across the parking lot toward a black Rolls-Royce. He did a double take. It was a short, squat man with a mane of thick white hair. Could that possibly be Antonio Buonsarde? Count Ercole Antonio Buonsarde, now felonious Count Buonsarde, pursued by the Securities and Exchange Commission, the Internal Revenue, the police, and God only knew who else? Yes, he'd recognize that mane of white hair, that suntanned, heavy face anywhere. Not to mention the black Rolls Royce. It was Anthony, all right.

The Rolls purred into life and glided slowly out of the parking lot. Maurice, without a second thought, followed the big black car out of the lot and onto a small country road.

Reckless Driving

AFTER MAURICE LEFT, GREG HURRIED TO CARLO'S office. After reading the newspaper squib on Munro's death, he'd finally decided what to tell Carlo: that he'd threatened Munro in the guy's car in the restaurant parking lot, as planned, then he'd left. He had no idea what happened after that. "Believe it or not, Carlo," he'd say, and look the man straight in the eye.

But the office was empty, the safe was locked, and no one knew where Carlo was. Oh, well, he'd come tomorrow, collect his money. Greg patted his pocket. He'd keep the snuffbox, he wanted to get home while it was still light. He didn't like Amanda's car. It fishtailed on snowy roads, tires didn't look good, and the steering mechanism appeared faulty. Knowing Amanda, she probably never brought it in for a tune-up, all those tranqs she gulped.

Gregory chuckled. Maurice the super asshole. "Man, you're smooth," he congratulated himself. He'd gained Maurice's trust. Now, he'd zero in. Just as he'd done with Lester.

Gregory drove onto Route 32, heading for the Rip Van Winkle bridge. Yeah, maybe he should stop by Hank Brown's garage, have him check the tires, the steering.

He'd already ordered a new Blazer, to be picked up as soon as he'd gotten the insurance company's okay. But that might take a few weeks.

Nevertheless, when Greg got to the straight stretch on the other side of the river, he stepped on the gas. Couldn't resist. Speed was erotic. He loved the feeling it gave him, flying down the road, like he was king of the

217

world. Let's see what this baby could do.

As the speedometer crept up, Greg watched the snowy landscape flash past. He weaved in and out, passing cars; on left and right, imagining that he was a racing-car driver at Le Mans.

Quicker than he'd thought, Brekenridge Corners loomed up. Greg could see a tractor-trailer turning right into his lane. He braked, then, when nothing happened, pumped the brakes harder. His foot was pressed to the floor, but the brakes didn't respond. Christ—had they locked? He panicked, felt his muscles seize up, couldn't breathe, couldn't get air into his lungs.

He swung the car into the fast lane to avoid the tractor-trailer, skidded, overcorrected, crunched into the back of the big truck that kept on going, swerved again, spun away from the truck, and crashed through a big wooden barrier into a pile of gravel, which had been dumped in the center of the traffic island. The car stopped with a shudder and Greg's torso ground into the steering wheel as his head hit the windshield. He lost consciousness.

Maurice Baleine felt like he'd seen a ghost. Was that really Anthony Buonsarde in the parking lot? Surely not. He'd assured Maurice that he had no connection with the Buonsarde crime family. He was a member of the Sicilian aristocracy—a nobleman. Would such a man lie?

Ahead, the black Rolls purred slowly on. It turned in at a pair of big stone gateposts, left-hand blinker flashing sedately. This, Maurice suspected, was Ugo Buonsarde's estate. Anthony was staying with his brother.

Maurice waited until the car disappeared around a

bend, then he backed out, heading back to Route 32. Now he knew where the enemy was. He'd decide what course of action to take after he'd thought about it. Should he see a lawyer? Telephone the SEC? No. He'd rather handle it on his own. He was smarter than all of them.

"Stupid fool," Maurice caught his breath as a nondescript car flashed its lights, then, when Maurice refused to move into the slow lane, flashed past on the right, then whipped back into the speed lane so quickly that Maurice had to slam on his brakes. He glimpsed a handsome profile, a ponytail of brown hair. Could that be Gregory Winlove?

Maurice heard an explosive noise, followed by a dull thud before he saw anything. It sounded far in the distance. Soon Maurice came upon a car, the same car that had passed him so unwisely, nosed into a pile of gravel. Cautiously, Maurice put on his right-hand blinker and pulled into a lay-by. He got out of his car and crossed the now-deserted roadway.

The jolt of car meeting gravel had caused the entire front of the automobile to be pushed in. Maurice wrenched open the driver's door with difficulty and looked down at the body of Gregory Winlove. The steering wheel was twisted sideways. Gregory's head lay back on the headrest and he appeared to be sleeping. A trickle of saliva snaked down his chin.

Maurice said, "Gregory, can you hear me?"

No answer. The man appeared to be unconscious. Without even thinking about it, Maurice snaked out his hand and patted Gregory's pockets. In the coat's left pocket, by the car door, he heard a rustle of tissue paper. He reached his hand into the pocket and withdrew a tissue-wrapped parcel. His snuffbox? He unwrapped the paper. The gold box nestled in his hand.

Maurice slipped the parcel into his own pocket. Then he slammed the door and hurried back to his Mercedes. A mile down the road was a tavern. He hurried inside— a horrible place stinking of beer—and yelled at the bartender. "There's been an accident just west of here, toward the bridge, on this road. Call 911."

"Okay," the barman said. "Folks still alive?"

"I didn't stop," Maurice lied. "Just call 911, quick."

Julius Prendergast drove to Gaitskill after lunch to visit an old bookshop. It was a twenty-minute ride, and while in the area, he'd planned on checking out The Country Squire where Charly and Rex had such a terrible dinner. But now, glancing at his watch, he saw that he didn't have time. So he got onto 32 eastbound and headed back to La Fermette.

As Julius neared Brekenridge Corners he slowed down, as this was a dangerous spot. He noticed that a car had plowed into a gravel pile in the center of the island and lowered his window. Someone was sitting in the driver's seat. Julius pulled over, parked his car, put on the blinker lights, and, looking both ways, crossed the intersection.

Julius knocked on the window and a man looked at him with a blank stare. *He's in shock,* Julius decided, and he wrenched open the car door.

"Are you all right?" Julius asked.

The man didn't reply. He stared at Julius with flat eyes.

"Are you hurt? Can you get out of the car? Want me to call an ambulance?"

Winlove turned toward the voice. Things were slowly coming back, and in his semi-conscious state he

220

muttered, "Brakes, crash."

"Your brakes froze and you skidded and crashed into the gravel pile," Julius translated. "That's what happened, didn't it?"

"Yuh," Greg said. "Then—car stops, guy comes over, opens door, steals something from my pocket."

He's rambling, Julius thought, but said, "What guy stole something from your pocket? What's your name?"

"Greg Winlove," the man said. "Guy who stole— Maurice the Princeton asshole. I could see 'im, couldn't talk. He didn't know I could see 'im." Gregory shifted in his seat and groaned.

"I'll call for an ambulance."

The man didn't answer. Julius called 911 on his cell phone, and the operator told him that the accident had already been reported. An ambulance was on its way. Julius, who was a responsible man, remained at the scene. He knew that once the car cooled down hypothermia could set in, and he wanted to make sure help arrived. Within five minutes he heard the wail of an ambulance. It pulled up to the car and two attendants jumped out. Then Julius drove on.

But was the guy serious about Maurice? *Our* Maurice? Stealing something from the man's pocket? "The Princeton asshole," the man had said. Yep, couldn't be anyone else.

In the kitchen of La Fermette Charly, Benny, and Mick were busy: Mick was washing pots, Charly was chopping a *mirepoix* of vegetables for the lobster stew: carrots, onions, celery, garlic. Benny was trimming leeks for the shellfish au gratin: only the whites would be used, the greens would be reserved for a soup.

"Oh, good, Julius, you have arrive," Charly said.

221

"You want to make me some salmon rillettes? The salmon filets are in the cooler."

"Something strange happened on my way back from Gaitskill." Julius told of finding Gregory Winlove, and what he'd said about Maurice. "Wasn't Greg Winlove the one who nearly ran you down?"

Charly nodded. "That young man, he is prone to accident, no? I did not know that he and Maurice knew each other. *Tiens.*"

"Maybe Maurice is organizing the antiques-theft racket," Benny said maliciously. Then he grinned. "I wonder if Barbara knows."

Julius and Charly and old Mick shook their heads. "He's too stupid to organize anything like that," Julius said.

"That man couldn't steal candy from a baby without gettin' caught," Mick said. "But if he lost all that money on the stock market, he's probably pawning his grandfather's gold watch or some such. That's what folks do when they're poor. And isn't Winlove doing something with antiques?"

Matthew Kendell sat in Dr. Soames's office that Friday afternoon, worried about his condition. He'd been feeling so strange, lately.

"I'm peeing all the time. At night, after dinner, I feel drugged. Not just tired, but like my limbs are stuck in glue. Like I felt when I took those tranquilizers you gave me, Doc. A friend told me to take calcium for my back, but it aches all the time even though I'm poppin' those things like candy. I wake, I'm aching all over, like a hangover, and I'm drinkin' hardly nothing."

"I don't like the sound of any of that, Matt," Dr. Soames said, scribbling on a pad of paper. "Those

222

problems aren't associated with Lanoxin, though it does have side effects. Now, let's go through your entire day, from when you get up. What you eat, how you feel. You're living alone now, aren't you?"

"No, I got Amanda's brother staying with me, Gregory Winlove. His oil burner's broke. He's been stayin' at the house since Amanda died. He's been fixing all my food, too."

Soames recognized the name Winlove. Mrs. Winlove used to be a nurse's aide at the hospital; she was always complaining about Gregory, her son, getting into trouble. On a whim, he pulled the telephone book over and dialed Hudson Valley Oil.

"Ted? Jerry Soames, here. Have you by chance got a Gregory Winlove buying oil from you? Yeah, check, would you? You have. How's his oil burner coming along, I hear it's on the fritz. No? He never called you? And he has a service contract? Okay, Ted, thanks a lot.

"You heard that, Matt, didn't you? Now, here's what I want you to do. Kick that brother-in-law of yours out, or else keep him but don't eat or drink anything that he gives you. You still have that Valium and the diuretic I gave you? Okay, throw them out. Dump the calcium. Didn't you read that piece of paper I gave you, telling you what not to eat or drink when you're on Lanoxin? Calcium's a big no-no."

"Uh, I think I lost it."

"No calcium, Matt. Not even those antacid tablets. We'll get Trixie to take a blood sample, and go pee in this cup, here. We'll test a few things. Hey, you smoking any pot?"

"Nah. Well, couple times, Greg gave me a hit or two."

"I see." Soames continued writing. That meant Matt

was probably smoking one, two joints a night.

"You think Greg's tryin' to poison me?"

Dr. Soames spread his hands out. He couldn't make accusations. He didn't want his insurance to go up. Folks loved to sue. "What do I know?"

After Kendell left the office, Jerry Soames called John Stark. Death by overmedication wasn't exactly an epidemic, but when the big, brutal husband of a sweet little lady suddenly dropped dead and his autopsy showed he had enough medication in his system to kill ten men, you tended to wonder who'd been doling out the meds.

"John, Jerry Soames. I've got a little problem. You got sheets on either Matthew Kendell or Gregory Wmlove? Kendell's had another heart thing. I'm worried. Great. If I'm not here, Trixie'll take the message."

Friday Dinner at La Fermette

"CALL FOR YOU, CHARLY." IT WAS AFTER FIVE, AND the kitchen of La Fermette was a whirlwind of chopping, stirring, sautéing. Elton Briggs, Sam Washburn, and Tommy Glade, tonight's waiters, sat at the big pine table eating meat loaf and mashed potatoes. Charly believed everyone worked better on a full stomach.

"Allo, allo, La Fermette, 'ere."

It was Jimmy Houghton. "It's a short contract, Charly, but I want you to approve it before I drop it off at Jonathan's office."

"Why not stop in," Charly said, "I treat you to dinner."

"No, tonight's my oyster stew night, and *Herbalgram* magazine's just arrived, I've been looking forward to reading it all day."

"Hokay. So read."

Charly listened. "Sure, send it to Jonathan. It must be final. No Maurice coming back, saying we promise this and this and do not deliver."

"We all know Maurice," Jimmy said.

Two hours later Win Crozier mopped bread around his Mediterranean lobster stew bowl, collecting last bits of sauce. "Marvelous, Charly."

"Howard Voss has gone home?" Charly asked.

"Absolutely. He wasn't going to stick around, have Officer Clem Hughes ripping him to shreds. We alerted John Stark, and he agreed Howard could go. Hughes calls it 'The Fag Murder' and is convinced Howard did it."

"Two day ago, he is convinced I do it," Charly told them.

Morty snorted. "Cop's a homophobe, hates foreigners, women, anyone with money. Stark says maybe it was a mistake, putting Hughes on the case."

"Robbie's murder is tied into the antiques-theft ring," Win said, "as anyone could see. But Hughes just ignores the theft angle."

"He is awfool man. But, changing subject," Charly said, "what do you know about Mr. Gregory Winlove?"

Win pursed his lips and looked cautious. "He buys his paints from us, plus varnish, beeswax, all sorts of things. A good customer. He not only refinishes, he actually makes furniture out of old wood. He uses old nails, wooden pegs. They're showpieces. You'd swear

225

they were centuries old."

"This remind me," Charly said, "of book I love. Called *Au Pays des Antiquaires* by André Mailfert. Monsieur Mailfert make furniture from old wood, then he store it in henhouse so chickens can scratch and make do-do on it, make it look old. Then he sell it to museum as antique furniture." Charly chuckled. "He say he have furniture in most museums in France."

"Well, I don't think Greg's that good," Win said, "but almost. He also goes to Europe to buy stuff, attends auctions, and he buys antiques from people, then resells them—sort of a broker."

Charly thought of Maurice. "People who need some cash, quick?"

"Could be," Morty said guardedly. "We really don't know . . ."

"Of course," Charly said, realizing they'd say nothing about a steady customer. An admirable trait, unfortunately.

Jimmy Houghton dined alone on oyster stew, then opened his issue of *Herbalgram,* the journal of the American Botanical Council and the American Herb Foundation. He read the monograph on Saint-John's-wort, an antidepressant, very au courant. Perhaps he could dig up some of the wild plants from Charly's fields this summer, see if they'd grow in his garden.

Jimmy, like Julius Prendergast, wanted to retire at fifty and start another life. Jimmy was collecting materials for his projected book, *Medicinal Herbs of the Hudson Valley.* He was always interested in hearing Charly's stories of French herbal medicines, for, like Charly, he had little use for the powerful pharmaceutical

226

industry. Jimmy was fed up with the money business. All that greed. All those gluttons.

Except that he'd miss working with people like Charly. Charly respected money, but he wasn't greedy. Charly's mania was the quest for justice. Right now he was trying to find out who killed Amanda Kendell, and who killed that friend of Win Crozier's, Robbie Munro. Ludicrous, stuffing the man in Charly's freezer. And stupid. Charly would move heaven and earth to find the killer, now.

What was it with Charly, this pursuit of criminals? He'd nearly gotten himself shot, the night that Jimmy killed Walter Maxwell, who had killed his father. But Charly? He wasn't related to these dead people. It was simply to see justice done.

Jimmy thought it went back to the Second World War, when Charly was a teenager. Charly had told Jimmy about four of his classmates, shot by the Nazis, and about a neighbor, a doctor. He'd been shot, too, after being tortured, for tending to the Maquis, the French guerrillas. You never forget things like that. They eat into your psyche, coloring your life. Stalking the predators, the bad guys: that's what Charly was doing. Getting even.

Jimmy Houghton, close to fifty, thin, sandy-haired, with grey eyes and pale blond lashes and eyebrows, pushed his wire-rimmed glasses onto his forehead and rubbed his eyes. Time to get out of the money business. There is no justice in the world, Jimmy decided, except for the rich, who could buy it.

But maybe people didn't deserve justice. *Oh, if I could make a million dollars, everything would be okay and I'd be happy,* the dummies thought. After they made the money, they were just as miserable. Oh, hell, why fight it? Jimmy sniffed, blew his nose. Maybe he had a cold coming on. *I'll brew myself some nice fenugreek tea,* he thought, *and go read in bed.*

Charly continued greeting his customers, but his heart wasn't in it. Kept thinking about Amanda Kendell, Matthew Kendell, Gregory Winlove. And Robbie Munro, stuffed in his freezer like a sausage.

Charly kept hearing voices: Winlove's "poor Amanda," said in a soft, whispery voice; Matt Kendell's tired voice saying he didn't do small haulage; Maurice, in that quacking voice, bragging about Count Buonsarde; that doctor in the hospital calling Kendell "big fella" in that fake-hearty voice that doctors used; Munro's spiteful little voice, going on about the Lalique vase; Amanda's little-girl whisper.

And what about Gregory Winlove trying to force him off the road? Gregory had seen Charly emerge from Kendell's house. Not a wise move. Did Maurice actually steal something from Winlove? Had Maurice sold Winlove something of value, that old snuffbox of his father's, for instance, then tried to steal the piece back? Charly's thoughts whirled on.

"Ah, good evening, Monsieur, Madame Crisp. Have you enjoy your meal? Madame is looking lovely. And, monsieur, a handsome tie. Would you care for a digestif?" Charly continued his rounds, but his heart wasn't in it this evening. Not while a killer lurked in the countryside.

Charly wandered back to his kitchen to find Tiger Cavett, Honoria Wells's farm manager, sitting at the pine table while Julius and Benny prepared two orders of lobster stew for carryout.

"Honoria just got back from a couple days in the city,

says she's too pooped to dine out," Tiger told Charly. "She and Father Evangelista are having a Kennedy evening, they've been reading that new book."

Charly liked Tiger Cavett. Tiger had integrity. Charly had originally gotten Tiger a job with Peter and Dinah Vann, but when Dinah asked Tiger to wash out her silk underpants, Tiger quit. Charly then recommended Tiger to Honoria Wells. This appeared to be working well.

"They need more than lobster stew," Charly noted, assembling ingredients for a salad. He also added two portions of saffron rice, two portions of string beans with butter and garlic, and a baguette.

"You've had a lot of excitement the last few days," Tiger told Charly. "Honoria told me about the body in your freezer, swore me to secrecy of course. My old enemy Robbie Munro. I always knew he'd end up badly."

"Old enemy? You know him?" So everybody knew about his body. Oh, well . . . how could you keep something like that hidden?

"Let's just say I've run into him in the course of my travels," Tiger said dryly. "I saw him in Steak Heaven the other night, and I said to myself, 'There's trouble.' Now that he's dead, I'll tell you this: a friend's apartment in New York was broken into, and the thieves took my friend's gold cuff links to Robbie Munro to sell them. By one of those wild coincidences, my friend went to Munro's shop to look for antique cuff links to replace the ones he'd had stolen, and there his were. My friend went to the cops and got them back. The cops told him they had their eyes on Robbie."

"And you see him at Rex's? Saturday night? The night he disappear?"

"Ummm—yeah, I guess it was Saturday."

229

"You're the second familiar face I've seen up here," Charly remembered Robbie's venomous little voice following him to the kitchen. He'd wondered who the first familiar face could be. Matthew Kendell? Gregory Winlove? But no, it had been Tiger's.

Charly thought for a bit. "Perhaps the man who kill Robbie he was at Steak Heaven that night? Do you remember who was there?"

"Let's see," Tiger said. "Kendell and Greg Winlove were there together, I avoided them. That's all I can recall."

"Why did you avoid them, *Monsieur Tigre?"*

Tiger giggled. "I love it when you call me *Monsieur Tigre.* Well, I avoided them because I don't like them. Winlove and Kendell, they're up to some monkey business, something to do with antiques. That's all I know. And I'm not going into what I suspect. But I'll tell you this: Greg Winlove, who's so greedy for money I can't believe it, has been pestering Honoria to lend him one of her library chairs so that he can copy it. It's colonial and worth a fortune, and Honoria won't lend it to him, because she thinks he'll either make a fake and sell it as a genuine piece, or else steal her original and return a well-crafted copy."

"Why," Charly asked, "was Winlove in her house?"

"Oh, he renovated something, an old desk, I think. He'd come highly recommended. And she said he did a beautiful job. But she didn't like him. She said he had funny eyes."

"Here's your grub, Tiger," Julius said, presenting a big shopping bag.

"Good luck with your detecting, Charly." Tiger paid and left.

"It give me furiously to think," Charly spoke aloud.

230

"What, Charly?" asked Benny.

"Oh, Benny. I am simply giving my brain over to thought."

Family Relations

"THIS'S JOHN STARK AT THE KLOVER POLICE. IS DOC Soames there?"

"No, Chief Stark," the receptionist told him. "Dr. Soames has already left for the evening. Dr. Wedgewood's in charge. Put you through?"

"Naw, this's personal. Look, just tell him to call me, will you? Tell him I found out some interesting facts."

Greg Winlove, lying in the Van Buren County Hospital, tried to piece together what happened. Brakes failed. Then the crash, plowed nose-first into that gravel pile, lucky it was there, really. What if it had been a brick wall. Or another car. Then that dumb guy reaching into his pocket, stealing back the snuffbox, Baleine, his name was. God, what a creep. Or crazy, maybe he was off his rocker. Then the ambulance, the emergency room, tests, X rays. Doc said he could leave tomorrow.

The tests and X rays had shown nothing broken, just a couple of cracked ribs. But think of the big fat fees they could charge his medical insurance. Lots of bruising, of course, and it hurt to draw air into his lungs. He felt like he'd been beaten up. Possible concussion, but probably not; no broken bones, pierced lungs, leprosy, cancer, tuberculosis, not even athlete's foot. They'd checked it all. "You're one lucky fella," the ambulance guys had told him. "But your ride's another story. It's at Brown's Garage."

"It's my sister's."

"Get a pickup, four-wheel drive, is my advice," one guy said.

"Yeah." He wanted to get over to Hank Brown's, inspect those brakes.

Greg was startled when he saw Matt Kendell's huge frame fill the doorway. "Hey, Matt? How'd you know I was here, man?"

"You told the nurse I was next of kin, hospital called."

"Oh, yeah. Well, you're my brother-in-law, no one else, now."

"Yeah, that's right. You okay? What happened?"

"Skidded on a patch of ice, plowed into a pile of gravel." Keep it simple. Guy wasn't too swift.

"Second accident this week. You okay? Or is someone out to get you, fix Amanda's car so it'd crash. Which you just took. Without asking."

"I was going to tell you, Matt, but I was in a rush. Naah, I don't think anyone's out to get me." But the brakes were definitely not working. Now—who'd want to kill him? He and Carlo were on good terms, or had been, until he'd squeezed that little faggot's neck too hard and the guy croaked. An accident. But then, making it look like an execution, he'd pumped a bullet into the worm's face. Brilliant. None of this could ever be traced to The Country Squire. Or to him. Carlo would understand. Accidents happen.

"Cops called me this afternoon," Matt continued. "Some antiques dealer turns up dead in a restaurant, had my telephone number in his pocket. Name's Munro. He's the guy wanted his own antiques stole, right? I told the cops he never called me, I didn't know nothing about it."

"Matt? Don't worry about it. Guy was an asshole."

"Yeah? And now he's a dead asshole. And Greg? I'm not puttin' you up no more. So when you get outta here, move your stuff out."

Greg shrugged. "Okay, Matt, whatever you say. I'm getting out of here tomorrow. I'll lease a car, come by, get my stuff. You mind my asking why?"

"I went to your house, turned up the oil burner, checked it out. There's nothing wrong with it. I broke your lock to get in, but I'm gettin' someone to fix it. I nailed it shut in the meantime."

Gregory changed the subject. "Hey, you ever hear of a guy named Maurice Baleine, lives around here?"

"Never heard of him."

"Says he owns a French restaurant."

"I only go to Rex's and the diner. Look him up in the phone book."

Matt still stood in the doorway, looking across at that lying, conniving piece of shit. Something was going on, he didn't know what it was, but he knew he didn't like it.

Gregory spent an almost pleasant evening in the hospital. He felt drowsy, even though they'd refused him painkillers because of the possibility of concussion. The beef stew was edible, and the bed next to his was empty. He spent his time planning vengeance on three people who didn't deserve to live: that little French snoop with the red van who was prowling around Matt's house; that Baleine guy, who'd stolen his snuffbox back; and Matt Kendell, though he'd bide his time with Matt, hoping that nature would take its course.

Ugo Buonsarde, his brother Antonio, Gianni, and Francesco were sitting in Ugo's kitchen eating air-dried

233

salami, brined olives, sourdough bread made in the Catskills, and drinking rough peasant wine.

"If at first you don't succeed," Ugo intoned.

"Yeah, boss," Francesco said. "He's in the hospital, a few scratches is all. This might take time, make it look accidental. Don't worry, though."

"I wasn't planning to worry. I never do."

"Ugo? My mind's made up. I'll leave from Atlanta," Anthony said. "They'll cover Kennedy, Logan, but not Atlanta, I'm sure. I'll go to London, stay in my flat a few days, then on to Sicily."

"They think you're there already, Tonio. Don't concern yourself."

"Who's concerned? I take precautions. I got the other passport."

"Edward Arnold, right?"

"Ed-wahd Jen-kins." Anthony made his voice sound flat, English.

"Oh, that's right. These Wasp names all sound alike."

"And," Anthony cautioned, "no more antiques for awhile. No more Winlove or Kendell, ever. It was unwise to bring in outsiders."

"I agree." Ugo nodded. "People who don't know our ways . . ."

"You sound just like Papa." Anthony smiled.

"You're leaving before our tripe fest on Monday?"

"I'm leaving Sunday morning, day after tomorrow, if you can spare Gianni or Francesco to drive me to Albany."

"Of course, *fratello mio.* But I'm sorry you're leaving so soon. I wanted you to taste Charly's tripe, see if it's as good as Mama's."

Anthony made a face. "You know something, Ugo? Something I never told Papa or Mama? I loathe tripe. I detest tripe. I think tripe's disgusting."

"Oh, Tonio." There was genuine distress in Ugo's voice.

"These late nights are killing you," Betty Stark told her husband.

"It's only eight o'clock. But I agree. It'll be over soon, though. I'm positive that either that trucker Kendell or Gregory Winlove did both killings, Amanda's and that antiques guy from New York."

"Then why not arrest them both, maybe one will tattle on the other?"

"I can't yet. Don't have enough evidence. I just have a gut feeling. Took Clem Hughes off the case, driving everybody crazy. Gave him the break-in at the school. Told him it was far more important and he bought it."

"Why do you think it's Kendell or the Winlove guy?"

"Jerry Soames called, he says Kendell's on his last legs, only has a few months before his heart gives out. I wonder if he's clearing up loose ends, old hatreds. And Greg Winlove? He's got a long history of petty crimes, on one of his sheets the school psychologist had a name for him. What do you call someone who's obsessed with himself?"

"A narcissist," said Betty.

"Yeah, that's it. Narcissistic personality disorder. I called old Doc Ross about it. He says people like that have no conscience, they'd kill you just as soon as look at you. They don't worry about being caught, they think they're smarter than you. Think they're God."

"Just like Uncle Phil," Betty said. "Fired his house for the insurance, then left his fingerprints all over the jerry can of gasoline, right in plain sight. Fire chief took about five minutes to decide Uncle Phil did it."

"Just like Uncle Phil. I called Kendell, he'd been in the hospital with a heart attack. He didn't want anyone to know, thought it would hurt his business. He says Amanda was scared of her brother. He was always trying to borrow money, threatening if she didn't pay. What's for dinner?"

"All your favorites. I've fed the girls, they're off to cheerleader practice. Pork chops with onion gravy, mashed potatoes, brussels sprouts."

"Betty, you're the best cook in the world."

Charly Makes a New Friend

CHARLY DECIDED TO CALL JOE OKUN, THE half-Passamaquoddy Indian who came from the same town as Matthew Kendell, up in Maine. Win Crozier had told Charly that Joe worked at The Paint Barrel, part-time.

Once, when Mick was ill, Joe had filled in as dishwasher at La Fermette. Charly was fond of the man. He was clumsy, he dropped things, broke dishes, but there was no shirking on the job. Joe had dignity. Besides, French people are enamored of the idea of *les peaux rouges,* American Indians. When Charly left France for the United States as a young man, many of his compatriots believed that America was one vast, lawless region teeming with *les cuvboy* and Indians. American movies had a lot to answer for.

Charly dialed Mrs. Wiggins's boardinghouse. He held the receiver away from his ear, knowing how Mrs. Wiggins answered the telephone.

"Wiggins," Mrs. Wiggins shouted.

"Charles Poisson, Mrs. Wiggins. Joe Okun, may I speak with him?"

"Sooeee, Joe Okunnn. Sooeee, Joe Okunnn," Mrs. Wiggins bellowed.

A quiet voice came on. "Uh, this is Joe."

"Joe, this is Charly Poisson. Do you remember me?"

"Ayuh,"

"May I talk with you about Matthew Kendell?"

"Ayuh."

"May I take you out for coffee? Pick you up at The Paint Barrel?"

"Bring my own coffee. In a thermos. Drink it at ten."

"May I come, talk to you at ten? I bring one of Patty's brownie."

"Bring two," Joe said and hung up.

By half past nine, lunch at La Fermette was under control and Benny and Julius were tackling Saturday dinner. They would preroast ducks, a couple of pheasants, and some chickens but keep them underdone, to be finished when ordered; roast the lamb, pork, and veal; make salmon rillettes and stuff some artichokes with a *mirepoix* of carrot, onion, garlic, and crumbled rosemary. Charly was marinating strips of pork and veal for several pâtés and while they rested in their marinade of brandy, olive oil, and herbs, Charly left in his little red van, but not for town.

Gregory Winlove lived off Route 32, east of Klover. Charly recognized the name of the road when he'd checked his telephone directory. And conveniently, Winlove was still in the hospital. Charly had checked that, too. He simply wanted to drive by. He wouldn't even get out of his car.

Allen Road, a dead end in the midst of fields, was a narrow dirt road, though the snowplow had been through. There were two houses at the entrance to the road, then nearly at the end, a handsome white clapboard farmhouse. A mailbox in front said Winlove. There were no cars in the driveway, though a modern, two-car garage stood to the left of the house.

Charly was surprised—he'd imagined Winlove living in a poor, run-down place. The house was freshly painted, probably a century old, with a handsome Palladian window at the front, brass side lights, and a flagstone path leading from the driveway to the front door, cleared of snow. Well, well, Charly thought. The place was clearly the house of a prosperous person. He could see, through the bare branches of the trees, what looked like a big red barn some hundred yards behind the house, and he noticed a plowed track that led from Allen Road to the barn. *Perhaps this is where he does his furniture work,* Charly thought. He was just about to disregard his previous vow and get out to peer in the windows of the house, when a pickup truck drove up and parked at the front of the house, nose-to-nose with Charly's van. He recognized Noah Van Gieson, the locksmith. Van Gieson walked over to Charly's van, smiling. Charly rolled down his window.

"Good morning, Mr. Van Gieson."

"Morning, Mr. Porson. If you're here to see Greg Winlove, he's still at the hospital, I hear. Been in a wreck, but he'll be getting out this morning."

"Oh, this morning?" Charly said, relieved he'd stayed in his van. "You are busy man, Mr. Van Gieson, changing all the locks at Mr. Winlove's."

"Only one. Mr. Kendell had to break in, Winlove wanted him to check the heat, didn't have no key. Oh,

238

look, that's Mr. Winlove, now."

Charly's stomach did a funny little dance as he noticed a black car inching up the road. The car turned into the driveway, stopped, and Gregory Winlove got out. He walked over to the two cars. "Well, isn't this a surprise," he said, staring straight at Charly.

"Good day, sir, I leave, now," Charly said, and rolled up his window. He started his van and drove hurriedly down Allen Road.

The first thing that Gregory Winlove did when he left the hospital Saturday morning was to call a taxi to take him to Honest Ed's Car Rentals on Route 9, where he rented a plain black Plymouth sedan. Then, he drove to Hank Brown's garage, where Amanda's wrecked car sat in a parking lot to the side, its front bashed in. He told Hank about the failed brakes.

Hank crawled under the car on a dolly, all Gregory could see was legs. Then Hank rolled out, looking grim. "Them fuckers were cut. Clean cut."

"What fuckers?'

"The brake lines. See, if they'd tore, they'd have jagged edges. But these don't. Cut clean. Whoever cut 'em's a pro. Prob'ly took him five minutes."

"How long would it take for the brake fluid to leak out?"

Hank thought for a bit. "Oh, 'bout ten minutes I guess. Maybe more, since it was cold out. Now you know, that's attempted murder, that is. If I was you, I'd call the cops."

"You're right, Hank. That's what I'll do."

Greg had no intention of calling the cops. There would be retribution, for sure, but he would handle it himself. Now, let's see, who was at The Country Squire yesterday afternoon, who could have cut his brake lines?

He thought about it as he drove to his house. Maurice? Possible. He was an idiot, but idiots sometimes possessed rare talents. Carlo? Ugo's legbreakers Francesco and Gianni? Well, they'd know how, but why would they? They couldn't run the antiques operation without him, he was the lynchpin, the world authority, the pro. No one could run it except Gregory Winlove.

Greg turned down Allen Road and noticed the pickup parked in front of his house. Van Gieson the locksmith. And he was talking to . . . Christ, can you believe it? That little frog who ran the restaurant, the one where he'd dumped Munro's body. Charles, or whatever his name was, the one he'd caught snooping around Kendell's house. Somehow he'd found out about Gregory. Oh, boy, Mr. Frenchman, say your prayers.

At five minutes to ten, Charly was parked outside the delivery entrance to The Paint Barrel. He'd asked Win permission to speak with Joe, and permission had been granted. "But I doubt you'll find out much, Charly, he doesn't exactly talk your ear off."

Charly and Joe didn't waste time with small talk. They sat in Charly's van. "Joe, I wonder if Matthew Kendell killed his wife," Charly began.

"Ayuh. Mebbe. He's a bad man. Up home, he was always gettin' into fights, beating up on us redskins. Hated us. Beat up one of my buddies so bad, he nearly died."

"He was a racist," Charly said.

"Whatever. A bad man."

Joe finished his first brownie and stared at Charly. He

240

had a granite face, short, squat body, as tall as Charly but three times as wide. His black, shoulder-length hair glistened. He might have been forty, fifty, sixty, hard to tell. His face was weather-beaten, and as wrinkled as a prune. But two lively brown eyes peered out at Charly. Eyes that noticed everything.

"When did you find out that Kendell had moved down here?"

"Saw the sign. Kendell Transports. Never thought it was the same fella. Went for a job, once. But I saw 'im there, so I left, pretty quick."

"You know why he left Maine?"

"Sheriff down to Machias didn't like 'im much. He kept the cops busy, always pickin' fights. I don't know why he came here."

Joe was now on the last brownie. When it was done, Charly knew Joe would go back to work.

"He had no respect," Joe said, looking Charly in the eye.

"And respect, it is important, is it not, Joe?"

Joe finished the brownie. "Lemme tell you about the People of the East, Mr. Charly." Joe sat up straight and looked through the windshield at the grey sky. "That's the Wabanakis Nation. Made up of five tribes: Passamaquoddy, Penobscot, Micmac, Malecite, and one other, I disremember the name."

"And all these tribe, they are in Maine?"

"Up in the North Country. See, we all have one thing common to us, and that's respect. We respect the Great Spirit who's in everything, in trees and plants and animals. And in us. So, no matter how poor we was, and the Indians where I lived was the poorest, we always had this respect."

"Respect for all living thing, because you are part of

241

the big scheme. I, too, have this belief."

"Yeah, I know you do, I can feel it," Joe said. "Made us act decent for our *n'musums,* that's our grandfathers."

"Our ancestors."

"Yeah. And we believe that every time we take a breath"—Joe illustrated by breathing deeply—"we breathe in the Great Spirit."

"And," Charly said, "Kendell did not have this respect."

"No, he did not. Like most whites. Always after money, that's all he cared about. Just like all the other white fellers."

The two men sat silently. "Thank you, Joe," Charly said.

"You're not like that. You have the *kchi,* Mr. Charly."

"The what?"

"The *kchi,* the greatness. You have respect, Mr. Charly."

"Thank you, Joe."

Without another word Joe opened the van door and walked away. All the way back to the restaurant, Charly murmured, "I have the *kchi,* I have the *kchi."* Would this power help him find the killer of Amanda Kendell and Robbie Munro? Without question or shadow of doubt.

Confrontations

TO CHARLY'S SURPRISE, JULIUS PRENDERGAST WAS IN his kitchen at half past seven Saturday morning. He usually arrived later.

"Julius, you are very early."

Julius grinned. "Wanted to talk to you, Charly. I want to quit my job up in Albany, work down here full-time as one of your cooks. Now that you're buying Maurice out, maybe you'll sell me some shares."

Charly stared, mouth open.

Julius continued, "I'll sell my town house on Lark Street, Aunt Honoria's offered me her little stone gatehouse. Now that she's getting older, I think she likes the idea of having me close by."

Charly stammered, "But your fine plans, the country inn . . ."

"I never knew running a restaurant was so complicated, Charly. I don't want to run anything. I just want to cook at La Fermette. I don't want to take Benny's job as sous-chef, I just want to cook, maybe buy some stock. Would you sell me a few shares, when you buy Maurice out?"

Charly sat down. His legs felt weak. "It sound great, Julius." Charly brushed a tear from his cheek. "Bit of dust in my eye. Yes, Julius. You are a gifted cook. Would you like to become my new partner?"

Maurice Baleine sat at his desk, his father's snuffbox clutched in his hand. Where could he hide it? He supposed that Gregory Winlove had discovered it missing and assumed the ambulance men had stolen it.

Too bad he didn't have a safe. He wanted to hide the thirty thousand dollars, too. If he put it in the bank, the IRS would know about it. He'd stuffed it under his mattress but mattresses and refrigerators, he'd read, were the first places that thieves looked. He wanted to keep the money hidden from Barbara, as well. The cellar? Yes, yes, the cellar. It was filled with boxes of books, cartons of china and glassware, cases of liquor from his drinking days. If thieves ever started on the cellar it would take them weeks to search.

Maurice took both the money and snuffbox to the cellar.

In the far corner were Maurice's cases of wine and liquor. He lifted off two cases and slit open the bottom case, which was filled with Beefeater gin. He took out six bottles and wedged the money and the box inside. He stood the bottles alongside. He dusted off his hands. Perfect.

Job number two was to call the Securities and Exchange Commission and tell them about Anthony Buonsarde's hiding place. He finally found the number (under "U.S. Government Agencies") in his Manhattan telephone book. But what number to call? There were nine departments listed, from Broker-Dealer Compliance to Complaints. Maurice was about to dial the "Complaints" number when his stomach gave a rumble and he glanced at his watch. It was past noon and he was ravenous. Maurice decided it would be best to deal with the SEC on a full stomach.

As he slurped canned soup and munched on a ham sandwich, a thought emerged: if Maurice called the SEC, he'd have to give his name. And if he did this, the IRS might start questioning him. Maurice's income tax returns did not always dwell in the palace of truth.

Like many dishonest people, Maurice saw trouble where no trouble existed: he was a slave to his paranoia. Where trouble really did exist, like Gregory Winlove, his eyes were blinkered. He couldn't look on Winlove as a danger, only as an annoyance.

No, he decided, calling the SEC was out. Now, how could he get his money back from Antonio Buonsarde? Well, he could get in touch with Buonsarde and *threaten* to call the SEC, if his money wasn't returned. But this would simply put the man to flight. A dilemma.

Maurice made a two-cup pot of Colombian coffee with his Melita filter and sat, sipping, in his big modern kitchen filled with every convenience that the noncook thinks essential—microwave, electric toaster oven, automatic ice crushing machine, blender, Cuisinart, KitchenAid, electric knife grinder, electric can opener.

As he sipped his black coffee, Maurice thought how tasteless it was without that delectable tot of Courvoisier. The doctors at the sanatorium had told him that one sip—one drop—of alcohol would probably kill him. He wondered if the doctor was right about that. Just one tiny tot? He felt poorly, not his usual self-confident self. He jumped as a door opened.

"Oh, there you are, Maurice. Listen, I'm ravenous, but I have to talk to you, the most amazing thing . . ."

It was Barbara, flinging open the back door so that a gust of frigid air blew in. "I didn't want to eat at Charly's, they're rushing around and the barroom is full. But—I can't believe this—Julius told me that he'd stopped to help a man who'd crashed his car yesterday and the man told him that you, Maurice Baleine, had taken something out of his pocket."

Maurice choked on his coffee and spent some time coughing.

Barbara continued, "Was he out of his mind, or what? Julius mentioned the man's name, Gregory Winlove, he's an antiques dealer. I won't touch his stuff. He deals in stolen merchandise, everyone says, and Mummy says he makes beautiful fakes, which he sells as originals. He also buys things from people who need quick cash, and he cheats them horribly."

Maurice, badly shaken, set down his cup. "Clearly,

245

my dear Barbara, this Winlove is out of his mind. Of course I didn't steal anything."

Maurice didn't try to pick up his cup: his hands were shaking too badly. He watched Barbara put together a sandwich of mayonnaise, pickle rounds, sliced chicken, and alfalfa sprouts.

"So," Barbara continued, "you don't know the man?"

"Never met the man in my life," Maurice squeaked.

"You're sure?" Barbara persisted. "Very handsome, very sure of himself. Oh, he's the brother of that woman who was murdered last week."

Maurice suspected that if he stood up, he'd pass out.

"Mummy says he's suspected of running a stolen antiques ring." Barbara finished her sandwich. "Well, I'm off to Win and Morty's to get paint chips and wallpaper samples, then up to Albany. Make your own dinner, there's chicken and ham in the fridge, I don't know when I'll be home."

Maurice sat, paralyzed, in his chair. He heard his busy wife revving her beige Cadillac down in the driveway. She had her own successful business, what did she care about him? Self-pity engulfed Maurice like a cloak.

Maybe just one, with my coffee, Maurice thought. He shuffled into the living room, where the laden bar table still stood. His hand shook as he reached for the Courvoisier, but he poured a healthy measure into his cup without spilling a drop. He took a good big swallow.

Ahhh, that was more like it. He felt the brandy traveling down his gullet and spreading outward, lubricating rusty parts. Magic. And, as if by magic, his cup had emptied. He poured more Courvoisier, feeling more and more like the old, self-confident Maurice.

Gregory Winlove turned right off Route 65, past La Fermette, the fancy-looking restaurant that Maurice claimed he owned, and drove slowly up Hubbard Road, which was Maurice Baleine's address in the telephone book. At a little crossroads he turned right. Here the road ended. A gravel driveway led up to a white modern stucco house. Ugly. Must be Maurice's place.

Gregory parked by the front door. No lights were on, the place looked deserted. The house was ugly, pretentious, cold, and not at all in keeping with the countryside.

He walked to the front door. He pressed the doorbell and chimes rang inside the house. He waited, then pressed the bell again. Nothing. He walked around the house, stepping carefully, and peered in the window of what must be the living room. Fancy place. He'd mentioned Maurice's name to Win and Morty at The Paint Barrel, and found out a few more things about the man: that he was married to Barbara De Groot, a well-known interior designer. She was a rich one, Barbara De Groot. He also found out that Maurice was, indeed, co-owner of La Fermette. And Morty mentioned, too, that Maurice had a little drinking problem.

Now, who's that lying on the couch, fast asleep? Gregory shielded his eyes and peered in the window. Looked like fat Maurice. Coffee cup on the table, bottle of booze on its side, on the floor. Well, well.

Gregory banged on the glass and shouted, "Fire! Fire!" then returned to the front door and rang the doorbell repeatedly. Finally he heard footsteps. The door opened, and Maurice, hair mussed, clothes awry, stood blinking. Gregory pushed Maurice aside and strode into the front hall.

"Yes?" Maurice said, slowly swimming to the surface. "Oh, Yes. Mr. Winlove. Good day to you, sir."

Gregory slammed Maurice against the wall. "The snuffbox, asshole. You stole it when I crashed. I saw you, just couldn't talk. Now get it, pronto, or I'll have the cops over here so fast you won't know what hit you."

Maurice's mind was functioning very slowly, but he did understand what was going on. "Of course, Gregory. It's a valuable box, I was afraid the ambulance men would steal it. I had no intention of keeping it. I simply took it for safekeeping, then I went down the road and called an ambulance."

"Mr. Baleine," Gregory said in a menacing voice. "Get the fucking box."

Maurice programmed his feet to move, and tottered down to the basement. He retrieved the parcel, stumbled back to the front hall, and gave it to Gregory, who tore off the paper.

"Now, Maurice," Gregory spoke slowly, as though to a child, "You know that stealing a box worth thirty thousand dollars is grand larceny, don't you?"

Maurice nodded, dumbly. He didn't know.

"And you understand that if I go to the police, they'll take you into custody, lock you up, put you in a cell. You ever been in jail? All those drunks, tryin' to get inside your ass? Can you imagine what that would do to your reputation? What your snooty wife would say? All your Princeton buddies?" Gregory spoke in a gravelly, steely growl, like a movie villain. It appeared to work, for Maurice blanched. You could say anything, Greg thought, if you did it in a convincing voice.

Maurice, believing every word, nodded his head.

"Well"—Gregory smiled pleasantly—"I won't go to

248

the cops on certain conditions. I want you to do something for me. Very simple. Lend me the keys to your restaurant. Get them for me, now."

Maurice turned like a sleepwalker and headed for his desk. He found his key ring and brought it out to the hall, unsnapping one key.

"There's only the one key?"

"It's the only one I have, the one to the front door," Maurice mumbled.

"You don't have the keys to Poisson's house?"

"No, no I don't," Maurice croaked. "Just the restaurant's front door."

Gregory pocketed the key. "This will remain our little secret, Maurice."

"What—uh—what're you going to do?"

"Oh, nothing much," Gregory said. "I'll return the key in a day or so."

He probably didn't need the key, Gregory thought, since it had been so easy to get in the back door. But it helped Maurice to know that he meant business.

Saturday Dinner and Danger at La Fermette

AT HOME, GREGORY WINLOVE EXAMINED THE KEY TO Charly's restaurant. Next, have a meal there, get a feel for the place. He'd worked in a restaurant one summer, and knew the chef's office was generally near the kitchen. Then late tonight, let himself in, leave a souvenir in Charly's desk drawer. The gun. Make an anonymous call to Clem Hughes. Hughes was convinced that Charly was Munro's killer. When

Hughes got the pistol, he'd insist on bringing Charly in. They wouldn't keep him, but this delaying tactic would give Gregory time to do one or two things and then get out of town. Without the little French snoop nosing around.

Gregory opened a drawer and retrieved the pistol. Pretty piece. Too bad he'd probably never see it again. The next item on Gregory's agenda was to reestablish a friendship with Matt Kendell, vis-à-vis the antiques business. Greg needed Matt's trucks, Matt needed Gregory's expertise. Couldn't they come to an agreement? If worst came to worst, Gregory could always offer to rent the trucks outright. But he hoped to get them a cheaper way.

"Hey, Matt, how're you feeling, fella?"

"Better," Matt said in a hostile voice.

"You check with the doctor? Your heart rate? Blood pressure?"

"What the fuck you want, Winlove?"

"I want to take you out to dinner, Matt. Want you to be my guest."

"Why? So's you can try and poison me some more? I saw Doc Soames, Greg, he told me a thing or two. 'Bout that Lanoxin, what I should and shouldn't be eatin' and drinkin' and smokin' with it."

"Dangerous stuff, Matt, that Lanoxin. You've got to be careful. No, I just wanted to treat you to a meal to say thank you for putting me up those few days. I've been worried about you since Amanda's death."

"Okay. Where you want to eat?"

"I thought that French place on Route 65."

"Why not!"

"I'll pick you up around six, at your house. That all right?

250

"No. I'll meet you there. 'Bout six."

Both men hung up feeling disgruntled: Matt, because he didn't trust the sucker one bit, and Gregory, surprised and annoyed that his ploys had been seen through. Maybe Kendell wasn't as dumb as he'd thought.

Patty Perkins noted Gregory Winlove's reservation and mentioned it to Charly, who was in the kitchen slathering Cornish game hens with his special mixture of French mustard, olive oil, bread crumbs, crumbled rosemary, and a suspicion of balsamic vinegar. It was late Saturday afternoon.

"I do not look forward to their visit. Not nice customer. And the older man, he smell, does not wash. Put them in corner at table fourteen, Patty."

"Okay." Patty sat down. "I'm making another apple brown betty and I'll poach some more pears. Hey, Mick, come sit down. You're looking grey."

Mick hobbled over. "Just for a minute, couldn't catch my breath, there." Indeed, the old man's face was drained of color, and his breath came in gasps.

Charly hurried up with some brown liquid in a tumbler. "Some Swedish Bitters, Mick. Drink. I think it is your heart. This will help."

Mick drained the potion. "This'll be fine, just fine."

"Go home, Mick. Is not busy tonight. You want me to call a doctor?"

"Nah, I'll be hunky-dory in no time. Listen, if I go home now, I'll just pace the floors, talk to Bruno. I'll stick around for a bit."

"Then you will have a glass of champagne, we will celebrate Julius joining La Fermette as a full-time chef, and perhaps he buy some of Maurice's old shares as well."

251

"I knew this was coming," Patty said, smiling at Julius. "He's already a member of the family, so it's no big surprise."

It wasn't a surprise at all, since Julius had discussed the matter with Benny, Patty, and Mick. But for Charly's sake, everyone pretended. Solemnly, Charly poured champagne into the goblets.

It was a small crowd for Saturday night, but, Charly thought, *What do you expect on a cold February night when more snow is expected?* The kitchen reflected this dreary mood: Benny halfheartedly sautéed the thick, juicy rib pork chops and Julius silently tossed pasta with mushrooms, shrimp, and scallops. Charly hadn't lost interest in the murders of Amanda and Robbie, but what could he do about them? He suspected that either Matt or Gregory was the killer, but had no proof. While Kendell and Winlove both appeared to be evil men, Charly felt that Winlove, at this point, was the more dangerous. Matt Kendell, with his heart troubles, didn't look like a killer. The trouble was, Charly admitted, he didn't know any of the players well enough—couldn't imagine what fires fueled their lives.

"You got the entrees for table fourteen?" Elton appeared in the kitchen. Table fourteen was the Winlove table.

"Yes, right here," Charly said. "Benny is plating the pork and I am finishing up the salmon with *sauce oseille.* Any special requests? Sauce on the side? Extra vegetables? They order appetizer?"

"No appetizers. And they haven't touched the bread. Winlove ordered a Coke, Kendell had a club soda. They're not happy campers tonight."

"Both just out of hospital, they probably don't feel

too good," Julius noted. "Maybe I should go say hello, since I found Winlove on the road."

"Good idea," Charly said. "Wear a toque, extra in my closet."

Julius plopped a tall white toque on his head. He'd be a co-owner soon, might as well look the part. He strode into the dining room.

"Good evening, Mr. Winlove, Mr. Kendell. Enjoying your dinner?"

Greg said, "Weird sauce on the salmon."

"It's sorrel—like a bitter spinach. The French serve sorrel with salmon because salmon's a fatty fish. Sorrel's supposed to cut the fat. But if you don't like it, I'd be happy to change it."

"No, don't bother."

"And Mr. Kendell? You enjoying your pork chop?"

"It's okay." The huge chop had barely been eaten.

Julius couldn't think of anything else to say. He certainly didn't have Charly's gift for small talk with the customers. "Well, enjoy your meal."

Back in the kitchen Julius told Charly, "I think this is the first and last time you'll have them as customers. They're not enjoying the food."

"Good. Customer like them I do not need."

"And," Julius said, straight face, "you think one of them's a killer."

"I know so. But—which one?"

"Gregory. He's not normal. And the trucker's a sick man."

"Sick men can kill," Charly said. "Why is Mr. Winlove not normal?"

Julius shrugged. "I don't know. Maybe the look in his eyes, maybe his body language. But I tell you, Charly, I looked at him and I felt goose bumps."

"I do not know these goose bump," Charly said. "But I agree."

Twenty minutes later Elton reported, "Table fourteen's left. No dessert, no coffee. Winlove paid. Left a lousy ten percent tip."

By half past ten La Fermette was ready to close down. Mick insisted on swabbing the floor and Charly let him, knowing the old man needed to feel useful. Charly, the last to leave, checked the dining room, the cellar, made certain the stoves were out, locked the back door. A light snow was falling and Charly was glad of an early night.

Upstairs in his little farmhouse, surrounded by cats, Charly, lying in bed propped up by pillows, turned the pages of a book that did not interest him. *Tiens, perhaps I should reread Les Lettres de Mon Moulin,* he thought, remembering Alphonse Daudet's charming memoir. Rereading favorite books was like visiting old friends. You knew the stories, but wanted to hear them again, just for the pleasure of it. He padded into the smaller of the two guest bedrooms, recalling that it was on the bedside table.

He picked up the book in the guest room, then walked over to the window. This side of the house overlooked La Fermette. Peering through the snowflakes, Charly was puzzled to see someone standing at the front door of the restaurant. Perhaps it was a trick of the moon? Of the snow? But—no. It was a person with a flashlight, bending down, trying to fit a key in the lock. Could it be Maurice, come to raid the liquor? This had happened before.

This person, however, appeared tall and thin. Maurice was much rounder. Now, the figure straightened up and disappeared into the restaurant.

Charly raced downstairs in his flannel pajamas, with a flashlight, put on his down jacket, and quietly opened the back door. He sped down the little road and crept up to his restaurant. He tiptoed to the dining-room windows and looked in, but all was dark. He crept around to a back window and saw a wavering light in his office. He looked through the window. A person was sitting at his desk. He heard the familiar creak of the swivel chair, and more creaks as desk drawers were opened. *What does he hope to find?* Charly wondered. Most people paid by credit card, and the cash was in the safe.

Charly crouched, watching. Yellow hands opened drawers. *He must be wearing kitchen gloves,* Charly thought. A gloved hand reached into a pocket, withdrew a parcel, and placed the parcel in a drawer. Then the figure rose, and Charly could see no more. He crept around to the front of the restaurant and crouched in the bushes. The front door opened and the person slid out, closing the door and locking it. The figure straightened up, and the flashlight shone full on the face. It was Gregory Winlove.

Winlove ran down the path, down Hubbard Road to Route 65. Charly heard a car starting up. He plunged his hand into his pocket and was relieved to find his keys still there. He opened the front door and hurried to his office.

He flicked on the light and opened the top drawer to his desk. A parcel was lying there. Charly tore open the paper wrapping. A pistol.

Charly wrapped up the pistol and sped back to his house. Into the van. Straight to the police station. Inside, bright lights and a blast of heat hit him. Vince Matucci was standing by a desk, talking to an officer Charly didn't recognize. Both men looked up.

"A man go into my locked restaurant and place a gun

in my drawer," Charly said breathlessly. "And the man is Gregory Winlove, I wish to report."

"Siddown, Charly," Officer Matucci said. "Tell us the whole story."

"I cannot stay, I am in my pajamas."

"Pretend it's a jammie party," said Officer Matucci. "And let's have it. The whole enchilada."

CHARLY'S SAUTÉED RIB PORK CHOPS

YIELD: 4 SERVINGS

4 rib pork chops at least 1 inch thick. Have the butcher bone
 the chops and bard them with pork fat. Secure with skewers.
¼ cup French mustard
¼ cup bread crumbs
¼ teaspoon salt
4 tablespoons olive oil
¼ cup balsamic vinegar

Let chops rest at room temperature for at least 20
minutes. Make a paste of mustard, bread crumbs, and
salt and smear thickly on both sides of chops. Heat olive
oil in large frying pan and sauté chops at medium-high
on both sides. Then cover pan, lower heat, and sauté
gently for 20 minutes, or until cooked through. Remove
chops from pan and keep warm. Add balsamic vinegar
to pan drippings and stir well. Serve chops with
dripping.

A Painful Sunday Morning

IT WAS SIX O'CLOCK WHEN CHARLY AWOKE SUNDAY morning. The police had accompanied Charly back to the restaurant last night, examined the office, and assured Charly that Maurice Baleine, who had the only other front door key, would be questioned in the morning.

Now, Charly had to scramble to be in the restaurant kitchen by eight. He sped through the cat rituals, his coffee, his cereal, his bath, in a distracted manner, and he was breathless with his exertions when he hurried into his kitchen at eight o'clock. He turned on lights, ovens, fans, hoping that Mick Hitchens was on his way: Mick was usually the first one in. No Mick.

At half past eight Charly telephoned Mick. Considering the man's poor health yesterday, Charly feared he might have the flu. But the telephone rang and rang. Benny and Julius arrived as Charly was dressing to go out. He explained. "Maybe he is too ill to call or to let Bruno out. I have"—Charly tapped his chest—"the funny feeling."

At Mick's old clapboard house all lights were out. No Bruno in the yard, though Mick's old car was parked in the drive. Charly walked up the neatly shoveled path and knocked. No answer, not even a bark. He twisted the doorknob and the door swung open. Charly marched in, calling, "Mick, Mick, Bruno, Bruno." No one answered.

With his heart thumping against his ribs Charly bolted up the narrow, steep stairs, knowing that whatever he found, it wouldn't be good. He stopped at

258

the open doorway to a small bedroom and looked in.

The bedroom had been painted white, but time had faded it to a brownish-grey. There was a double bed, a pine bureau, a wooden chair, everything old, tidy, dusty. A woven wool rug lay on the floor. A pair of trousers was hanging on the wooden chair.

Mick lay in bed, on his back, covered in a down quilt. Only his head was visible. He appeared to be asleep, eyes closed, but the stench of urine and excrement and the pallor of Mick's face, told Charly that Mick was dead. Bruno lay at the foot of the bed, a look of pain on his face. Charly felt his muscles turn to jelly and he thought that he might faint, but he took a deep breath and closed his eyes. "It was his time," he told himself.

Charly opened his eyes. "Come, Bruno," he said, slapping his thigh as Mick used to do. Bruno heaved a great sigh and followed Charly down the steps, his big black body hunched in grief. *He must be bursting, the poor dog,* Charly thought, opening the front door. The dog hurried over to the tall grass beyond the little lawn.

Charly shut the front door and waited. Then he turned to the kitchen and found the telephone, where he dialed 911, the only number he could remember in his distress. Mick had known. That's why he'd asked Charly, only a few days ago, to be sure and take Bruno if he died. Oh, yes, Mick knew death was coming. Charly was convinced of it.

Charly mounted the steps again and went to the bedroom door. He looked down at Mick and told him, "Bruno and I will never forget you, my old friend," then he opened a window. The cold air blew into the little room, drawing out the bad smells and bringing in the metallic, fresh odor of the frozen fields. Charly touched Mick's icy cheek. Then he went to call the dog.

While he waited for the doctor to arrive, Charly found a bag of dry dog food and fed Bruno. The tears rolled down Charly's cheeks and he realized that he was crying for the dog, so humbly eating his dry food, as well as for the old man.

Charly thought of the people who would welcome Mick: parents, friends, relatives, Charly's father and mother, his Tante Jeanne with her tumbler of cherry brandy, his school chums killed by the Nazis, Dr. Jean Michel, crucified for tending the wounds of the Maquis, the guerrillas, nailed to a rough wooden cross and left to rot. And the old priest in the mountains—the SS had forced him to disrobe and climb into an outdoor bathtub of water, to freeze to death. Why? Why? He thought of cats long gone, of Maurice Baleine Senior who dropped dead in his own restaurant, sitting at the bar with his *coup de blanc,* a glass of white wine. A good death, like Mick's.

"Yes, yes, Bruno, yes, yes," Charly repeated as the big dog laid his head on Charly's thigh. "We will go very soon, now."

"Seventy?" Dr. Hiram Bingham snorted. "He told you that?" They were standing in Mick's kitchen. "He was well over eighty, and he had a heart condition. He knew he could go at any minute. A fine man. Lost his job when the mills closed down twenty years ago. But he never grumbled. He found odd jobs to do, and then he started working for you. You'd just opened up. You kept him alive, Charly. He'd have been dead long ago, but he told me you needed him and that's what kept him going. Now, what about his dog? Want me to drop the pooch off at the pound?"

"Tchah!" Charly said, horrified. "What an idea. No, I

promise Mick, if he die, the dog is mine. No question. Bruno is already a member of my family. I will take him with me, now. You will let me know what to do. I will pay for funeral, burial, whatever. Any bills, I will pay. Mick was my friend."

Charly took the bag of dry dog food and a leash. "Come, Bruno," he said, slapping his thigh. They walked over to Charly's van. He opened the door on the passenger side. Bruno put his front paws on the seat, then turned and looked expectantly at Charly. He was too massive to make the high jump. "Allez-oop," Charly cried, grabbing Bruno's tail and lifting him into the van. Bruno turned around, sniffing, then sat on his haunches looking out through the windshield, as if he'd been riding in Charly's van all his life.

During the drive back to the restaurant Charly spoke to the dog. "You will become a part of our family, Bruno. There are four cats and they will not like you at first and you will not like them. But we will accommodate ourselves, yes?" The dog looked over at Charly, interested in his voice. "We will have enough to eat, and you will be a good dog."

At the restaurant Bruno and Charly walked side by side to the kitchen door. The big dog and the small man looked like they belonged together. Charly carried the leash in one hand, and kept his other hand lying flat on Bruno's neck. The dog exuded heat, like a small furnace.

"Mick is dead, a peaceful death in bed," Charly told Benny and Julius. "We must rejoice that his death is without pain. It was his time."

"I can't believe I'll never see him again," Benny said, and started to cry.

"Oh, God, he was one of the good ones," Julius said.

261

"I thought something bad had happened when you didn't come back, so Benny and I washed the pots and got some things going. He was a fine man, Charly, one of the best. A gentle man."

"I'll miss him a lot," Benny sobbed.

Charly poured three thimblefuls of brandy and handed two over. He held his high and said, "To Mick."

"To Mick," Benny and Julius echoed, and sank the shots.

"And for Bruno, some Ignatia, homeopathic remedy for grief," Charly said, and went to his office where he fumbled in a desk drawer.

"Ha, what is this?" In the drawer, wedged in a crack, was a torn slip of paper—the duplicate, which is given to customers, of an American Express charge for $54.55, signed Gregory Winlove. It must have fallen out of Winlove's pocket, and thinking that it was a paper of Charly's, Winlove had shoved it back into the drawer. It was the bill from last night's dinner. Just another proof that Winlove was here, Charly thought as he slid the dupe into an envelope for the police.

In the kitchen, Bruno was being fed bits of meat by Benny and Julius.

"You'd better keep him in your office during meal service," Julius said, "I think there's a health department regulation about dogs in restaurants."

"Help me roll up my rug," Charly said. "I want to give him a bone, but outside it is too cold."

"Charly," Julius said tolerantly. "The dog's over a hundred pounds. He's half Lab, half Bernese mountain dog, Mick told me. He'll love it outside. We'll tie him to the big maple tree with this rope I found."

The three men looked down at the dog, and the dog looked back and wagged his tail feebly, knowing he was being talked about.

The back door burst open and a muffled figure burst in, banging against a rack of utensils. "Oops, sorry," said Joe Okun as pots crashed to the floor. "You'll be needin' me, Mr. Charly, won't you?"

"Joe," Charly gasped. "I was just going to call. How did you know?"

"I knew," Joe said.

"Welcome, Joe," Charly said. He couldn't think of anything else to say.

Tripes à la Mode de Caen

WHAT IS THAT STRANGE NOISE? CHARLY THOUGHT, opening one eye at five o'clock Monday morning. It was a cross between a snort and a snuffle, as steady as a metronome. Bruno. Charly raised himself on an elbow and looked around the dark bedroom. There were no cats. Only Bruno, lying on the little oriental rug, snoring.

Four puffed tails and a lot of hissing had greeted Charly and Bruno when they'd returned to the house last night. Bruno had wagged his tail, but the cats kept their distance. "They will become accustomed to you," Charly now whispered to his new dog. "Eh, Bruno?"

At the mention of his name, Bruno gave one final snort, lifted his head, and wagged his tail. "No trouble," Charly said. "I will not permit it."

By the time the cats had gone out and come in, been fed, Bruno had gone out and come in, been fed, and Charly had drunk three cups of Puerto Rican coffee, bathed, and eaten his hot cereal, the cats were in truce mode, keeping a wary distance. Bruno was stretched out on the kitchen floor. "It may take as long as a week," Charly noted. Two cats were sitting close by, ready to bolt if the dog made a move.

Today might be Charly's free day, with the restaurant closed, but there was much to do. First, there was the meeting with Maurice in Jonathan Murray's office for the restaurant ownership transfer—an historic day. Toward noon he must drive over to Ugo Buonsarde's house with the container of tripe. Charly had a feeling that this meeting would go well. Ugo might be an outlaw, but he was a gentleman, and, above all, he loved Charly's cooking. His manners and outlook were those of a fellow Italian, and Charly was certain that they would find many points to agree on.

At eight o'clock Charly called Noah Van Gieson, the locksmith, then he called Maurice to remind him of their meeting.

"After this morning you are no longer with the restaurant, Maurice, so I would like to remind you to bring your front door key to Murray's."

Maurice cleared his throat. "I—I've been looking for the key, Charly, and I can't seem to find it."

"It is on the same key ring with your car key and your house key," Charly said sternly. "I have seen it many time."

"Yes, uh, that's right, isn't it? I wonder, uh, what happened to it?"

"Maurice, very late last night someone with a key to the front door came into the restaurant. And that person did a bad thing. There are only two front door keys to the restaurant, yours and mine. Were you the person who came?"

"What? Good God no, Charly. Someone came in? That's terrible. Oh, what? Excuse me, Charly, Barbara says there's someone at the door for me."

"Then let me speak to Barbara while you attend to your visitors."

Barbara came on the line. "What's going on, Charly?" she whispered. "Two policemen are at the door asking for Maurice." She sounded more amused than worried. "What's he done now?"

"Listen to what the men from the police say to Maurice," Charly advised. "In less than one hour, Maurice and I will meet in the office of Jonathan Murray. Like little divorce. In one hour, my dear Barbara, Maurice belong to you and you alone."

"Perhaps not for much longer, Charly."

"*Tiens, quelle surprise.*"

"Well, that's it, gentlemen," Jonathan Murray said. The meeting had run less than thirty minutes and Charly and Maurice were sitting in leather armchairs facing the lawyer's walnut desk. The documents had been signed, papers had been notarized, and Charly had presented Maurice with a check. Quite a large check. Maurice got up and turned to go.

"Let me shake your hand, Maurice, and wish you good luck," Charly said. "And you will, I trust, get your key back *from wherever it has gone.*" Charly raised an eyebrow significantly as he spoke in italics.

"Yes, yes, Charly, of course. Good-bye, Jonathan. Good-bye, Charly, I'll stop in at the restaurant later on today." Maurice was in a fever to be off.

"Today is Monday, Maurice, and the restaurant is closed."

"Oh, ah, of course." Maurice bolted.

Jonathan said, "Charly, if you have a minute?"

Together they waited until Maurice's footsteps

retreated. "Hy Bingham called me yesterday," the lawyer said. "My condolences, Charly. You lost a fine gentleman in Mick Hitchens."

Charly nodded.

"Mick asked me to keep his papers, Charly. He made a will, he left his savings to you, twenty thousand dollars. For the care of his dog."

Charly opened his mouth, but nothing came out. He sat back in the big leather chair and closed his eyes. Finally, he drew a sobbing breath. "Is not *nécessaire*. The money, I do not need. How can I accept?"

"Listen, Charly, I knew you'd feel this way. And I've been thinking. Why don't you put the money in a money market account, Jimmy Houghton will advise you, and use it for the care of other animals? I know an old lady, for instance, she has only her social security to live on, and she worries that she doesn't have enough money to care for her old dog properly. He's the only reason she's staying alive."

"Then we will give her the money."

"There are others, Charly. You could pay several people small monthly sums to help them out. Would that be agreeable?"

Charly nodded. He didn't trust himself to speak.

"I'll make a list, send it to you," Jonathan said. "How's that?"

Charly nodded again.

"And how's Bruno? Getting used to your cats?"

Now, Charly smiled. He wiped his eyes with his linen handkerchief. "He is *splendide,* Jon-a-tan. Already member of my family."

"And, uh, Charly, I wouldn't count on Maurice returning those keys I heard you discussing."

"I have already called Noah Van Gieson. He changed

266

all locks this morning. Maurice give the key to Gregory Winlove. I do not know how Winlove could force him to do that, but I suspect many thing."

"Yes, Charly," said Jonathan Murray. "I'm sure you do."

Charly took another sip of the dry Sicilian Corvo. The light wine went remarkably well with the tripe, a surprise, as Charly would have chosen a heavier, more full-bodied red. "Is *splendide,* Signor Buonsarde."

"A good accompaniment to your tripe, don't you think?"

"*Mais oui.* The bouquet . . . " Charly sniffed. "Very delicate."

Immediately upon Charly's arrival Ugo had placed the large earthenware pot of tripe in the oven to become piping hot, while he and Charly, Francesco and Gianni, nibbled on bread, olives, and air-cured salami, made without chemicals, just meat, salt, spices, and herbs.

"My father," Charly said, "would be interested. He was a *charcutier* you know, a maker of sausages . . . "

"I did not know. And what were his specialties?" Ugo asked. An hour quickly passed, then another. The tripe was eaten, and savored. Charly asked for the air-cured sausage recipe and Ugo chuckled.

"After you've made it a hundred times, you might, just possibly, get the knack. I never did. Or maybe American air is too thin. This comes from my aunt in Sicily. It's all in the quality of the air—the salami has to be put to hang where it will sway gently in a slight breeze.

"A *courant d'air,* " Charly murmured.

"Yes, yes, a current of air, but only very slight. And you must turn the salami every few days, so that the drying will be even. Otherwise the meat will rot. To make it is an art. Of course we must bring it in secretly, since the U.S. Customs do not approve of home-cured salami. The poison you buy here, aggh . . . " Ugo made a face. "I cannot eat it. So filled with chemicals."

"The American people, they love the chemical," Charly agreed. "The chemical industry is very powerful. And if the newspapers criticize, the chemical industries threaten to remove all advertisement, so the newspapers do not print the truth."

"Ah, always greed," said Buonsarde. "Greed is one of the seven deadly sins. And do you know why?"

Charly sipped his wine and shook his head. He was enjoying himself. Of course he knew why, but he also knew that Ugo wanted to tell him.

"Why?"

"Because"—Ugo tapped his index finger on the table for emphasis—"the gluttony, the greed, this unnatural craving for money, will turn upon the glutton and destroy him. I see it in my business all the time."

"Ah-ha! Exactly, Signor Buonsarde. I am in total agreement."

Ugo turned to Gianni and Francesco. "Is this not so, gentlemen?"

"It's so, boss," the men said in unison.

Charly now spoke of Mick's death and the monies to be contributed to the elderly pet owners. Ugo spoke of his help to various churches that gave money to the poor. There was a lot more warmth in the room than that provided by the tripe and the wine. After salad, an oozing, perfectly ripened Gorgonzola, ripe figs from Ugo's greenhouse, and espresso, Charly stood up. It was late, and he had to get home to Bruno and his cats.

"This has been one of the most *sympathique* days of

268

my life," Charly told Ugo. "It is a day that I will always remember."

"And I too, my friend. Come, I will walk with you to your car."

Ugo and Charly beamed as Gianni and Francesco helped them on with their outerwear, then accompanied the two men to the courtyard.

"An exceptional day, a day of friendship. . ." Charly had just begun his little farewell speech when the crack of a rifle sounded, then another, and a bullet thunked into the roof of Charly's van. Charly screamed.

Temperatures Rise

AT THE FIRST SOUND OF GUNSHOTS GIANNI AND Francesco had thrown themselves against Charly and Ugo, tumbling them to the ground. Neither had been hit. The pair shielded the two older men as they crawled to the other side of the van, away from the shooter. Here they waited, then Ugo and Charly scuttled into the house, protected by the bodyguards.

"Get the Land Rover and your rifles," Ugo instructed his men. "If he was shooting from the top of that hill, he's probably parked on Lake Road around the corner. Maybe you can head him off."

Back in the warm kitchen Ugo poured small measures of grappa into two tumblers and presented one to Charly. The rough brandy traveled down Charly's gullet like fire. "We have—little situation," he told Ugo. "The wife of Matthew Kendell is killed, and then I find a dead antiques dealer named Robbie Munro in my freezer. Both have been murdered. Do you know these people?"

269

"I've heard the name Robbie Munro," Ugo said cautiously. "And Matthew Kendell I've known for many years. We've leased his trucks on several occasions. Kendell was the man I visited at the hospital."

"Do you know the man Gregory Winlove?"

Ugo pretended to search his memory. "I think he sells antiques to Carlo Calamare, my general manager. He also works with Matthew Kendell, something to do with antiques." Ugo lowered his voice. "Kendell thinks Winlove murdered his wife. She was Gregory Winlove's sister."

Charly said, "I thought Kendell killed his wife."

"I doubt it," Ugo said. "Matt used to be a wild man, but he's calmed down, and he's had a serious heart condition for the last five years."

"I did not know," Charly said.

"I've met the wife," Ugo continued. "A bit slow. Matt said he wrote a will, left everything to her, but with two of his lawyers as trustees, so Gregory couldn't steal any of it. Matt sees death staring him in the face every day, he told me. Terrible way to live, uh?"

"Terrible," Charly agreed. "But he hit his wife. I see her eye, all braised."

Ugo said, "He's a violent man. He's also a coward, like most wife-beaters. He's not a man to call your friend."

Gianni and Francesco came into the kitchen. "We think we hit him, and we think it's Winlove," Gianni said. "He'd reached his car, you was right, he parked on Lake Road, but he drove off before we could get near enough."

"You didn't follow him?"

Gianni said, "We decided to come back, you might

need us here, boss."

"If we followed him, it could take hours," Francesco added. "We couldn't—uh—deal with him out in the open."

"I know where he lives," Charly said. "Perhaps I can call the police and they will pick him up, there."

"The police can't hold him," Ugo said. "They have no proof and neither do we. He'll get a lawyer, be out in an hour. No, *mon ami*, the police are useless. Now, I know you must get home, Chef. Gianni and Francesco will follow you, and they will help you search your restaurant and your home, in case Winlove is hiding. Perhaps you could point out Winlove's house to them. Then you must stay inside. To have anyone die is a tragedy. But one of the world's greatest chefs? No, no."

Charly agreed with this sentiment wholeheartedly.

Gregory Winlove had felt a bullet nick his ear, which bled a lot, but he'd slowed the bleeding with paper towels he'd found in the rented car. It had terrified him. One millimeter to the right, and he'd be a dead man. It was a shock to be on the receiving end. Gregory liked to deal the cards.

He knew Ugo's goons were out to get him, and now he knew why. It was because of Robbie Munro's body, he'd finally figured it out. He'd followed Charly over to Ugo's, surprised that the restaurateur and the gangster were friends. Charly must have told Ugo about the body in his freezer, and about Greg's trying to run him off the road. Ugo must have told Charly about Greg's antiques business. So there you were. But now they were together. Gregory would kill them both.

But it was frigid on the little hill up from Lake Road, and Greg's hands were so stiff he had trouble handling

271

the rifle. Also, his foot slipped on a patch of ice as he was firing. One shot was all it took to announce his position, and now the mob was after him.

Where could Greg hide? The bodyguards would stalk his house, and probably guard Charly's house and restaurant, as well. Ugo had an army of goons. Gregory didn't worry, though. He knew he was invincible.

It was dusk. The best thing was to wait, car hidden in bushes, at Kendell Transports. After dark he'd drive home, park in the woods, get his stuff from the house, and run. He'd fill his leather duffel with clothes, money, traveler's checks, his three passports (each made out to a different name but with his photo on all three), and, of course, Maurice's snuffbox, and sneak out again. He'd drive up to Albany Airport and get the first flight out— to Philadelphia or Atlanta or Boston or Kennedy. From there, he'd fly to Paris. There was an important auction next week, where he could sell the snuffbox. No one would trace him to Paris.

"No one at all," Gianni told Charly. The three men had searched Charly's house, his restaurant, even his tool shed, and Charly drove with the men to Allen Road and pointed out Gregory's house, which was locked and dark. Now they were back in Charly's kitchen, and Charly was setting out food for Bruno and the cats. Francesco and Gianni had nailed black plastic garbage bags over the kitchen window, and now they tacked dark towels over the plastic. Charly promised the men he wouldn't move from his house.

"You got a gun, Mr. P? Mr. B'll send some men to Winlove's as soon as he can. We'll stay with the boss, in case Winlove tries again."

"I have no gun. But I have knives, and Bruno, he will

272

bark."

As soon as the men left, Charly telephoned Stark and told him about Winlove's attempted murder. He didn't mention Ugo.

"Just stay inside, Charly," said Stark. "Don't open the door for anyone. I can't help you now, we've got a big accident over by the Taconic Parkway and the State Police need us. Plus, we've got a crazy on our hands, he's inside his house, holding the baby hostage. I've called everyone in. Can't spare anyone."

The telephone rang. It was Rex Cingale.

"Bad news, Charly. About Bobby."

"Yes?"

"Carlo Calamare's made Bobby head daytime bartender. Bobby'll be working there full-time. He's moving over there, one of the employees offered him an apartment to rent. It looks like he's gone for good."

"You know what I think, Charly?"

"What?"

"I think Carlo's training Bobby to be a full-time hood."

Charly thought so, too. "Ah, Rex, maybe not. Besides, what can you do?"

"Not a fuckin' thing, Charly. Know something funny? I miss the guy. He used to get on my nerves something terrible, all that Mr. Cool business, always combing his hair. But whatever happened, Bobby was up. Smiling. Know what I mean?"

"I know what you mean, Rex."

An hour passed. Then another. Charly was restless. He was not only restless, he was bored. He couldn't believe that Gregory Winlove would come to his house. Winlove was smart. At this very moment he'd be on his way to an airport. But had he left, yet? *Maybe I should drive to Allen Road, just to see,* Charly thought. If the house was lit up, he'd drive home and call Ugo.

It was dark. Greg saw the lights in the main office of Kendell Transports flicking off. Time to get moving, before Ugo assembled his army and marched on Casa Winlove.

A lot of Gregory's bravado had left him. Now, he was frightened. He'd always come out on top, even when they sent him to reform school he'd gotten out before his allotted time. He'd pretended to be a model citizen, an act he could play very well. What had happened, here? The antiques business had been going splendidly, and then two things happened: he'd lost his temper with his idiot sister when she refused to lend him money, and he'd broken into her house and found those notes she was writing to her dumb friends. She was getting out. Divorcing Matt. He'd been counting on her cash. And that idiot Robbie. What a dumb move.

Gregory sat in the car and flexed his powerful hands. They seemed to operate independently of his mind, sometimes. Something would short-circuit in his brain, everything shrouded in fog, then he'd black out. And when he came to, he couldn't remember what happened. First his sister, then Robbie. But no one could get him. Gregory told himself, *I'm a genius, and no one can touch me.* Part of him actually believed this.

It would soon be over. He'd drive home, put on his disguise, and he was off to Paris. Credit cards, his several passports, traveler's checks, that envelope of French francs—Gregory ticked off a mental list. He checked his gas gauge—plenty, he'd filled it this morning. He'd call the rental place from the airport, if he had time. Tell them to pick up their car, there.

Gregory was a master at planning.

"I will not be gone long, Bruno," Charly told the big black dog. He hurried out to his van and drove to Allen Road. He parked at the top of the road and using his flashlight, crept through the snowy fields until he got to Gregory Winlove's house.

The house was dark, and there was no car in the driveway. But Charly saw flashes of light in the house and decided it was someone using a flashlight. It must be Gregory.

Charly gasped when a woman emerged from Winlove's back door. She was tall, with long dark hair and a Russian Cossack's fur hat, wearing a dark cape and boots. Was this a lady friend, come to pack for him? He must be hiding elsewhere.

From his hiding place Charly watched the woman—she was carrying a duffel bag—stride through the weeds, her flashlight pointing to the ground. She passed within twenty feet of Charly. He could smell a lemony scent. Suddenly she gave an "umpf" of annoyance, and Charly nearly cried out as the entire top of the woman's head lifted up—it looked like she was being scalped. Her hat, with long hair attached, had caught on a branch.

Charly clapped his hand over his mouth as he realized that the woman was wearing a wig, which she now tugged at, finally disengaging it from the branch. She replaced the wig, pulling at it so that it fit snugly, then put on the hat, while balancing the flashlight with her knees. Suddenly the flashlight slipped and the light shone into the woman's face. The light lit up the strong, slender nose, the full lips. Charly was looking at Gregory Winlove in drag.

Fatal Decisions

EVER SINCE BOBBY MATUCCI HAD GIVEN CARLO THE thousand dollars that he'd found, Carlo had eyed Bobby with more and more approval. The signs were scant, but telling: "Hey, Bobby, call Gianni for me, will ya?" Letting him into the family. Or, "Hey, Bobby, here's the keys to the main liquor cellar, get me couple Canadian Clubs, uh?" Trusting him with the keys. Or, even more personal. "Here's the keys to my Caddie, Bobby, go see if I've left my glasses on the dash, wouldya?" Like that.

Now, late Monday afternoon, Bobby was down in The Country Squire's main liquor cellar with a clipboard and list, checking the inventory. Now that he was head daytime bartender, he had a lot of responsibility. He was flattered that Carlo thought so much of him, but when he told Kimberly, expecting excited praise, all he got was a "Huh, big deal."

Now that he saw Kimberly every day, Bobby noticed her bulk. Would she become a tubbo like her mom? Another thing: she'd started bossing him around, treating him as she did her parents: "Hey, Bobby, get me a Coke, lotsa ice." Not even a "please" or a "thank you." Un-unh, he didn't like the way things were going, there.

Gino Teresa, manager of the hotel-motel, offered Bobby a furnished apartment over his garage, only two hundred a month. "Apartment" was a fancy word for a room with a kitchenette and a midget bathroom, but the place was clean, furnished in maple furniture, double bed with firm mattress, well heated. Gino told him there was all the hot water he'd ever fuckin' need, even if he showered five times a day. Good deal, huh? "A giff,

276

kid," said Gino. Some gift. One room.

So here Bobby was, in the cellar of The Country Squire, doing the liquor inventory: racks of booze, wine, margarita mix, Tom Collins mix, Bloody Mary mix, peanuts, maraschino cherries, pearl onions, olives, tins of pretzels. Everything dusted and labeled. Suddenly Bobby jumped. He heard voices.

"Big upset," mumble, mumble. "He wants five men, that means . . ." mumble. "I said I gotta stay here, the place's gotta keep running, uh? The hell with accident, he says, just take Winlove out, I don't care how."

Bobby looked around but could see no one. He circled the perimeter of the big room. The voices became louder just over here, under this vent. Bobby realized that the voices were coming from Carlo Calamari's office, just above, that the men were moving around, and when they moved close to the vent, he could hear them. Suddenly he pricked up his ears as he heard "that Matucci kid." He stopped and held his breath.

"Not . . . bad kid. For an outsider."

"Grandfather came from Palermo. I've been checkin' up." Carlo.

"Mr. B likes the look a' him." Who said that?

"Don't know how far he'll go. Soft. Not . . . tough guy."

"But when he's hitched to your daughter, uh, Carlo?"

"Good match. She's strong, he's weak. He's a follower." Carlo again.

"So they hit Winlove, then what?"

Bobby had heard enough. He threw down his clipboard, his black apron. Sprinted upstairs. Knocked on Carlo's office door. "Mr. C? An emergency at home, I gotta run. Matter of life an' death. I'll be back."

Like hell he'd be back. Like, never. He grabbed his jacket, grateful that his bags were still in the car, that he hadn't moved into Gino's room, yet. His car started right up. Bobby fled The Country Squire.

The man at Parkeby's spoke to Maurice respectfully. He spoke to everyone respectfully. You never knew who was on the other end of the wire.

"Of course, Mr. Baleine, hard to give a price without seeing it, but I could venture a guess. Gold, with a painted enamel top, eighteenth century, it sounds like eighty thousand to me. This is based on past auctions."

Maurice's throat had gone dry. He squeaked, "I thought the fad for snuffboxes had died down."

"Oh, dear heavens no, Mr. Baleine, quite the contrary. It's at its peak right now. I've never seen such prices, far beyond our estimates."

Maurice thanked the man at Parkeby's, and said he'd be in.

"That would be splendid, Mr. Baleine." The voice was plummy.

Maurice felt faint. He picked up the receiver to call Winlove, but put it down again. No, he'd call in the rooming. Early. Get the man out of bed.

Matthew Kendell woke with a start. He didn't know what time it was, but it was dark. He was in his study, lying on the couch, he'd taken the afternoon off because he felt terrible. Not bad, terrible. He ached all over, his head throbbed, his eyes felt funny. Maybe this was it. He was dying. He thought a lot about death, these days, and decided it wouldn't be too bad. It would be better on the other side, though, if he could avenge his wife's murder. Her brother Gregory killed her, he was sure of

278

that. Now, he was going to Greg's house, kill him with his bare hands. He'd take his Colt along, just in case. But he wanted to feel his fingers choking off that worthless life.

Matt got his pistol, loaded it, checked the safety, thrust it into his jacket pocket. The decision made, he felt a surge of his old energy. He went outside to his car and got in, loving the smell of the leather interior, the soft purr of the powerful engine. "You're the only thing I'll hate to leave," he told the car. He knew his life was ticking away. An hour left, or maybe a day, or even a week. But he knew. Not long, now.

Charly watched Gregory Winlove dressed as a woman hurry down the road. Gregory was fleeing, no question. He wouldn't bother Charly tonight. Charly trudged over to his van hidden in the bushes and backed cautiously out. He looked both ways on Route 32. The road was clear. As he drove along, Charly saw a big black Land Rover speed past. It looked like the car Gianni and Francesco were driving earlier. Then a minute later, a black car passed him with a woman at the wheel. Winlove? Did he forget something? Charly wouldn't get involved. Or should he? Charly pulled over to the side and thought about it. Should he or shouldn't he? Charly turned his van around and drove back toward Winlove's house.

The snuffbox. Gregory hadn't driven a mile when he remembered that he hadn't packed the snuffbox. He'd packed his money, his passports, his clothing, and left one of the main things behind. He pulled over to the side of the road. Should he turn around and go back? Take a chance that Buonsarde's goons weren't there yet? Yes. And even if they were, so what? He, Gregory Winlove the genius, would win out. He always had and always would. Gregory tuned his car around and headed back to his house.

Cautiously, he turned off his headlights and drove down Allen Road. Good, no cars. Buonsarde probably wouldn't send his men until tomorrow morning. He didn't know Gregory was running out. He turned into his driveway, cut the engine. He unlocked the back door.

The snuffbox was on the front hall table. He was just reaching out for it when there was a noise, a click, and he heard footsteps in the kitchen. He reached into the hall table's drawer and withdrew his Llama automatic. He'd put it there before leaving the first time, knowing that he couldn't carry a firearm on the airplane. He flicked off the safety.

Two figures emerged into the faintly lit hallway. It was Gianni and Francesco. There was an intake of breath and one man said, "Christ, it's a broad," and the other man said, "No it's not, it's the fucker in drag." Both men raised their pistols and started firing as Gregory pressed his finger on the trigger of his own gun. He saw both men fall.

Filled with the triumph of shooting the intruders, Gregory didn't realize, at first, that he'd been shot. Something exploded in his chest as he pulled the trigger again and again, and his eyes clouded over as he watched the two men spiraling to the ground.

Charly, arriving near Winlove's house, again parked his van in the bushes and crept to the front door. Good, lights were on. He peered into the window and saw three bodies, Gianni, Francesco, and Winlove in his dress.

Charly tried the front door. It was locked. He ran around to the back. This door was open. He hurried into the front hall and peered down at the three men. He was certain they were dead. He'd seen enough corpses during the war. All three had their eyes open, gazing sightlessly at the ceiling.

Looking down at the bodies, Charly felt faint. His body was flooded with perspiration. He took off his beret and hung it on the newel post, and mopped his face with his handkerchief. Soaking wet. He spied, on a table, a small parcel wrapped in tissue paper. Unwrapped it. Maurice's snuffbox. Charly put the snuffbox in his pocket and left the house. As he reached the top of Allen Road he saw a car turning in. It was a Jaguar. Kendell? It didn't matter. For once in his life, Charly had detected enough.

Matt Kendell's pains were coming steadily, now, and his heart was cramping as if a giant hand were kneading it. He parked in Winlove's driveway and stumbled from his car, pistol in hand. He zigzagged to the front door. He didn't bother to ring. He twisted the knob, and when the door didn't open, he gave a mighty kick and the door burst open, wood splintering. He looked down at the three bodies, and then he collapsed.

Charly was still shaking as he opened his back door. Bruno was lying by the refrigerator, and he got up as Charly hurried in. Two cats lay nearby. From now on, Charly vowed, he'd stick to his animals. People were too much trouble. Still, he must make one telephone call.

"Signor Buonsarde?" Charly spoke into the receiver. "Bad news. I have just come from the house of

281

Winlove. Winlove, Gianni, and Francesco are dead. They lie in the front hall. I wanted you to know. Yes, I will do whatever you say. No, I will not call the police. You will take care of it? Very good, sir."

Much later, as Charly slept, the telephone rang. He sprang up, snatched the receiver. It didn't even interrupt Bruno's loud snoring.

"Chef Poisson," Ugo Buonsarde said. "We have removed Gianni and Francesco, they will receive a proper burial here in the mountains. The funeral director is a cousin of Mr. Calamare's. I wanted you to know."

"You have my silence, Signor Buonsarde. Nothing will be said."

"Thank you, Monsieur Poisson. I knew I could count on you. Oh, and another small thing. There is a black beret in your mailbox. We found it in Mr. Winlove's front hall."

TRIPES À LA MODE DE CAEN

YIELD: 10 SERVINGS WITH LEFTOVERS

10 pounds beef honeycomb tripe, cut in large cubes

2 cups tomatoes, peeled, seeded, and cubed*

4 carrots, peeled and sliced

8 large onions, peeled and coarsely chopped

8 cloves garlic, peeled and chopped

2 calves' feet, have butcher saw into 4-inch rounds. Blanch 5 minutes and drain

½ cup apple brandy or Calvados

2 cups white wine or hard cider

2 bouquets garni: parsley, 4 thyme sprigs, 2 bay leaves, bound with thread

At end: salt and pepper as needed

Layer all ingredients except salt and pepper in large earthenware casserole with top. Either seal edges with a paste made from flour and water or wrap entire casserole in tinfoil.

Bake in 200° oven for 10 hours. Let cool and taste for seasoning, adding salt and pepper as needed. Serve with boiled potatoes.

*The classic recipe for Tripes à la Mode de Caen does not call for tomatoes. This is Charly's preference.

Dear Reader:

I hope you enjoyed reading this Large Print mystery. If you are interested in reading other Beeler Large Print Mystery titles or any other Beeler Large Print titles, ask your librarian or write to me at

Thomas T. Beeler, *Publisher*
Post Office Box 659
Hampton Falls, New Hampshire 03844

You can also call me at 1-800-818-7574 and I will send you my latest catalogue.

Audrey Lesko chooses the titles I publish in Large Print. Our aim is to provide good books by outstanding authors—books we both enjoyed reading and liked well enough to want to share. We warmly welcome any suggestions for new titles and authors.

Sincerely,

Tom Beeler